RELEVANT REIGN

ALEATHA ROMIG

NEW YORK TIMES BESTSELLING AUTHOR

Book four of the Royal Reflections Series

Aleatha Romig

New York Times, Wall Street Journal, and USA Today
bestselling author

D1275021

Dedication

The Royal Reflections series is dedicated to my husband's grandmother, Lucille. (And yes, she's read my books!) At ninety-seven years of age, she remains a bright and beautiful part of our lives, the lives of our children, and of our grandchildren. She has shown us that blood doesn't dictate who we love—the heart does that.

Thank you, Grandma Lucy, for the example you've shown. You will always be regal and royal in our hearts.

Relevant Reign

"Your greatest threat will always come from the inside. Never forget that." **Omar Navarro,** *Ozark*

Molave's survival is at stake. The monarchy is faced with betrayal that could end Molave and remove the kingdom from the map. With so much on the line...

What price is too high?
Will the Godfrey monarchy go on?

Don't miss this dramatic conclusion of the Royal Reflections series as the bonds of family are tested and family itself is reevaluated. The prince and princess must decide if Molave is worth the risk or if returning to America is in their future.

Have you been Aleatha'd?

From New York Times bestselling author Aleatha Romig comes a brand-new contemporary romantic-suspense series, Royal Reflections, set in the world of the royal elite, where things are not as they appear.

*RELEVANT REIGN is the much-anticipated conclusion in the Royal Reflections series. Royal Reflections must be read in order: RUTHLESS REIGN, RESILIENT REIGN, RAVISHING REIGN, and now RELEVANT REIGN.

PROLOGUE

L eaving the infirmary, I barely spoke to Lord Martin as I rushed to our apartments. Lady Buckingham met me on the grand stairs. "Where is the Princess? Is she upstairs?"

"No, Your Highness. She's with the queen."

The queen.

Changing directions, I headed toward the king's offices. He'd told me not to rule with emotion, but at this moment that felt impossible. The emotions were bubbling within me, reaching a boiling point.

"Sir, what is happening?" Lord Martin asked.

"I need to see Lucille. If I can't, I must speak to the king."

"I will call for an appointment."

"Fuck that," I growled.

Lord Martin stayed at my side, stride for stride, as

1

we hurried past faceless people in the corridors. Some greeted me and others bowed. I didn't slow. Pushing my way into the king's outer office, I said, "I must see the king."

"Your Highness," one of his secretaries said, standing. "He isn't expecting you."

"Is anyone with him?"

"No, sir, but..."

I didn't bother waiting for the guard to open the door as I pressed on, pushing open his office door.

"Roman?" King Theodore said, looking up from his desk. "What is this about?" He waved off the guard.

I waited until the door closed. "I just came from the infirmary."

"The princess is expecting," the king said with a smile as he stood. "I'm elated."

"No. Yes." I shook my head. "Inessa Volkov is hiding from her brother because—"

"She's pregnant with your child. The guards found the pregnancy test. There's no need to worry. We have her now."

"It's not mine—the baby. I've never met her." The words he'd just spoken registered. "You have her. What does that mean?"

"Son, it means a great day for Molave. You have two heirs on the way."

CHAPTER
1

The Queen of Molave
In the past

I woke with a start, searching the shadows of my bedchamber for answers.

Is our son all right?

Is he injured?

I ached for any shred of news.

As if designed to keep me in the dark literally as well as figuratively, heavy drapes covering the windows kept what was left of sunlight away—if indeed the sun was still in the sky. Peering around the room through puffy eyes, I took in the opulence hidden beneath the shadows. The finest furniture, made for a queen, created the perfect bedchamber. My temples throbbed as I fell farther and farther down the black hole of sorrow.

Time passed unmarked by anything of substance since we'd received the first call. Minutes crept while hours flew. The numbers on the clock at my bedside either wouldn't move or spun without reason. Nothing made sense.

Willing myself to move, I managed to scooch up and sit against the pillows and headboard. I turned to my right, seeing beyond the sheer curtains shrouding my bed. The telephone on the bedside stand sat silent.

I longed for more news.

An accident at university.

As soon as we were told, Theodore flew to Kristiansand. That was hours ago or maybe days.

The last word was that our son, the Prince of Molave and our heir to the Crown, Roman Archibald Godfrey, was alive.

My Roman—my handsome son, the one God gave to me after we lost Teddy. Roman wasn't our only surviving child. Five years after Roman's birth, I'd had another successful pregnancy, our only daughter, Isabella. Due to the high number of unsuccessful pregnancies between the births of Roman and Isabella, the royal physicians advised that we stop trying.

And now, nearly twenty years later, I felt the despair I'd felt when I'd been told about Teddy...and the lake. This time it was Roman and the crash of his glider.

My cracked lips and dry throat reminded me of the tears I'd shed.

Throwing back the blankets, I willed myself from

the bed. Pushing back the draperies, I stared out at the royal gardens a story below. The dimming sunlight cast shadows from the palace walls. Upward, the sky was filled with a crimson hue, creating a vivid explosion of color reflecting up on the low-lying clouds.

Instead of concentrating on the beauty before me, my thoughts went back nearly two decades. Upon Theodore III's—Teddy's—passing, I could have assigned blame to his nanny or to any of the other servants in the vicinity as Teddy waded into the lake. During sleepless nights and joyless days, I'd imagined what my baby had experienced before he was spotted, floating in only decimeters of water. Theodore, my husband and the king of Molave, was livid.

I supposed his rage was enough for the both of us. I couldn't express mine. It was different. My anger was not for those who were present, but at the one who wasn't.

Me.

As Teddy's mother, it was my responsibility to keep him safe. Oh yes, he was supposed to grow and move beyond a mother's care, but not before his second birthday. The crushing pain of awakening each morning without a child was unbearable.

Our marriage suffered.

I resented my husband, Theodore, for his grief, for his fury, and finally, for trying to see past the pain. In all fairness, it was my self-loathing that carved a hole in our marriage I was certain would never mend. The only shred of happiness that kept me going, kept me eating, drinking, and sleeping was the knowledge that within me was another child.

Perhaps it was wrong of me to wonder if I deserved another chance. For that reason, I kept the news of the pregnancy a secret for as long as I could. One would think that I couldn't have hidden it from Theodore. The truth was, I could barely stand to look into his dark eyes. Each time I did, I saw the contempt.

He wasn't told of my condition until I was nearly six months along.

It was nearly half a year after we laid Teddy in his final resting place before my pregnancy could no longer be hidden. My husband and the country were joyous at the news. Three months later, our miracle son was born.

Roman Archibald Godfrey.

The last Archibald to reign Molave was Theodore's great-grandfather.

With dark hair and deep brown eyes, Roman was in every way our golden child.

The sound of the door to my bedchamber opening pulled me back to the present. Turning, I expected my mistress, Lady Kornhall. Instead, it was my husband.

My body chilled as his gaze met mine. Securing my

own hand, I tried in vain to stop the onset of trembling. Without a word, he came closer, his expression stoic, not giving me a clue to his findings. By the time Theo reached me across the room, my entire body shook as sobs bubbled from my throat.

"Is he...?" I couldn't even say the words.

Theo reached for my shoulders. "He's alive."

As my knees gave out, my husband's arms encircled me. His strong embrace kept me standing. I looked up into his eyes. "I want to see him."

"He's injured."

"He's alive. That's all that matters."

Theodore walked me back to the bed. "I've ordered the physician to give you something to help you rest. This is all too much for you."

As I sat on the bed and lay back, I held tight to Theodore's hand. "Our son will live." It wasn't a question, but at the same time, I needed his reassurance.

"Yes, my love. Roman is too strong to leave us." He kissed my forehead. "Lady Kornhall will see to your needs. Mr. Davies will be here to give you something to help you relax. Trust me, Anne."

"I do."

"Isabella has been sent to Annabella. My mother is with her."

"Why?" My forehead furrowed. "I should be with our daughter."

"There's no need to burden her with news of her brother."

"But surely, she'll hear. He's the prince."

Theodore shook his head. "I've forbidden anyone from giving out information. There is nothing that would come of making this public." He inhaled. "This is a family matter."

"Thank you, Theo. I don't think I could go on with losing another child."

His Adam's apple bobbed in his throat. "We will not, not on my watch."

Nodding, I exhaled.

As Theodore stood, the door of my bedchamber opened, and Lady Kornhall appeared carrying a tray.

"Eat, Anne. And know Roman is safe."

CHAPTER 2

Roman
Present time

King Theodore's booming voice issued the order. "Take a seat, Roman."

Emotions this man told me I shouldn't feel were surging through me at the speed of light. Failing to obey his command, I paced the confines of his private office as I tried to collect my thoughts. Each notion was but a particle in the swirling cyclone within my mind.

Baby.

Babies.

Pregnancy test.

They had her—Inessa.

What did that mean?

I thought back, recalling the game of charades I'd played this morning with Francis. A child was coming —a Godfrey. Memories of what happened next consumed my thinking.

As I walked away from Francis's cell, I returned to

Noah's. Two medical personnel were caring for him. Their eyes opened wide as I burst inside. Noah lay completely nude, the nurses working on the bath I'd demanded.

"Get out," I shouted.

The two nurses bowed their necks and scurried away, leaving their patient fully exposed.

Without a shred of clothes or modesty, Noah's dark eyes met mine as he lay prone on the damp sheets. He was the first to speak, "You know."

"Is it true?" When he only smirked, I went closer. "Is Inessa pregnant with your child?"

His gaze left me, looked down at his exposed body and back to me. "I wasn't sure I could produce a kid. After all, Lucille..." He shook his head. "Truth is, I never wanted to have a kid, with either of them."

My molars were in danger of cracking as I applied more and more pressure with each word he spoke. When he finished, I asked one more time. "Is Inessa Volkov pregnant with your child?"

"She said she was."

"When did she tell you?"

"It was during the Eurasia disaster tour." He shook his head. "That whole expedition was fucked from the beginning."

"Do you know if Alek knows?"

"He didn't then." Noah's sinister smile grew. "Seems like it's your problem now."

My thoughts were all over the place. "Do you think the princess was hiding from Alek because of the pregnancy? Did you see her at Forthwith? Do you think Alek threatened her? Did she tell him?" I paced back and forth in the small cell. "This is why Aleksander II thinks I took her."

"He thinks more than that."

"What the fuck does he think?" I asked, spitting out the question.

"Get me unchained from this bed, and I'll tell you more."

I'd already authorized that.

"Tell me first."

Noah shook his head. "Listen, Roman" —he used the name mockingly— "I have all the time in the world or as much as Theo decides to grant me. You on the other hand...the clock is ticking. Unchain me and get me more of my meds."

Meds.

They weren't meds but drugs to feed his addiction.

I ran Noah's last few statements over in my mind. "Inessa told you during the tour, when you met in Oslo?" I asked. "That was last summer." It was about the time I'd seen Lucille and him on the television, right after I'd

11

learned of my character's demise. My thoughts continued to spiral. My demise—that of Lord Divisto...was it the Firm? Had they known they needed me? Were Noah's days already numbered? "So, she's what...four or five months?"

"I don't know. Do the math. I'm done talking."

"Fuck that. Your bath is done. I'll command the nurses to drop the temperature in your cell. How long do you think it would be until you suffered from exposure?"

Noah shook his head. "That's not you talking. You wouldn't do that. Theodore—yes. You, no. For some reason you give a shit and torturing me isn't on your agenda."

"Neither is having a child with a woman I've never met."

He inhaled. "In Oslo, I told her my marriage was over. I promised more than working with Alek—I proposed marriage."

My stomach dropped as I reached for the end of the bed's frame. My knuckles on my left hand blanched as the weight of his promise fell heavily on my shoulders. "That's why she was upset that I—you—never contacted her. But I didn't know. How was I supposed to know?"

"I left clues." He shrugged. "I was pissed about the whole thing. If I'd been king..."

"You will never be king."

"Did you say she was at Forthwith?" His lips

pressed together. "Shit, I didn't know that. I haven't seen her since Oslo."

I recalled something King Theodore had said. "Where were you? You were gone for months between when you were supposed to die and when you came back to Forthwith. Where were you?"

"I told you, I went back to Norway, to my life."

"And you saw your tombstone?"

"Yeah."

"Someone had to help you."

"I was on my own. That's my story. Hell, I'm going to die anyway. I'm not taking anyone who doesn't deserve it down with me." He quirked his lips. "Those who do, hell yeah."

I scanned his naked body and the thinness of his wrist attached to the bed. His hair was wet from being washed, and he was still in need of a shave. "Forgive me if I'm not concerned about your threats."

"I'm not the one you need to worry about."

As the knowledge of Inessa's pregnancy churned my stomach, I centered my energy on the thoughts of one person.

Lucille.

I needed to tell her what was happening.

Turning, I inserted my key and unlocked the door. One last look over my shoulder and I said, "You're wrong."

"*About?*"

"*Too many things to discuss. You're wrong about me. Your care is done for now.*" With that, I opened the door and once back in the corridor, I locked the cell. The view through the window dimmed.

"*Your Highness,*" one of the medical staff said.

"*Are these rooms individually temperature controlled?*"

The man nodded. "*This wing is old. Basically, there is cold and almost warm.*"

"*Don't waste heat on this patient. Forget my earlier orders; he remains chained. And leave him as he is. No one enters for any reason until I return.*"

"*He's only been given one meal, earlier today.*"

I looked through the glass. "*If he isn't exactly as I left him, there will be consequences.*"

The man wearing scrubs bowed his head. "*Yes, Your Highness.*"

"Roman, sit," King Theodore demanded, pulling me to the present.

Releasing a gust of air, I lowered myself onto one of the chairs placed before the king's desk. "Noah proposed...to her."

King Theodore inhaled and leaned back against his chair. "When?"

"In Oslo." My response slowed as the earlier adrenaline waned. "It happened during the Eurasia tour. The princess told him she was pregnant."

"You'll need to break it off with her."

A new burst of energy. "I don't fucking know her." Exasperation seeped from my declaration. "Noah said he hasn't seen her since Oslo."

King Theodore exhaled, his nostrils flaring and his eyes momentarily closing. "If he's being truthful, that lessens a bit of the complication."

"Everything seems pretty damn complicated."

"Think about it, son. The girl hasn't seen you since Oslo. She'll have no reason to doubt it's you."

"We've never met."

"She must never know that." King Theo's dark eyes focused on only me. "This is a delicate situation. I'm asking you to do what's right for Molave and for the Godfrey monarchy."

I ran my left hand through my hair.

Doing so was a nervous habit I'd worked to eradicate as it wasn't something Roman had done in videos. When playing a role, I had the ability to fully take it on. Since, apparently, one hand in a cast didn't cure me of this habit, I could only surmise that at some point playing a role and living my own new life had merged.

My gaze met the king's. "I don't know what's right anymore."

"You do. You feel it." He lifted his fist to his chest.

"Here. Tell me you don't." Before I could speak, he went on, "Lucille is also pregnant."

I nodded. "We wanted to tell you together."

"News has a way of finding me—I won't rob her of the pleasure of sharing the news. The two of you may tell Anne and me at dinner tonight. Anne will be overjoyed." He stood, walked past the large bookcase filling one wall from floor to ceiling, and came to a stop at the ornate polished highboy. Lifting a decanter, he poured two fingers into a crystal tumbler. "I'm elated the procedure worked," he said before taking a hearty drink.

The small hairs on the back of my neck stood like lightning rods.

What if neither of the two pregnancies are truly Godfrey heirs?

"It seems so," I mumbled.

The king lifted another tumbler. "I'll pour you a glass. Celebration is in order."

"It isn't even noon."

"Good scotch knows no restriction of time."

The king walked toward me with the second crystal tumbler in his hand. As he extended his hand, I noticed the way the liquid quivered within the glass.

Is he trembling?

Taking the glass, I asked, "Are you well?"

King Theodore filled his chest with air. Instead of

answering my question, he held his glass toward the window. "Single malt, the best." He lifted his glass toward me. "To the continuation of the Godfrey monarchy."

Our glasses touched, the clink of crystal echoing within the office.

My sip wasn't as hearty as the king's. While I was a connoisseur of bourbon and whisky, scotch was never my thing. The bitter fluid burned my throat. Yet the numbing sensation was welcome in my right hand. I attempted to flex my fingers in the splint.

"Your Majesty," I said, weighing my words. "Noah isn't Roman."

"No. Of course he isn't. You are."

"Inessa's pregnancy is from Noah. I say I deny that it's mine. Once the child is born, we demand a DNA test. That test will prove my innocence to the world."

He shook his head. "King Aleksander II will be furious."

"He'll be furious when he learns of her whereabouts."

"Yes, and he'll be even more furious believing the child is a Godfrey." The king took another drink, seemingly contemplating his response. "No, there won't be a public declaration. We have no reason to make the girl out to be a liar. It won't matter. That child will not be allowed to return to Borinkia. I'll forbid it."

"You can't keep the King of Borinkia's sister in Molave indefinitely."

"Of course not. The girl can leave."

None of this was making sense. I recalled his earlier claim. "You said you have Inessa. Where is she?"

"Here, son. She's being kept in the palace."

My stomach twisted. "The rumors are true. We've kidnapped her."

King Theodore returned to his chair. "It's not like that. She just recently arrived. We were honest at the Fifteen Eurasia Summit."

"Where did you find her?"

"The positive pregnancy test was found at Forthwith. She was found at Annabella."

Annabella.

"What?" I panicked. The princess was at Lucille's and my home. "Sir, I confided to you that Isabella asked Lucille if she and the children could go to Annabella. She said she was frightened."

He nodded. "I'm glad you did. As for your sister, the ministry guards are bringing her and her children to Molave today. I told them not to disturb the children's sleep."

"Isabella was hiding Inessa at Annabella?" I asked, hardly believing my own assessment.

"It is how it appears. Of course, your sister will have an opportunity to explain."

I shook my head. "Why would there be a pregnancy test at Forthwith? Inessa informed Noah she was pregnant months ago."

King Theo leaned back in his chair. "You're right."

I let out a breath. "It was Lucille's. She took a test at Forthwith."

The king hummed. "That doesn't need to be shared with the ministry. If memory serves me, Anne preferred to keep the news to herself until later."

"I agree."

CHAPTER
3

Lucille

"She's showing," Queen Anne said.

My eyes closed. I didn't need the picture to know that the princess was pregnant. I'd recalled that in my dream last night. I'd been too focused on her presence; her physical appearance hadn't registered until later. I looked up at the queen. "I know it doesn't make sense, but it isn't my husband's child."

"That child she's carrying is a Godfrey."

I stood. "I'm sorry, ma'am, but it's not. I can't explain—"

Queen Anne shook her head. "We need to face facts. Your child will of course be heir, but the other one is a Godfrey. You must understand, we cannot allow a Godfrey to be raised in Borinkia. If she were from somewhere else...but she isn't."

"What are you saying?"

"I'm saying that it's best for the Crown if Inessa is

kept in Molave until the child is born. At that time, the princess may return to Borinkia if she wishes."

"She is here?"

The queen nodded.

"In the palace?"

Another nod.

"What do you mean that she can return to Borinkia if she wishes? What about her child?" I asked.

"If the child is a male, he will be raised in Molave."

I couldn't fathom what the queen was saying. "You can't take her child."

"We can, my dear. The Firm will find a good and respectable home with parents who can be trusted."

"No." I shook my head. "I don't know the princess, but what you're suggesting is horrible."

Queen Anne inhaled and straightened her posture. "Lucille, please sit. We have much to discuss."

It took all my willpower to do as she said. The mere thought of someone taking my child was beyond my comprehension. I couldn't and wouldn't play a part in the same thing happening to another person, even if she was a person I had every reason to dislike. Perching myself on the edge of the sofa and moving my crossed ankles beneath the seat, I laid my hands in my lap and looked Queen Anne in the eye. "Please explain."

She pressed her lips together for a moment before lifting her chin. "I had hoped this would never be a conversation we needed to have. I'd hoped that by the time you'd been married for five years we would have at least two children from you. I understand your plight better than most. I was in the same position."

I nodded.

Queen Anne was in the position that one day would be mine. I laid my hand on hers. "You've had three children."

Tears came to her eyes, the liquid emotion teetering on her lower lid. "Losing Teddy was absolutely the most devastating time of our lives. It was a tragedy that no one should have to endure. I was inconsolable."

Taking my hand back, I nodded. "I'm so sorry."

"Yes, everyone was and is. What kept me going and the reason I couldn't stop living... I was pregnant with Roman. I hadn't announced it, not even to Theo." A smile curled her lips. "I knew. Roman was my secret—until I couldn't keep him a secret any longer."

My cheeks rose as I smiled. "I didn't realize the timing."

A knock tore our attention away from one another as Lady Kornhall entered, curtsied, and carried a tray toward us. Along with a china pitcher displaying the royal crest and matching cups and saucers, there was also a plate of scones. Our conversation remained on hold, silence resting thick as a fog, as Lady Kornhall added hot tea to each cup before offering the cups and saucers to first the queen and then me.

"Thank you," Queen Anne said, "That will be all for now."

Another curtsy and soon we were again alone.

I placed my cup and saucer on the table. "I'm sure King Theo was overjoyed—about Roman."

After a sip, Queen Anne set her cup and saucer beside mine. "What I said at dinner the other night is accurate. All marriages have difficult patches. Losing Teddy created one such difficult time. I could have chosen to resent my husband for the things he did. And he could have decided to resent me for the way I behaved. Being the king or queen does not make one infallible. We both made mistakes."

"I'm not certain why you're telling me this," I admitted. "Roman and I are committed to our marriage. Our roughest patch is behind us."

"Oh, my dear, we don't know what tomorrow holds in store. I pray you're right, but if you're not and there are rough times ahead, the only way to make it work is by being partners in every way."

"And keeping my husband's mistress in Molave until she gives birth will help—how?"

Queen Anne shook her head. "The woman isn't the issue. Never give too much thought to her. The child is the focus."

"I don't understand."

"Did you inform your parents of your condition before they left?"

I nodded. "I'm sorry we didn't tell you and King Theo first..."

Queen Anne lifted her hand. "That isn't important. What is important is that after your first trimester, the Firm will announce the wonderful news to the citizens of Molave and the world. Everyone will know that the Godfrey family is strong and growing."

Exhaling, I reached for my tea and peered down into the cup, hoping to find the words to explain that my Roman didn't father Inessa's child. When my gaze again met the queen's, I sighed. "Roman isn't the father of the Borinkian princess's child."

"That will be confirmed after the child is born."

"We can't hold her, keep her from her family. And we can't take her child from her. That child did nothing wrong."

The queen stood with a smile. "That's the same thing I told myself. It was what helped me get through the dark days and nights. The child was innocent." She took a deep breath. "You and Roman will have a child in the next year. Either yours" —she nodded toward my midsection— "or the one who will be born in our care. To the world, the child will be yours."

After setting down my tea, I stood. "I will raise my

child. Mr. Davies said everything is progressing normally. I'm not setting up a contingency plan for a failed pregnancy."

"No one wants disaster. Think of the princess's child as insurance, for sooner or later."

"I'm sorry, ma'am, I can't do that. I can't go along with replacing one person with another."

"You already have."

Her words hit like a punch. My circulation dropped to my feet as I staggered and reached for the back of a chair. "Your Majesty?"

Queen Anne came closer and reached for my hand. "Lucille, you're pale. My goal isn't to upset you but to help you see that things happen for a reason. Inessa has confessed that she and Roman had a sexual relationship."

"Who did she tell?"

"She told me."

"You spoke with her?"

Queen Anne nodded. "I needed to see her for myself, to talk to her. She's younger than I realized. As you can imagine, she's frightened."

I thought of the secret door in the queen's parlor and the cells beneath the infirmary. "Where is she?"

"She's secured here in the palace. Her needs will be met."

"I can't go along with this."

"My dear, we aren't asking your permission."

Closing my eyes, I sighed.

Queen Anne spoke, "Theo likes to protect me. He worries. I suppose there was a time I gave him cause. As I said earlier, I'm much more aware of the happenings in my home and country than I appear."

Roman.

She knows about Roman.

Yet even if my instinct was correct, I couldn't articulate the questions running through my head, not without confessing that I too knew my Roman wasn't the man I married.

Instead, I questioned, "Does the king know that you know the Borinkian princess is here?"

Queen Anne nodded with a smile. "Some things must be shared. That said, this subject will never be dinner conversation. You must not tell anyone that you know of her presence. I told you for one reason—the child."

"I have to tell Roman," I said.

"Only if it becomes necessary, then you'll both need to embrace what has been presented to you."

"Another woman's child."

"Your husband's child." She again reached for my hand. "Lucille, you're a beautiful woman, inside and out. You have shown your compassion for the people of Molave, a country that you accepted as your own. I have no doubt that you have the capacity to love unconditionally. Whether an infant is placed in your arms or one day, a child or even an adult calls you mum, you won't turn that soul away. You will love because loving is what we as mothers must do. It's innate and our capacity is infinite. It's programmed into us."

Not in every instance.

"There are people who have failed," I said. "Children who are left hurt and abandoned."

"Would you do that?"

I swallowed the tears as I shook my head. "No, I couldn't."

Queen Anne lifted her cool hands to my cheeks. "This is why Roman loves you. Theo and I do too. Never turn that love away."

Tears escaped my eyes.

The queen wiped them with her thumbs. "I'm glad you understand."

My eyes opened to her caring expression. "I don't," I replied honestly. "I'm trying."

"Give yourself time."

CHAPTER 4

Roman

I met Lord Martin outside the king's offices. He spoke low as we hurried toward my office apartments, passing by people I recognized and others I didn't. My mind wasn't on their faces or protocol as they bowed in my presence.

"Your Highness," Lord Martin said, "your appointments are waiting."

My appointments.

It felt as if the entire world was imploding—a catastrophic, cataclysmic annihilation—and I had meetings waiting. Meetings to discuss the assignment of representatives from each province to my new council on interior affairs. Then there was the appointment with the engineers who had dismantled the drone from Forthwith. Mrs. Drake left over ten text messages about wanting to speak to me, and she wasn't yet on my schedule. That list didn't include the impending mess with Isabella or the other seven to ten appointments.

I hadn't been untruthful when I said kidnapping the Borinkian princess didn't fit into my schedule. It didn't. Neither did going to speak with her in the far wing of Molave Palace, although that was the mandate King Theo had given me.

"I'm already late," I said, glancing at my watch as we entered the grand foyer. My attention went to the large staircase. "I'm going to speak to Lucille. I'll be back as soon as possible."

"Sir, they're waiting for you."

"And they can continue to wait. Tell Dame Williamson that my audience with the king lasted longer than expected. She can deal with the appointments."

"Yes, I'll let her know you apologize for the inconvenience."

I stopped walking and turned to my assistant, creating an obstacle as people walked around us. My response was more of a growl. "Do not put words in my mouth. I'm not sorry. I'm the prince, and I will see to those people when I'm ready. That you may relay. Their inconvenience isn't my concern."

Lord Martin bowed his neck. "Yes, Your Highness."

With an abrupt turn and a nod to the guard at the bottom of the stairs, I headed up the staircase to the second floor. In a few moments, I was in the corridor leading to the princess's and my apartments. Turning the handle to our connected parlor, I recalled Lady Buckingham saying Lucille had been with the queen. I hadn't checked to see if she was back.

Opening the door, I stopped as Lady Buckingham came from Lucille's apartment, her eyes meeting mine as she dipped into a curtsy.

"Is the princess present?"

"Yes, Your Highness. She's resting."

"Resting?" My pulse quickened. "Is she not well?" I opened my eyes wider, all other concerns evaporating as my thoughts focused on Lucille. "Is it the baby?"

Lucille's mistress smiled with a shake of her head. "No, sir. She's simply tired. It is to be expected in her condition. I was about to call for her lunch."

"Call for mine as well."

Lady Buckingham nodded. "Yes, Your Highness."

I removed my phone from the inner pocket of my suitcoat and sent Dame Williamson a text message. I was getting better with using my left hand; however, I was ready to lose the cast and splint.

"I WILL RETURN AT 1 P.M. RESCHEDULE MY APPOINTMENTS FOR THEN."

Was I sorry for the inconvenience?

No, not at all.

After placing my phone back into my pocket, it vibrated with a response. In another life I would have checked to see if my wishes would be granted. That was another time. As prince, I made the rules. My word was law with everyone except the king.

I opened the door and entered Lucille's parlor, expecting to find her on her sofa or lounge chair. The fire in the hearth crackled behind the screen, but the room was empty. Without hesitation, I continued down the hallway toward her bedchamber. Pushing the door open, I met the gaze of the beautiful woman sitting on a soft chair before another fireplace. A blanket was over her legs, and a book was in her lap.

"Roman?"

She closed the book.

I didn't stop until I was at her side, and I brushed her lips with mine. Staring into her blue orbs, I grinned. "Princess."

Crouching on my haunches, I covered her hand with mine. "When Lady Buckingham said you were resting, I began to panic."

Her smile faded. "Why?"

"I was afraid something had happened...with you" —I moved my hand to her lower stomach— "with the baby. Did you see Mr. Davies?"

"I did," she said, covering my hand with hers. "He said everything is good—perfect. He did an ultrasound, and I saw the baby's heart beat."

"You saw an ultrasound?" I didn't mean for my disappointment to be audible, but it was.

Lucille tilted her face. "Oh, my prince, I thought of waiting until you were there, but I know how busy you are."

"I'll be present for the next one and each one after. I don't care who I'm scheduled to see. You and our baby come first."

Her smile returned, growing larger. "I'm just under four weeks."

"Okay."

"The procedure was three weeks ago."

Rising from my crouch, I sat on the edge of her ottoman. "The baby is mine?"

Lucille nodded. "I think so. I want it to be so. I'm also scared."

"Don't be scared. No one will know."

Her chin fell. "I have so much to tell you."

"I too have much to tell you. I also have a horrendous schedule of meetings. I knew I wouldn't be able to concentrate on them until I spoke to you." The book in her lap caught my attention. "What is that?"

Lucille smiled. *The Girlfriends' Guide to Pregnancy.* Mary gave it to me, right after we learned I was expecting."

"Didn't you tell me you learned of the pregnancy at Forthwith?"

She lifted the book to her chest. "Yes, Mary said she'd kept the book with her for years, waiting for the right time. That makes it even more special."

I let out a long breath. "The ministry guards found a positive pregnancy test at Forthwith."

"Oh." Her blue eyes opened wider. "It was mine."

"They thought it belonged to someone else."

"Who?"

"Inessa Volkov."

Lucille inhaled, her neck straightening. "She's pregnant, but much further along. She wouldn't need a test. You can tell by looking at her."

"You know?" I asked.

The princess nodded as her smile disappeared. "Queen Anne told me."

"She knows?"

"I think she knows much more than we thought. She said she spoke to her—the princess."

Shaking my head, I stood and walked back and forth before the fire. "Papa isn't aware that Mum knows."

Lucille lifted her hand, beckoning me closer. "Roman, Queen Anne knows about you. She basically told me. If I would have let on that I knew what she was saying, she would know I know."

"Mrs. Drake said Mum knows. The chief minister said it dismissively, as if I would already know that."

"Everyone is lying to one another."

I again sat on the ottoman and placed my hands on Lucille's blanket-covered knees. "I've never lied to you."

"The princess is here," she said, "in the palace."

I nodded.

"Who told you?"

"The king. He wants me to talk to her." I sighed. "Noah admitted he proposed to her in Oslo, during your tour. She told him then that she was pregnant. Now it makes sense why Francis said she was upset that I hadn't contacted her."

"Queen Anne said the baby is a Godfrey, but if she knows about you, she would have known about Noah. She would understand that the child isn't yours and isn't a Godfrey."

"Tonight at dinner we will announce the baby."

"Queen Anne knows."

"The king does as well."

Lucille scoffed. "That doesn't sound like much of an announcement."

"Papa wants you to think we're telling them for the first time. I promise, he's happy."

"Roman, they want to keep Inessa's child, a backup if something were to happen to ours."

"That's ludicrous."

Lucille squeezed my hand. "I've never spoken to

her. It goes without saying that I don't like her. She tried to ruin my marriage." Moisture glistened in her blue orbs. "But I can't be a part of taking someone's child." She shook her head. "I won't. You need to help her escape."

"Fuck, Lucille. This is so fucked up."

A grin lightened her expression. "Yes, Your Highness. I believe that's an accurate assessment. I won't take another woman's child from her, not unless it's what she wants. You need to talk to her and learn her thoughts. Regardless of what I think of her, she is that child's mother."

Once again on my feet, I spun in place. "I wish the Firm had found me sooner." When I turned, Lucille was looking up at me. "If I were here earlier," I tried to explain, "maybe some of the mess Noah made would never have happened."

"I don't know why they found you when they did. We can't turn back time. Instead, together, we can try to right the wrongs. Think about it. How unlikely of a pair we are. And still you've given me the love and trust I always sought. You're giving Papa the heir he's proud of and Queen Anne a son to cherish. If you had arrived earlier, maybe things wouldn't have worked the same. The important thing is that you're here now."

A knock came to the door.

"Enter," I called.

"Your Highnesses," Lady Buckingham said with a curtsy. "Your midday meal is in the parlor."

My focus went to Lucille. "Would you rather eat in here?"

Her smile blossomed. "I get to eat with you. I'd do that anywhere."

Offering her my hand, Lucille stood and laid the blanket back on the chair. She was dressed in the same skirt and blouse from this morning.

As I peered toward the floor, I saw that she was wearing stockings, but no shoes, making me grin. "Always without shoes."

"I can put the heels back on," she offered.

"Are you cold?"

"No."

"Then there's no need to be uncomfortable." I bent my arm.

Her small hand came to my elbow. "Your Highness."

"Come, Princess. I want a few more minutes with my wife."

She turned and looked up at me. "Your wife."

"I like the way it sounds."

"I do too, Your Highness."

CHAPTER 5

Roman

Minister of the Interior, Lord Rowlings, was the only person waiting when I made it to my offices. He and the secretaries stood as I entered a minute or two before my promised time.

"Your Highness," Dame Williamson said with a neck bow.

"My other appointments?" I asked, looking around.

She smiled. "I have numbers, and I will text."

I lifted my eyebrows with a nod. "I like that."

"I thought it was better than a room filled with impatient people."

"It's a good policy. It's time we modernize a few things."

"I have a few other ideas," she said.

"Bring them to me when I'm free. Be sure to send yourself a text."

"I will, Your Highness."

"Give me thirty minutes with Lord Rowlings, and you may text my next appointment."

Dame Williamson nodded.

I turned to Lord Rowlings. "Join me."

"Your Highness."

Soon we were alone in my office.

The plan to create the commission I'd initiated was in progress. The first round of representatives would be appointed by the Crown. Lord Rowlings had his list of suggested candidates from each province.

"The people are excited about this direct means of communication with the Crown."

I looked over the list, my finger moving from one to the next. I looked up. "The names are all males."

"Yes, sir."

"Why?"

Lord Rowlings's forehead furrowed. "I don't understand your question."

"The list only contains men's names," I said, standing. "Why haven't you proposed women?"

Lord Rowlings got to his feet. "Well..." He looked down at the list before him and shuffled a few papers.

"Our chief minister is a woman." I said. "I'm confident the men you've chosen are respectable citizens, but I want this initiative to better represent the people of Molave, men and women."

"Sir, I've personally contacted these men. They

have all agreed to represent their respective provinces. I can't uninvite them."

"You can." I pointed at the list. "You weren't supposed to contact anyone until I approved your selections. Now, inform fifty percent of these gentlemen that the Crown is thankful for their willingness to serve. We will keep them in mind for future endeavors. And return to me by next week with a list representing our citizens. I want a breakdown on demographics: age, gender, occupation..."

"If I may?"

"Say what you must," I said.

"The men on this list are friendly to the Crown. They'll work to inform their neighbors of any plans we have without question."

"Then start from scratch. I want an entirely new list."

"As you're aware, there are citizens who are less than supportive of the monarchy."

I nodded. "I am. Those people deserve to be represented. The point of this commission is to provide an avenue allowing those with concerns to be heard. Appointing a list of yes-men will only accomplish a façade. Nothing will change."

"The king—"

I lifted my hand. "I'm the prince. This commission

is my idea. Bring me a new list next week." I lifted the papers from my desk. "I will keep these."

Lord Rowlings squared his shoulders. "Your Highness, I apologize for contacting the gentlemen, but my intention was honorable. I wanted to bring you a list with people eager to work with you. Now, if I inform them that they won't...well, it could be taken badly. A poor reflection on this commission."

Feigning a grin, I lowered my tone. "You yourself said these gentlemen are friendly to the Crown. I'm sure they'll take the news well. Bring me what I asked for or I'll find someone else to do it." I looked down at my watch. "You, sir, are dismissed."

"Your Highness," he said with a neck bow.

I'd barely had time to add the interior minister's list to a folder before Dame Williamson knocked and announced my next set of visitors, Mr. Meade and Mrs. Dawson. The two engineers had impressive resumes, both citizens of Molave and graduates of MIT. Mr. Meade returned to Molave four years ago and was approached by the Firm to work for the Crown. A slight man, he was personally responsible for many of the recent advancements and personally reached out to Mrs. Dawson to work with him.

They both greeted me with a neck bow. "Your Highness."

I motioned to the conference table. "Please take a seat. I'm anxious to hear what you've learned."

The two looked at each other as they pulled out two chairs beside one another.

Taking the seat at the head of the table, I pushed forward. "You have learned something?"

Mrs. Dawson spoke first. "The drone was not armed, but it had the capacity."

"The drone could have done what?"

She continued, "There are instances of drones dropping hand grenades, mortar shell, or other improvised explosives. This one wasn't carrying such things. It did send an aerial view of what it could observe."

"Could you access the footage?"

"No, sir. There wasn't recording. The footage would have immediately been broadcast to the person or persons in control of the drone. Unfortunately, the transponder was too damaged to determine where it was being sent."

I shook my head. "What else?"

Mr. Meade responded. "The drone itself contained parts from various origins. The casing has characteristics unique to Israel." He paused. "While the serial numbers were ground off, the GPS system is definitely from the US."

"The United States?" I repeated questioningly.

"Yes, sir," Mrs. Dawson replied, "as were the GPS

transponders found in the wheel wells of multiple cars in the royal fleet."

"Are you suggesting the drone was being used by Americans?"

The two looked at one another. "We're still trying to determine where the signals were being sent. The transponders that were used have a limited range. Even the nearest US base would be too far away."

"What is within the range?" I asked.

"Within Molave," Mr. Meade said. "And parts of Norway and Borinkia."

"Sir," Mrs. Dawson said, "with the death of King Aleksander I, Borinkia's borders are closed. However, the drone incident was before his death. Norway and Molave have open borders. The operator may have been within one of the countries but not loyal to either."

"You're telling me we don't know," I said.

"We know that there's been noise buried deep on the internet of stolen arms shipments. Military supplies as well as artillery. If someone didn't want the origin of the drone known, utilizing stolen parts to make an unidentifiable drone would fit that bill. Israel has reported loss of equipment."

"So have many other governments including Molave's military," Mr. Meade added. "Without the serial numbers, we can't confirm that the parts were stolen."

What we were discussing was way out of my realm of knowledge and too important not to fully understand. "You don't have enough for the Crown to make an accusation." It wasn't a question.

They both exchanged looks. Mrs. Dawson spoke. "At this time, no, sir. We're learning more from the transponders than the drone. And we're still working on them. We would like to set up a mission."

"What kind of mission?"

Mr. Meade answered, "With your permission, we will work with the operational head of the military, General Dickerson, to set up a decoy. If the Crown would announce plans of your continued tour with the princess, we will be sure to utilize cars with the transponders still attached and watch for another drone. We may also be able to track the transmission from the transponder back to whoever is watching them."

"The princess and I have decided to postpone our tour."

Mrs. Dawson sighed. "We hadn't heard."

"I'm not sure it's been announced."

"One more stop, sir," she said. "Now that we know what we're dealing with, we could intercept the transmissions and hopefully learn more than we now know."

"I won't approve the princess being used as bait."

"Sir, the cars are safe."

I laid my left hand flat on the shiny table. "I'll do it —alone."

CHAPTER
6

Lucille

"Ma'am, I'll accompany you to the dining room," Lady Buckingham offered.

Pivoting, I looked up to the mantel, spying the hands and reading the time on the antique clock. "I don't know where Roman is."

"Perhaps the prince was held up with work. I heard his schedule was quite full."

Raking my lip with my teeth, I turned toward the door, the one that led out of our apartments in Molave Palace, willing the door to open. I looked up at my mistress. "We're supposed to tell the king and queen about the baby tonight. I don't want to do that without him." Tilting my head, I asked, "You haven't heard that he's left the palace, have you?"

"No," she replied with a shake of her head. Her hazel gaze again went to the mantel clock. "The king and queen..."

Nodding, I acquiesced. The monarchs would soon arrive to the dining room. Protocol said all others attending dinner should arrive before them. Even ordinary evening meals were laced with protocol. Part of me longed to be back to Annabella, the other part was satisfied with the safety and security that came from being within the walls of Molave Palace.

As I had throughout the day, a brief thought regarding the new guest within the palace walls came to mind.

Is Roman with Inessa?

Is that why he's late?

Inhaling, I straightened my spine. "Yes, we shouldn't be late."

Only a few months ago, most of my journeys to the dining room were made alone, whether here in Molave City or back at Annabella Castle. Rarely did Roman retrieve me and if he did, our walk throughout the corridors and down the grand staircase was tense. As Lady Buckingham and I made our way down the same hallways, I recalled what it was like, that sensation of walking a tightrope. One wrong move and I'd unleash the wrath of my husband, tumbling from the air to the net below.

A quick turn of my head and I met Mary Buckingham's gaze. "Thank you."

"Ma'am?"

I reached for her arm. "I simply want you to know that you're appreciated. When things were difficult between Roman and me, you were always there—with whatever I needed." My grasp tightened. "You truly are my lifeline."

Lady Buckingham bowed her chin as we continued to walk. "Thank you, Your Highness. I'll always be here for you."

"And for our child," I said softer so as to not be overheard.

At the bottom of the staircase, past the guards, I looked around the grand foyer and toward the direction of Roman's offices. While people milled about, there was no sign of my husband. Lifting my chin, I nodded to my mistress, and we continued toward the private dining room.

It was as we drew closer that I realized the people farther down the hallway were Princess Isabella with her nanny, Lady Sherry, and the young prince and princess. While the children were holding onto the women's legs, Isabella was in a hushed discussion with Lady Sherry.

"Thank you for your escort," I said, dismissing Lady Buckingham. "After dinner, I will either walk to our apartments with Roman or alone. I'll let you know when I arrive."

"I'll be waiting."

As my gaze met my sister-in-law's, Lady Sherry reached for each child's hand and escorted them away from the dining room. Isabella stood taller, her jaw clenched and her gaze focused on me. In that moment, her dark stare reminded me more of Noah's than of my Roman's.

I scanned my sister-in-law. While she wasn't as disheveled as she'd been after Francis and Roman's accident, she was obviously distraught. Her long hair was secured in a low ponytail, and she was wearing a jumper and wool slacks. Her clothing suggested she hadn't changed since traveling to the palace.

"Isabella," I said, coming to a stop before her. "I didn't know you were in Molave City. Did you recently arrive?"

"As with my last trip, coming here wasn't of my doing."

"Did Roman again send for you?"

"No. It was Papa."

I tilted my head. "Maybe it's because you wanted to be here with Francis."

"You promised," she replied in a hushed voice.

"What did I promise?"

"Annabella. You said we could stay."

"You did—you may. Of what were you afraid?"

Within the dining room the clink of dishes and table settings alerted us that butlers and maids were busying about, making last-minute perfections for tonight's dinner. The long table, set for seven people, was currently unoccupied. Isabella reached for my arm, tugging me away from the doorway. Once we stopped, I pulled my arm from her grasp. "Isabella, tell me what happened."

"I told you that Forthwith was searched."

"Did they find something? You said on the phone you believed Francis was—"

"They wouldn't tell me anything," she interrupted. "I know they didn't find who they were looking for."

"Who?"

Inessa.

With a deep breath, I questioned, "Was there a problem at Annabella Castle?"

"You told, Lucille. Why did you tell Papa where we were?"

"I didn't." I exhaled. "I told Roman." Like pieces of a puzzle sliding into place, I saw a picture of what had occurred forming in my mind's eye. The guards had searched Forthwith for the Borinkian princess. They didn't find her. But now she's here in the palace. My eyes opened wide. "You took Inessa Volkov to Annabella?" My question came out too loud.

"Shh."

My tone took on a new venom I wasn't aware I could spew as I narrowed my eyes and spoke through clenched teeth. "You took my husband's mistress to our home. How could you do that?"

"I thought she'd be safe."

"And if King Aleksander II would have found her there—in our home—in *Roman's* home... What then? There would have been proof that Roman kidnapped the princess."

"Alek didn't know where she was. I don't know if he's been informed that she was found."

Shaking my head, I closed my eyes and exhaled. When I opened them, I met her dark gaze. "Tell me, what do you have to say for yourself?"

Isabella stood tall. "I say I was helping a friend."

"How long was she at Forthwith? Did Francis know she was in your home?" Did you know Noah was also there? I didn't voice the final question.

Crossing her arms over her breasts, Isabella paced back and forth like a caged animal. With each step, her heeled boots clicked on the marble flooring. "She came to me for help."

Inessa went to Isabella and Noah had gone to Francis. Either the duke and duchess were renowned for their generosity to people in need or something else was at play. Either way, I had no comment.

Isabella spoke slower. "I didn't know about her and Roman, but I do now...I know more."

"You know she's pregnant," I said, deadpan.

Isabella spun my direction. "How do you know that?"

"I told you; I saw her. Remember? You denied that she was at Forthwith."

Isabella shook her head. "I'm sorry. I've been torn." She again reached for my hand, her gaze meeting mine. "I wanted to be completely honest, but when I learned about the baby...Alek is furious."

"He knows?" My mouth dried with the question.

She shook her head. "Not about the baby. He knows about their relationship and that Roman made promises he hasn't kept. By the time Inessa started to show, she left Borinkia." Isabella shrugged. "I don't know where she was specifically before coming to Forthwith. But when Borinkia closed its borders, she got scared and came to me."

That was only a few days ago—after the announcement of the king's death. My lips came together with the revelation that Isabella was still lying. Inessa was at Forthwith before the borders were closed.

Voices reverberated through the old corridors as more people approached.

We both looked toward the dining room.

My words were but a whisper. "Out of everyone in the world, why would that woman come to you?"

"She feels alone, Lucille. Haven't you ever felt that way?"

I had. I had also been honest with Isabella, unlike what she was being with me.

Isabella continued, "And now the ministry guards —from Molave—took her. I'm scared for her." She spoke faster. "There are archaic laws about people illegally entering Molave."

"Molave has open borders."

"Not for citizens from sanctioned countries."

"You're saying you were hiding an exiled princess in my home?" Asking Isabella if she knew where the guards had taken the princess was on the tip of my tongue.

"I was helping a friend."

The sound of Roman's voice caused me to turn. From a distance, I saw that he was walking with King Theo and Queen Anne toward the dining room.

I straightened my shoulders. "Say nothing of this at dinner."

"You sound like Papa."

Placing my hand over my midsection, I shook my head. "The truth is that I'd rather not speak of her while eating. She's upsetting to me."

"I can't promise. That is the reason I sent the children with Lady Sherry. Papa knows they found Inessa at Annabella; we've spoken briefly. If Roman knows..." She sighed.

"If he knows...what do you fear?"

"He'll be livid." She gestured toward me. "You are.

Forgive me, but I didn't want the children to witness his rage."

My Roman wouldn't cause a scene at dinner. I knew that.

Would Noah?

Yes, he would.

I reached for Isabella's elbow. "We must hurry."

Together, we stepped into the dining room seconds before the king, queen, and Roman reached the doorway.

CHAPTER 7

Roman

"Your Majesties," Lucille and Isabella said in unison with curtsies as we entered the family dining room. The two ladies turned to me. "Your Highness."

My gaze lingered on Lucille's stare as a rosy hue filled her cheeks.

Before anyone could respond, Mum stepped forward, her eyes on Isabella. "Oh heavens," she said, opening her arms to her daughter. "Why wasn't I told you were back in Molave City?"

"One of many surprises," Papa replied as Queen Anne embraced Isabella.

"Where are the children?" the queen asked.

Isabella's focus was on Papa and me. "I thought it better if they dine upstairs with Lady Sherry."

"Well, I will be up after dinner to see them," Mum said as she took her seat. A butler was at the ready to help her with her chair.

I made my way around the table to sit to Papa's left

and Lucille's right. Once I was seated, Lucille reached under the table for my hand. I gave hers a squeeze as others continued their conversation about Isabella's children.

There was something in Lucille's blue stare that I tried to decipher. Leaning close, I whispered, "Have you changed your mind about the announcement?"

She shook her head.

"What's bothering you?"

"Later, Your Highness," she replied softly.

The woman beside me was resolute in her resolve. My mind swirled with possible reasons from her demeanor. I wondered if she and Isabella had exchanged words or if it was about the baby. Whatever it was, Lucille was radiant as our food was served.

The conversation from across the table began to register.

"No," Isabella answered Mum. "I haven't received permission to see him yet."

Him.

Francis.

Her dark stare pleaded to Papa.

"Tomorrow is another day," Papa said, dismissing the subject. "In the future, I want the children present for dinner."

"Forgive me, Papa," Isabella said. "The children

are still upset and tired from the recent activity." She feigned a smile. "Tomorrow is another day."

Upset.

Activity. She was talking about the search of Annabella, the one that followed the Forthwith search I authorized in conjunction with Mrs. Drake, the one that found Inessa Volkov.

That reality was the elephant in the room.

Isabella did her best to make it a topic of conversation; however, no one took the bait.

The meal progressed without another word about Francis and with no mention of Inessa. It was as if when in Queen Anne's presence, the concerns of life were veiled, leaving us to discuss mundane subjects with superficial thoughts.

As dessert was served along with a glass of sweet wine, Lucille again reached for my hand. Turning her way, I grinned and nodded. "Papa, Mum..." I met Isabella's stare. "Isabella. Lucille and I have an announcement."

"Do tell," Queen Anne said, her gaze fixed on both of us.

Lucille spoke. "Mr. Davies has confirmed what we hoped. I'm expecting a child."

Mum clapped.

Papa lifted his glass. "A toast." His stare met

Lucille's as a smile broke out across his face. "You may take a small sip, my dear. It won't hurt the baby."

Isabella was the last to lift her glass.

Papa's voice boomed through the dining room. "To Roman and Lucille and to the Godfrey name, may it forever reign."

Lucille's and my gaze met as we brought our glasses to our lips. From the corner of my eye, I noticed how a splash of the king's wine dribbled from his chin. When I turned, he had already lifted his napkin to his lips.

Isabella cleared her throat, garnering everyone's attention. "Congratulations. Surely you didn't know when I asked you."

Lucille sat taller. "I did. I hadn't yet informed Roman. I wasn't ready to share."

Isabella nodded. "I see. There are times when misrepresenting yourself is not considered lying."

Lucille met her stare. "I replied that I was forever hopeful. That wasn't a lie. I hadn't yet seen the royal physician."

"What is this about?" Papa asked.

Isabella turned to the head of the table. "Nothing. I'm just trying to figure out how half-truths differ depending upon who is speaking."

My skin prickled with the knowledge this conversation was upsetting Lucille. "If you have a point to make," I said, "by all means, speak."

"Thank you for your permission, Your Highness," Isabella responded mockingly.

My chair screeched across the floor as I abruptly stood. "Yes, sister. I am to be addressed as Your Highness...for now."

She glared my direction. "For now."

I looked to Papa and back. "One day, it will be Your Majesty."

Isabella shook her head and turned to the queen. "Forgive me, Mum. I'm rattled by recent happenings. I believe I will be going up to my apartments to be with the children. Will you be joining us?"

She was once again fishing for our sympathy. When it came to what she'd done, I found myself in short supply of it.

"Isabella," Papa said.

"Yes."

"After dinner, we have things to discuss in my office." His voice softened. "Anne, I'm sure Lady Sherry will welcome your visit with the children while our daughter is delayed."

Turning, I offered Lucille my hand. "I believe that means our dinner is done." I noticed the cookies on her plate. "Would you like those brought upstairs?"

She shook her head. "My stomach is a bit queasy."

"Oh, Lucille," Mum said, "Dry toast helped me while I was pregnant with Roman and Isabella. Ginger tea too. Have your mistress have both at the ready. Morning sickness is truly a misnomer. It can occur at any time of day or night."

"I was never ill," Isabella said. "Pregnancy agreed with me."

Ignoring Isabella's comment, Lucille stood and addressed the queen. "Thank you, ma'am. I'll alert Lady Buckingham."

"Roman," the king said, "you will join your sister and me."

Mum pushed back her chair. "Lucille, I believe that leaves the two of us. Shall we go upstairs?"

Isabella sat with her neck straight and her jaw clenched while Lucille and the queen exited and the king and I stood. Once we were alone, she looked from one to the other. "May we forgo the formality of your office, Papa, and resolve this matter here and now?"

"My office is not formal, child. My office is private." With that, he dropped his napkin at the bottom edge of his plate and turned toward the door. "Follow me."

I gestured to Isabella. "After you."

"Oh no, brother. Protocol puts me in last place. You made that perfectly clear again tonight."

We walked without speaking, a parade of royals

filing through the mostly empty hallways on our way to Papa's office. Once inside the front apartment, a single secretary stood, greeted us, and opened the door to the king's private office. Throughout the short journey, I recalled what I'd been told about Isabella and Papa's earlier meeting, the one upon her arrival.

She admitted to hiding the Borinkian princess at Forthwith and then moving her to Annabella. According to the king, Isabella showed little regret or misgiving at her decision to help a friend. Nothing was discussed about Borinkia or the death of King Aleksander I. Papa was saving that for when I could be present.

The reason I wasn't involved in the first meeting was that on top of a day overpacked with appointments and meetings, I made a return visit to the lower level of the infirmary.

As the key turned and I entered Noah's room, a potent, rancid stench filled my nostrils. The two medical workers had followed my orders, leaving him exactly as I left him: naked, no blankets, and still chained to the bed. I'd been away for at least six hours and during that time, the temperature of the room had plummeted—cold enough that even in my suit coat, I felt my skin prickle at the chill.

Shivering uncontrollably, Noah turned his dark eyes toward me, the circles of darkness growing more purple beneath each orb. *The sheet beneath him was wet and discolored from his urine. While this man had outweighed me months ago, he'd shrunk to an emaciated version of himself.*

"Fucking kill me," he said, his voice hoarse and his lips cracked.

"What's the fun in that?"

He closed his eyes.

"No, Noah. Look at me."

Inhaling, his lids slowly opened, and his voice remained low. "I wasn't in on a plan to kill Aleksander I."

"I believe you. You were in on the plan to kill King Theodore. What was the endgame?"

"Reign." *He looked down over his quivering nude body.*

Stepping closer, I lifted a blanket off the floor and laid it over him.

Noah's eyes closed as he hummed.

"Keep talking and I'll get you cleaned again and unchained."

"I did some research on the cherry pits."

I waited.

"Even though Theodore didn't die—which he deserves to do after what he did to Lord Avery and all the Romans before me—he hasn't escaped the damage. The first time I tried the poison was a few years ago. I watched him get sick and then after I quit, he was better." Noah shook his head. "But each time he loses a little more."

"Loses what?" I asked.

"He's slower, not as astute. Last thing I noticed were tremors. The poison has affected his brain. The tremors are from the damaged cells." He shrugged. "If I could have held out, I would be king today."

I too had noticed some trembling of the king's hands. "I don't know him well enough to see a decline."

"It's there." He grinned. "When he'd correct me or tell me how I fucked something up and his words came slower than normal, I would relish knowing I was the cause."

"And when you were king, what would you do?"

He smirked. "I told Francis I'd go along with his and Alek's plan. I'm not sure that was true. Hell, I could have burnt the entire monarchy to the ground. I just wanted..."

"You wanted what?" I asked.

"To be free of him, Lucille, all of it."

"Tell me about the baby," I said. "Inessa's."

He lifted the back of the bed and peered around the room. "There's a glass on the sink. Get me some water."

Turning, I saw the glass. "Is this water safe?" I asked as I filled the glass from the faucet.

"I fucking hope not," Noah replied moments before

I took the glass to his lips. When he drained the entire glass, he lifted his gaze to mine. "I sure as hell didn't mean to get her pregnant. Seems I put you in a shitty position."

I took the glass back to the sink. "Now help me get out of it."

"I think she's lying."

"Who?" I asked, crossing my arms over my chest.

"Inessa."

"No, she's not lying. She's pregnant. I was shown her picture after I confronted Papa about it."

"I don't think it's mine."

"You admitted to having sex."

"Yeah, I fucked Lucille too and no kid. The steroids lowered my sperm count. If Lucille couldn't get pregnant, how did Inessa?"

"How did you get away with the steroids without Mr. Davies knowing?"

Noah chuckled. "Idiot. He asked for samples. I gave him Lord Avery's samples, not mine."

"When Inessa told you she was pregnant, did you question her as to the paternity?"

"No." He shook his head. "I was miserable. That tour was fucking awful. The kid seemed like a possible escape. I've had time to think since then."

"Any idea whose kid it could be?"

"She's a handsome woman in her own way.

Wealthy, from a powerful family. I would suppose she could fuck anyone she wanted."

Noah's stomach made a loud, gurgling sound.

"Why would Inessa ask Isabella for help?"

Noah's eyes opened wide as his forehead furrowed. "She wouldn't. She doesn't like Isabella."

I took a step forward from where I'd been resting against the wall. "Isabella said they have been friends for years."

"That's a lie. Isabella hated her too. Hated Alek also. From the way Francis talked, she was jealous. Hell, she'd get pissed when Francis spent time with either of the Volkovs. He used me as cover more than once. If Inessa went to someone at Forthwith for help, it would have been Francis."

"Anything more you can tell me?"

"Keep your promises: clean bed, clothes, food." He rattled the chains. "Get rid of these, and I'll give it some thought."

Isabella and I took the seats across the grand desk from Papa. As my gaze met that of the king's, we silently confirmed what we'd discussed right before dinner. Someone was lying, and as upsetting as it was that it could be Isabella, we needed answers.

CHAPTER
8

Lucille

Once Queen Anne and I were on the grand staircase, I spoke softly, "May I ask about the Borinkian princess?"

"It isn't good for you to concentrate on her. Think about your child."

"It goes without saying that I am. I'd like to speak with her." Perhaps if I obtained the queen's permission, Roman wouldn't see my behavior the same way he saw my trip to the infirmary. It wasn't that I hated Roman's punishment, but rather as princess I had rights I could exercise.

Queen Anne pursed her lips.

I continued at a little over a whisper. "I know you can't put yourself in my place, but I have this need to understand what she did and why."

"My son is a handsome man." The queen lifted her cheeks in a smile as we reached the top of the staircase and stopped walking. She gazed up at the portraits lining the tall walls. "So much like his father at his age. Why wouldn't the princess be attracted?"

Being as we were alone in the corridor, I spoke louder. "Because he's married."

Queen Anne nodded as her eyes met mine. "Lucille, you're understandably naïve. Your good nature isn't shared by all women or men. Monogamy is an ideal created by men for women, not the other way around. That standard has been enforced by the church, another entity where historically men prevail. I dare surmise that you were questioned regarding your intimate history after Roman proposed."

Swallowing, I nodded.

"Do you think Roman was asked the same?"

"I've often wondered."

"If my experience taught me anything, it was that Roman wasn't questioned. I went through the same thing when Theodore asked me to marry him."

My chest ached with the revelation. "We share so much."

Queen Anne nodded. "We do."

"Why haven't we ever spoken about this?"

"Because, my dear, there is a season for everything. I dare say you weren't ready for these conversations before. You are now. I see your resolve and your resilience. You will survive whatever the future brings because you've chosen to survive. That girl isn't your future or your past. What she and Roman shared means nothing more than the procreation of a Godfrey."

"I still feel as though I should talk with her," I said.

"She won't have sufficient answers, Lucille. Trust me. You want to blame her and not Roman. That's natural. She does share responsibility. He does also."

Inhaling, I nodded. "My mother said the same thing." It was difficult to explain the truth to either woman. Even I sometimes found it hard to separate the Romans in my life. I guess I wanted to ask the princess about the Roman who hurt me.

Was he kind to her?

Why her and not me?

Is this wrong to fixate on those feelings when my Roman wasn't the man who cheated on or abused me?

Queen Anne continued. "Times have changed in the world, even if the Molavian monarchy hasn't kept up. The young princess is simply a product of the times. In some ways, I feel it would be liberating to live as she has."

"To sleep with a married man?" I asked, unsure how I was feeling about the way our conversation was progressing.

"To feel free to explore one's desires unimpeded by tradition or expectations."

"Would you?"

"Heavens, no," Queen Anne said with a shake of her head. "One need not partake in the dessert to appreciate the appetite."

I wanted to argue and say that I believed in monogamy. However, as the words came to my tongue, they left a sour taste. I was guilty of loving a man other than the one I wed. My circumstances were different, but nevertheless, I entered into a physical relationship with Oliver, knowing he wasn't Roman.

"You love Roman," the queen said.

I nodded.

"Do you trust him?"

"I do." I trust the man who I stood beside while we both received the church's blessing.

"Let the powers-that-be handle the girl."

"With all due respect, she's a woman and a princess."

Queen Anne nodded. "You too are a woman and a princess. Are you less than her?"

I thought about her question. "No, I'm not less. I'm also not more."

The queen shook her head. "That is where you're mistaken, Lucille. You are more. You are Roman's wife, something she will never be. You will one day be the queen." Her lips curled in a grin. "I have faith that you will make a wonderful queen. And I hope to be around to see you standing beside Roman at his coronation.

I'm also willing to help you in any way that I can. Right now, my advice is to forget about the girl and at present, don't think about your husband's other child. But, my dear, do not forget that the child exists. I promise, it isn't easy to do what I say, I know that. However, no one should ever suffer the loss of a child. Take reassurance that another will exist."

"You know this...firsthand?" My eyes opened wide as a seed of curiosity was planted in my thoughts.

"What is important is that you're safe and healthy. I've asked Theo to speak to Roman about the two of you remaining in Molave City through the holidays and into the new year."

"Our home is at Annabella Castle."

Queen Anne looked around the corridor. "Your home is here in Molave. I know about the incident with the drone." Her head shook. "Theodore thinks if he doesn't tell me something, I won't know it. Men are so simple."

I smiled.

"Safety and family. I didn't realize Isabella was here, but now that she is, I'll also insist that she and the children too remain here. I'm sure it will help with Francis's recovery." Her eyes widened. "I know. You can spend time with Isabella and the children. She's truly a wonderful mother. She can share so much with you."

My teeth clenched beneath the façade of a smile. "Where we reside will be at Roman's discretion."

"Yes, of course. I know Theodore appreciates Roman's assistance. He simply gushed over the Fifteen Eurasia Summit." She squeezed my hands. "He's the right man."

Right man?

"Your Majesty?"

"When the time comes, Roman is the right man to take Theodore's place. I'm more confident than I have been."

What is she saying?

"Because he's your son." My statement sounded like a question.

"He's the heir. Don't you agree, Lucille?"

"That Roman is the right man? Yes, I agree."

"Won't you join me with Prince Rothy and Princess Alice before they go to bed?"

"I'm sorry. My stomach..." I laid my hand over my midsection. "I believe I should rest."

"Yes, of course. Tell Lady Buckingham about the dry toast and ginger tea. Oh, and I remember craving carrot cake as Roman's arrival grew closer. Mr. Davies will warn you about calories, but if you want something, eat it."

I nodded. "Thank you."

CHAPTER
9

Roman

As I made my way into the infirmary, each step was an effort, my mind and body wracked with exhaustion. The damn day felt as if it would never end. My left arm ached and my right hand cramped. The after-dinner meeting in Papa's office was the icing on the shit-cake day that still wasn't complete.

Isabella had done everything from denial to shouting to crying to pouting, her arms crossed over her breasts as she stood staring out the windows into the darkness. My temples pounded from the confrontation. If this had been a scene in a movie or play, I would have to argue that Isabella's script was riddled with inconsistencies, as if it had been scripted by multiple writers with no preparation on their part to read what was written before.

At one point, we'd all raised our voices.

In retrospect, it was interesting how to-the-heart I'd taken this role—my new life. I truly wanted success, not for only me and Lucille, but for Molave. I saw the king's visions and understood his desires for the country and monarchy.

What Isabella had done in hiding Inessa wasn't only an affront to her family but dangerous for our country. Instead of telling her that I'd been fed information from the man who previously was me, I went into the meeting as the same brother she'd known her entire life.

Leaning back in the chair, I turned toward Isabella with a smirk. "You're lying. You and Inessa aren't best friends. You can't tolerate her."

"That's not true," Isabella replied, obviously shocked by my confrontation. "I've known Inessa since I taught classes at the university—probably ten years ago. And you don't know a damn thing about me. You haven't been interested in me since you left for university. You came back a different person."

Interesting timeline.

That would need more investigating.

One thing was certain—I was currently a different person.

I smirked again. "Then Inessa must be the person lying." I turned to Papa. "I suppose after a heated night of passion women lie as much as men."

No, I hadn't slept with her, but Roman had. Isabella didn't know there was more than one of us.

"You're awful," she snapped. "You claim to love your wife."

"I do love my wife," I blurted out. "I also know Inessa doesn't like you. I know you bitched at Francis for spending time with either Inessa or Alek. So why would she come to you for help?"

Papa sat back, gripping the clawed ends of the chair's arms. His attention varied as if he were watching a tennis match as I pushed Isabella in an effort to learn what was really happening.

"She came to me because my brother knocked her up."

I shook my head. "I'm not claiming responsibility until we have DNA proof."

"God, you're a horrible person," she said, standing and pacing near Papa's desk. She spun, bringing her attention back to me. "I can't believe you have Lucille fooled. You're a snake."

"Isabella," Papa interjected. "Roman's behavior isn't the subject of this meeting."

"Of course it isn't." Her fingers balled to fists as she brought the fists to her hips. "You're upset because I helped her, not that he slept with her."

Papa spoke as the calm in the eye of the current storm. "That topic has already been discussed. Take a seat and tell us when the princess came to Forthwith."

With a huff, Isabella took the chair she'd just

vacated. "It was after the Borinkian borders were closed."

"Think again," I said.

"Excuse me?" Her face snapped toward me.

"Lucille saw her the day after Francis and I were ambushed at Forthwith. The borders weren't closed until King Aleksander I died three days later."

Exhaling, she shook her head. "Okay, I'm mixed up. There was a lot going on."

Papa leaned forward. "Was she at Forthwith when Roman and Francis were attacked?"

"Yes, but she couldn't have had anything to do with it."

"Why are you defending her?" I asked.

"Because she came alone. No guards. No escort. Unless you now say she was the one who shot you and Francis, she wasn't responsible."

I stood and gripped the back of my chair. "She was at Forthwith the night after we were attacked." I turned to Papa. "She was on the property after you sent more cars and guards for Lucille's speech."

"The transmitters," the king said, following my train of thought.

I nodded.

"No," Isabella said. "Lucille mentioned something about transmitters and told me to have the cars checked before we traveled to Annabella. There weren't any transmitters. Inessa wouldn't do that."

I wasn't convinced.

The timing was too suspicious.

"You invited Lucille and me to stay at Forthwith knowing Inessa was there."

"I invited you before she arrived. I didn't think you'd cross paths. I'm only your sister, but Forthwith is a big castle, too. You don't have the monopoly on castles, Roman."

Ignoring her childish remarks, I asked, "Did you invite her or did Francis? He'd offered to set up a meeting."

Isabella shook her head. "Lucille said that too. You're the one lying. Francis wasn't involved with your and Inessa's affair. You just can't take personal responsibility for your actions. You never could."

The pieces to the puzzle were within reach.

Francis told me at the time of the state dinner to plan a tour stop for Forthwith. He said he'd arrange a meeting. Inessa was at Forthwith before we arrived.

What happened to derail that meeting?

Was it the arrival of Noah that sent Francis's plan into a tailspin?

Isabella continued, "Inessa called me from town. It was right after your speech claiming your recommitment to your marriage. You and Lucille were on your *way. I sent one of our butlers to find her. I didn't even see her before the news of your ambush came. I was with the children. We barely spoke that night. It wasn't until after Lucille left for the speech that we finally truly talked, when I saw..."* She shook her head. *"She asked for my help. I couldn't deny her."*

"I assume," Papa said, *"there is record of her calling you."*

Isabella's lips gaped. *"Are you truly going to have the Firm investigate me, Papa?"*

"We're investigating the connection between Borinkia and Molave. I'm disappointed that you're involved. There is talk of retaliation from Borinkia. This is bigger than your interference."

"Interference?" She repeated the word, each time louder. *"I've told you all I know."* She inhaled. *"Now you two tell me about my husband."*

Her husband.

My last stop for the night.

The guard at the door on the main level stood to attention as I approached. "Your Highness."

I nodded.

Too many words had been said in the last twenty-four hours.

After the guard opened the door, I made my way down the stairs to the secluded corridor of medical cells. I offered another nod to the nurse sitting by the monitors.

"Your Highness," he said, standing and bowing his neck.

I slowed. "Yes."

"The patient in the far room..."

Noah.

I came to an impatient stop.

He went on, "We did as you bid. He's no longer chained to the bed. I thought you'd want to know if you were planning on visiting him."

"Bathed and fed?" I asked. "Temperature of the room?"

"The temperature is comfortable. Yes, sir, he's been bathed, shaved, and fed. Pajamas, too."

I nodded. "What about his medications?"

"Mr. Davies authorized oral medications. He had one dose about an hour ago."

"And he's cooperating?"

He nodded.

"Thank you." I began to walk toward the occupied rooms.

"Your Highness," the nurse called.

Sighing, I turned back. "Yes?"

"It's been advised that a guard be present during any interaction since he's now able to move about."

The male nurse before me was obviously capable

of handling Noah on his own. The guard was undoubtedly for visitors such as me. I almost scoffed. Hell, I beat the shit out of Francis. I could most certainly hold my own with Noah.

"I'm visiting the other patient," I said.

"He's scheduled to be moved soon."

"After our conversation I'll inform you if those plans change."

He offered another neck bow. "Thank you, Your Highness."

Walking past Francis's room, I peered through the window of Noah's. From the light of the monitors, I saw him. No longer in the bed, his frail form was seated in the uncomfortable chair I'd sat in during our meetings. He wasn't chained, but he was still attached to an IV, the silver stand at his side glistened in the artificial light.

I almost felt pity for the man.

With as many fires as I'd dealt with today, he was sitting alone with only the sound of the monitors for company, staring into oblivion. It was a numbing sight to see a fellow human without stimulation of any kind. The books in his bedchamber came back to me. While the real Roman may have only spoken English and Norwegian, Noah was capable of more. This cell wasn't only a prison holding his body but one holding his mind.

Shaking my head, I went back to Francis's room, inserted the key, and twisting the knob, pushed the door inward. The automatic lights illuminated the room. While Francis was also unchained, his ability to move was hampered by the contraption holding his leg in the air. Even without the ability of speech, his light blue eyes glared my direction as his lips came together.

"Isabella and the children are back in the palace," I said, forgoing common pleasantries.

Francis blinked twice with a nod.

"She wants to see you."

He nodded.

"Here's the thing." I pulled the chair to the side of his bed. "Isabella was caught hiding Inessa Volkov."

Francis blinked once with a shake of his head.

"The ministry guards found the princess, and Isabella has admitted to it."

His eyes opened wider.

"She admitted her part to Papa and me. The guards found her at Annabella where Isabella and the children were also staying."

Francis's nostrils flared as he laid his head against the uplifted bed.

"Isabella said she was hiding Inessa because they're friends. I think she's lying."

He lifted his head, meeting my gaze. Two blinks.

"You agree she's lying?"

Two more blinks.

"Why?" I asked.

He lifted his left hand and pointed to his chest.

"She's covering for you?"

Two blinks.

"Was Inessa at Forthwith to meet with me?"

He shrugged his shoulders.

"Isabella is in trouble."

Lifting his left hand, he turned it palm up.

"You want to help her? Isabella?" I confirmed.

Two blinks.

"You will convey the same story that I told you to Isabella and everyone."

Two blinks.

"You will never utter a word about Noah or about me or anything that would bring my identity into question, to anyone."

Two blinks.

"If you fail, you won't be the only one who suffers."

He dropped his chin to his chest in a sign of defeat.

"I'll do what I can for Isabella. Don't make me regret it."

Francis lifted his chin and met my stare. No longer did I see hatred in his cool blue orbs, but a new emotion—fear.

"What are you worried about?"

He lifted his hand with all four fingers pointed up to the top of his head.

"King."

Francis nodded.

"Papa?"

He shook his head.

"Aleksander II," I said.

My stomach twisted as Francis blinked twice. "Did you know of a plan to kill Aleksander I?"

CHAPTER
10

Lucille

Beyond the windows of my bedchamber, the moon glistened in the dark sky and specks of stars were visible through a thin veil of clouds. In the last few days, temperatures had plummeted, clearing the air and coating Molave City with a glittery frost. Placing my hand on the pane, the outside cold radiated to my palm as the window filled with condensation.

Three times I'd gone out to the connecting parlor looking for Roman. I hadn't seen him since dinner. Within his bedchamber, Lady Caroline had set out his night clothes and left. Even Lord Martin was absent.

I found it unnerving how much I longed to be near Roman. It was an addiction unlike anything I'd ever known. The desire came from my heart and soul, sprouting need that consumed my mind and infiltrated my senses.

The spicy aroma of his cologne, the taste of his lips, the sense of his hard body near mine were all triggers fueling my dependency. Even at dinner, in the presence of the king and queen, I couldn't stop myself from reaching beneath the table to simply touch his hand or thigh. As overpowering as those feelings were while in his company, outside of his presence they were exponentially magnified.

My thoughts would focus on a kiss, a touch, or even the timbre of his voice. That one memory would elicit a visceral response. My heartbeat quickened, my palms grew moist, and my core twisted. If I allowed myself to indulge too long, my nipples would bead and my bloomers would dampen.

Instead of a thirty-three-year-old married woman, I was a teenage girl in lust. If I were a person who wrote journals, I would be drawing hearts and sketching our initials. Truly the desire was greater than I'd ever before experienced. It was young wonder combined with a mature understanding.

If Roman were his predecessor, I would relish the seclusion and isolation brought on by his busy schedule. Instead of pining, I'd count the stars in the sky as signs of my good fortune.

Laying my hand over my midsection, I leaned against the window frame and stared down at the pavement and empty streets. This late at night the palace guards had the gates secured, keeping traffic and tourists away.

In the Monovia region at Annabella Castle, my apartments looked out onto forest and lawn. With December near, no doubt the castle was again buried in snow. It's a wonder the guards were able to transport Isabella and the children. I pushed away thoughts of Inessa in my home.

When Roman and I were first married, I entertained snowbound fantasies with my prince.

As years passed, I spent my days and nights precariously vacillating between loathing the isolation and abhorring my prince's presence. Now, as I stared into the night, my mind again wandered with thoughts of being snowbound with my Roman. In reality, there would never be a time when we would be alone—just the two of us. Nevertheless, in our home with only our trusted staff was as close as it could get.

Closing my eyes, I pictured one bedchamber instead of two, a place where we could come together after our long days. The uncommon traditions of royal living had me yearning for the simplicity of two ordinary people. My fantasy wasn't comprised of castles, crowns, or tapestries, but of two people in a minimalistic surrounding.

The opening of my bedchamber door pulled me from my fantasy. "Roman," I exclaimed as he entered. "I was afraid I wouldn't see you tonight."

"Princess."

Exhaustion dulled his dark eyes as he, with a grimace, shrugged off his suit coat and tugged at his tie.

Hurrying to him, I reached for his tie as his left hand fell to his side. Untying the knot, I pulled the satin from around his neck. Placing my hands on his shoulders and stretching my toes, I pushed upward until my lips met his.

A growl resonated from his chest as his left arm snaked around me, pulling me to him. My tender breasts flattened against his hard chest as he tugged my hips to his. Despite his tired appearance, his kiss was the oxygen bringing life to the simmering embers of our mutual desire.

My fingers threaded through his dark mane.

His kisses moved lower, along my sensitive skin, behind my ear, and down my neck. His chin, rough with a day of beard growth, abraded my flesh, sending chills down my spine and prickling goose bumps in its wake.

Palming his cheeks, I lifted his face until our gazes met. "I've missed you."

A smile curled his lips. "You're the best fucking part of the day."

"It's nearly midnight. Are you just now getting back to the apartments?"

With a sigh, Roman nodded. "This day wouldn't end. I told Lord Martin I'd put myself to sleep. There was no sense making him stay awake." He kissed my nose. "I expected to find you asleep." His hand met mine, our fingers intertwining as he moved me to arm's length. Sparks returned to his dark orbs as he scanned from the top of my head to my toes. "You're perfection, Lucille. Absolute perfection."

"Spend the night with me," I proposed. "You're tired. I can tell. We can simply fall asleep in one another's arms."

"That's the best proposal I've heard all day."

As he reached for the buttons on the front of his shirt, I stepped closer. "Let me help. I have two hands."

With a tweak of my fingers, the small buttons slipped through the holes, one by one. With each centimeter of opening, the shirt gaped, until it hung from his wide shoulders. His white t-shirt was absent. Weaving my fingers through the soft dark hair, I ran my touch over his chest and lower, feeling each indentation of his toned torso. Back upward, I splayed my fingers. Beneath my palms, Roman's heart thumped a steady rhythm.

I looked up. "When I think about what happened, that I could have lost you..."

"I'm in this forever. You won't lose me without a fight."

Easing the cuff links from the shirt's cuffs, I gently

teased the shirt from his shoulders. "The bandage on your arm is smaller."

"I saw Mr. Davies today. He said the gunshot is healing properly." Roman lifted his right hand. "He wanted to do another x-ray of my hand, but I couldn't fit it in my schedule. I'll see him again in a few days."

As I lifted his right hand, Roman's expression pinched, and his lips pressed together in a straight line.

"Your hand hurts?"

He nodded and looked down. "Worse than before," he replied, stretching his fingers.

I noticed how swollen his digits were. "Where is your brace?" It was the sling he'd been wearing.

"Mr. Davies said that's why it hurts, but that damn sling is a nuisance. And there's too much happening to take pain medications."

"Roman, you have to take care of yourself."

He lowered his forehead to mine. "I'd rather take care of you."

"Heal and you can take care of me with two hands."

Roman smiled as he walked me across the room. Step by step, I moved backward until I reached the edge of the bed. One quick tug of the sash from my dressing gown and it gaped open, revealing my thigh-length nightgown. "I can take care of you with no hands." He licked his lips.

Warmth filled my cheeks as I grinned. "I don't doubt your abilities, Your Highness."

"I don't mind proving myself."

"You're tired."

"I was."

Shaking my head, I reached for his belt. "Let me at least help you ready for bed."

"When I'm totally healed, I'm going to be the one to undress you each night. Lady Buckingham is fired."

Unbuckling his belt, I looked up through veiled lashes. "Not fired. Replaced is a better word."

"No, Princess. My plans for you are not limited to replacing what your mistress does. Bringing you pleasure is my job alone."

Crouching down, I removed his shoes and socks. Next, I unfastened his trousers, allowing them to fall to the floor. The dark hair from his chest reappeared lower, creating a dark trail to the edge of his boxer briefs. Regardless of the fatigue in his eyes, in his limited attire, it was obvious that he was aroused.

My pulse increased as I stared at the bulge beneath the satin boxers.

'I've imagined you on your knees.' It was one of his options to punish me for visiting the infirmary alone. Now, as I reached for the waist of his boxers, I wasn't thinking about punishment or the man below the infirmary. As my core dampened and my insides twisted, I

was thinking about what my Roman had said, that bringing me pleasure was his job.

It was a task I'd willingly give to him for eternity.

Still on my knees, I lowered his boxers, freeing his cock.

My tongue darted to my suddenly dry lips.

"Lucille."

My name was a growl, octaves lower than normal, as his breaths quickened, and his fingers brushed the top of my head. I peered upward, encouraged by the intensity in his dark stare. No longer dull, his orbs swirled with desire, and his clenched jaw tightened, stretching the muscles along the side of his handsome face.

The thump of my heart echoed in my ears like the beat of a bass drum. My head felt light as I leaned closer. Roman's musky scent filled my senses as I licked the glistening end of his cock. The salty taste was uniquely my Roman's.

He reached for my chin.

My eyes opened as I looked up.

"You're the princess," he said hoarsely. "I bow to you."

"My prince, I will always bow to you, too." Closing my eyes and opening my mouth, I sucked the end of his cock between my lips.

His skin tightened as his erection grew.

Veins popped to life through the velvety flesh.

Lifting my hands, I surrounded the length with one hand and reached for his balls with the other. A low chorus of curses filled my ears as I worked to take more of him. Bobbing my head, I moved up and down his hardened shaft as he intertwined his fingers in my hair. His guidance wasn't dominating but encouraging. My jaw began to ache, but with only one glance upward, I refused to stop.

The sheer bliss of his expression was intoxicating.

My prince had come to me after his long day and under my care, he was being rewarded for being the man I loved and trusted.

Roman's thighs tightened as he rocked with me, his speed increasing.

Wrapping my arms around his thighs, I held tight, refusing to stop before he found his release. Within my grasp, his body convulsed, and his cock throbbed as warm liquid filled my mouth.

I'd never swallowed.

Never.

I'd never considered it.

On my knees at my prince's feet, for the first time, I did.

I swallowed.

Gulp after gulp.

"God, Lucille..." His baritone tenor rumbled through me.

The sound of a pop reverberated through the bedchamber as I fell back on my heels.

Roman offered me his hand. Pulling me to my feet, he said, "That was..." His lips came to mine, his tongue searching for his own taste.

When we pulled away, the sight of his grin brought a smile to my face. "Your Highness, it's my job to bring you pleasure."

Cupping my cheek, he shook his head. "I'm glad you weren't asleep."

CHAPTER
11

Roman

Time passed. Days filled with work and nights of passion combined, creating weeks. Despite the chaos within the palace and beyond the Molavian borders, Lucille and I were able to enjoy what some would call the honeymoon phase of our relationship. With the church's blessing, we both saw ourselves as married in every sense of the term. Any lingering feelings of guilt were gone, blown away by the winter winds.

Changes also occurred that were more visible. While our belongings remained separate, Lucille and I made the unofficial move of spending our nights together. Without a formal announcement, Lady Buckingham and Lord Martin quickly fell into line. Our individual nighttime routines were shortened, giving us more time together. In the morning, a knock would proceed the opening of either of our bedchambers.

Lucille's zest for sex was nothing resembling the things Noah said about her. With the pregnancy hormones raging, she was insatiable in a way I found equally arousing. We'd progressed leaps and bounds beyond vanilla missionary. The fact that my princess was open to trying new things was not a secret I would share.

The increased libido was her state as we retired or frequently on and off throughout the night. Mornings were altogether different. Despite my efforts and those of Lady Buckingham, mornings—especially—were the time of day I'd find the princess on her knees and not in a way I enjoyed.

Mr. Davies assured me that nausea was normal and positive. It meant Lucille's body was adapting to her pregnancy. Another change to Lucille's schedule was a late-afternoon nap. Without it, she could fall asleep during our evening meal and once nearly did.

Rothy and Alice were now constants along with Isabella. To the observer we were the happy royal family, at least during the evening meal.

The palace was beautifully decorated for the coming holidays and a new year was soon to arrive. Some mornings I'd wake with my mind moving in a million different directions, all involving the Godfrey monarchy. Other times, my reality would hit me as if even I were surprised to remember I had a life before this one.

My hand was still splinted but improving. The gunshot wound in my left arm was healing remarkably.

The other two patients were also improving. With Isabella and the children's arrival to Molave Palace, Francis was permanently moved upstairs in the infirmary, leaving only one patient in the locked cells. While Francis was still unable to speak clearly, he'd found a way to communicate with signs and noises. His interactions were monitored. To date, he'd maintained the Firm's story of our ambush.

Noah's self-inflicted trauma was mostly healed.

It was ironic how his addiction had both influenced his unhappiness and saved his life. Without the tremors he would have successfully shot himself.

A week or so ago, I caved and took a stack of books from my bedchamber to his cell. He was as excited as a child on Christmas morning.

Admittedly, it was a strange relationship the two of us were forming. As Lucille's official husband, I wanted Noah to suffer for what he'd done and the way he'd treated her. At the same time, we shared an unusual bond, that of being the same person. I visited his cell daily, extracting information that, while possibly available in his journals back at Annabella, would without him never be known.

It was interesting to admit that I no longer dreaded my visits to the basement of the infirmary; on some days, it was almost pleasant. Our most recent conversations centered on the Borinkian princess. I needed to fully understand their relationship if I had a snowball's chance in hell of convincing her I was Roman Godfrey.

"She's not Lucille," Noah said.

"Do you want to be more specific?"

He smirked. "Not really."

"You said she was a better lay," I prodded.

"Rougher. Feisty. She likes it that way, dirty. She's not my type, but it kept things interesting. Better than boring."

Most days Noah was willing to talk—sometimes too much. Other days, he was more reserved. I reminded him that as long as the information was flowing, I would continue to lobby King Theodore for Noah's current status. Whatever it was to be labeled.

Prisoner.

Patient.

Death-row inmate.

King Theodore never visited Noah. All the king's information came through me. I saw what Papa was doing, creating space so that one day it would be easier to make a final decree.

When it came to the foreign princess, the time had finally arrived when I would face her. It had been nearly a month since the ministry guards brought her from Annabella to Molave Palace. I was briefed daily on her health and well-being. I was also told of her recurring visitor—my sister.

"My old apartments," I said to Mrs. Drake, who was seated across from me in my office. My thoughts went back to my stay in the far wing of the palace. While it had only been months, it seemed like years since I was there.

"She's comfortable," Mrs. Drake said.

"More so than Noah."

Mrs. Drake's stare met mine. "You shouldn't say his name."

"Do you want me to call him Roman? Would that be the second or third?"

Her lips pressed together. "Your Highness, what you speak of is extremely sensitive information. He shouldn't be..." She let her words trail away.

"Alive," I offered.

"It would be better."

"I'm learning from him. He has five years of memories to share, information that without him I would never know."

Taking a deep breath, she pressed down on her thighs and exhaled. "The king and I have spoken at some length. I'm aware that you are the reason he survived his accident. I respect your decision."

I lifted my eyebrows, unaccustomed to praise from the chief minister.

She continued, "His presence is nonetheless dangerous. If the wrong people were made aware of what has been done—with him and with you—it would cause irreparable damage to the monarchy. We must think of the good of Molave."

"I understand. However, my difficulty comes in not thinking about the good of the one man in our care."

"You have done well, Your Highness. You're intelligent and a fast learner."

"Be careful, Mrs. Drake, I may begin to think you approve of me."

Her lips curled into a smile. "I do. Forgive me if I'm leery. If the scheme to assassinate King Theodore had worked, the man in the cellar would now be king. You can admit that chain of events would have Molave in a precarious position."

I nodded. "I'm aware of his guilt."

"Well, yes, reigning is a lonely and ruthless job. It is also dangerous. Finding people to trust is not easy. The Firm has worked to make your role as pleasant as possible. You and the princess are...well, the princess is your reward."

Inhaling, I stood, a rebuke on the tip of my tongue.

Before I could speak, the chief minister continued, "Reigning requires difficult decisions. One man is a liability that can be easily removed. The more interaction he has with others, the more people who know the truth."

"The medical personnel know him as Noah—our attacker. They don't know he was someone else. Not when they see me daily."

"I have heard the resemblance is not what it was."

I nodded. "The steroids have aged him."

"When the time comes, when you are king...King Roman, you will be required to make decisions that you personally may find abhorrent; that isn't reason enough to risk what has for centuries been solid."

"That is what I don't understand."

Mrs. Drake sighed. "What don't you understand?"

"Why replace Roman Godfrey in the first place? Why replace Noah?"

"Noah made poor decisions, personally and publicly. He wasn't interested in following the plan. As you've been made aware, King Aleksander II has called together troops guarding the borders between Borinkia and Molave, Norway, and Sweden. We must work to de-escalate the situation."

I'd been briefed on the troop buildup. "Give him back his sister."

She exhaled. "Today's meeting is the beginning. You must be the one to convince her."

"The thing I don't understand is that as prince, Noah could do whatever he wanted. The same with me or if I don't follow your instructions, do you have another Roman waiting in the wings?"

"You, sir, are Roman Godfrey."

"As long as I do what you and King Theo want. What if I don't believe that ruthlessness is best?"

"I will be here to advise you."

"Was there a real Roman?" I asked, finally verbalizing a question I'd wrestled with since I first traveled to Molave.

"Yes."

"And did he make unacceptable choices?"

"In a way," she said.

"Is he still alive?"

Mrs. Drake pressed her lips together.

"I need to know if one day a man matching my appearance will claim he's the rightful heir."

"That won't happen, sir."

"You can guarantee that?"

One nod. "Without a doubt." She took a deep breath. "Are you ready to visit the princess?"

I asked, "You've visited her." I knew that from my daily reports.

"Multiple times."

"Is she guarded?"

"Her exits are under constant surveillance for her own protection."

"She can't leave."

Mrs. Drake met my gaze and shook her head. "Princess Inessa isn't a prisoner. She is the guest of the Godfrey monarchy, one granted political asylum."

What?

"Asylum? Isn't that granted to people who fear persecution from their own country? When did her status change?"

"Upon our early interviews, we learned that she was hiding for her safety."

"Inessa fears Alek?" I shook my head, recalling what Noah had shared. "That wasn't what I was told."

"I'm sorry you were misinformed."

Was I misinformed or did I assume that she was a prisoner?

Noah's knowledge of Inessa was historical, not current. The princess's other visitor would know more—my sister.

"What about the child?" I asked.

"When the child is born in Molave, he or she will have Molavian citizenship."

"Is King Aleksander II aware of Inessa's status?"

"Her pregnancy or asylum?"

"Both," I said. "Either."

"The princess wanted to speak to you first. She's been asking for you since her arrival."

"I'm still not sure I will convince her of who I am."

"You've convinced Princess Lucille. Certainly, this will be easier."

I convinced Lucille with honesty. That wasn't my plan with Inessa.

A few minutes later, I was alone, walking the same corridors I had in the late summer. My sense of confidence was low. I hadn't felt this unsure about myself since I walked these same corridors for Rothy's second birthday.

Taking a deep breath, I stopped at the doorway to the apartments that used to be mine and knocked.

CHAPTER 12

Roman

The door opened from within.

"Princess Inessa," I inquired.

"Your Highness," a lady-in-waiting said with a curtsy. "I'll inform the princess you've arrived."

Pushing my hands into my pant pockets, I stood in the front parlor. Slowly turning, I took in the décor. Everything was the same as when I'd lived in these apartments. I turned in time to see Princess Inessa coming my direction. This was the first time I'd seen her in person. While she was young and pretty, she didn't evoke the visceral response I'd experienced the first time I saw Lucille.

Inessa's smile beamed as she came closer. In a quick scan, I assessed that the princess was petite, even too lean. The white gown she wore did little to hide the growing baby. If anything, the clinginess of the material accentuated it.

Her hair was a pale yellow, and unlike in the

picture with Noah, currently her locks were plaited into a long braid draped over her slender shoulder.

"Roman." Her Borinkian accent was thick, sounding very Slavic.

"Inessa."

She laid her hand over her stomach, her light blue gaze coming to mine. "It's taken you long enough. I suppose it's a long walk from your apartments and that Letanonian cunt?"

A chuckle resonated from my throat, blocking the rebuke that would not facilitate my goal. Inhaling, I pulled my hands from my pant pockets and gestured toward the seating area. "We should talk."

Inessa tilted her head. "And I thought you were here to fuck."

My neck straightened as I tried to rein in my utter shock and sheer repulsion that she'd managed to elicit in only a few seconds. "Inessa, I owe you an apology."

"You owe me more than that," she said, making her way to a loveseat and taking a seat near one end. "Sit." She patted the cushion to her side.

Instead of accepting her invitation, I sat on the edge of a soft chair facing her. With my knees parted, I leaned forward. "Tell me about the request for political asylum."

She shook her head. "Ah, yes. It's all part of the plan."

Noah hadn't mentioned it.

"I don't recall—"

"Het," she said, interrupting. "If you'd called. You didn't. We said we'd work together. I had to make decisions and I did."

I inhaled. "Forget all I've said in the past. I've decided to make my marriage work."

She laughed. "Come, Roman. We've always been honest with one another."

"I'm being honest. Lucille and I had a rough patch. We're working on things. I can't leave her."

"Can't. As in your papa won't allow it." She smirked. "And here I thought you'd finally taken control of your life."

I stood. "I have taken control. I want to stay married to Lucille."

"You're a good actor."

My face snapped her direction. "Excuse me?"

Inessa stood and sauntered closer. With each step her dress parted. High-heeled shoes accentuated her shapely legs as if choreographed for a sensual tango. The sweet scent of her perfume filled my nostrils as she shimmied up to me. Her red lips curled. With one hand, she reached up and dragged her fingernail over my cheek.

Fuck.

That hurt.

Without thinking, I wrapped my fingers around her wrist, yanking her hand away.

"There you are," she cooed and lifted her other hand to my shoulder. "I thought they'd replaced you with some mild, boring version." Her icy blue stare bore into mine as she pressed her body against mine.

"I lied to you," I said, my grip of her wrist still tight.

"Or you're lying now. Tell me you haven't missed me."

Pushing her away, I raised my voice. "I haven't missed you."

"You want me to believe you've suddenly developed an affection for fucking that dead fish."

My tenor lowered to a growl. "What the fuck do you expect from me?"

"I want what you promised. You proposed."

"In Oslo," I said. "Yeah, things were bad. That tour was a disaster."

Her smile reappeared. "I have fond memories of that night. The only disaster was you telling me you would marry me and then disappearing. I called you. Francis called you. Even Alek tried."

Shit.

"I got rid of the phone. Working on my marriage."

Inessa inhaled and walked around the parlor, running her fingers over the furniture. "I want to be your queen." Every now and then, she'd look up, making sure she had my full attention as a seductive smile would curl her lips. "I want what we dreamed together. My father is gone. Two more and we will have the wealth of Molave and the power of Borinkia."

I shook my head. "That's no longer my dream." Not that it ever was.

She ran the palm of her hand over her midsection. "The queen, she likes me."

"Mum?" I knew that Queen Anne had visited Inessa.

"She's very interested in your child—*our* child."

"Not in the way you think."

"I don't think we should kill her. She'll be a good ally. I imagine her standing at our son's baptism. The world will approve."

"King Aleksander I. Was it you or Alek?"

"Not me. I haven't been in Borinkia since October."

"So it was Alek."

Inessa shrugged. "Maybe it was old age. Otets, he was sick."

"You're hiding your grief well."

"I've grieved. Today I want to celebrate."

"We aren't celebrating."

She paused near the fireplace, appearing to inspect the crystal objects decorating the mantel. Craning her neck, she peered over her shoulder before turning back and lifting one of the figurines. The room echoed as she threw the object into the fireplace. Like gunfire, she threw a second and a third. Each object shattered in the flames leaving shards of crystal littering the ashes.

"Stop," I yelled, rushing to her and turning her to me. "What the fuck?"

Her blue orbs shimmered as she pressed her baby bump against me. "Celebrate with me," she cooed as she lowered her hand to the front of my trousers—taunting and rubbing.

"You're crazy." This was not the reunion Noah described.

"For you, my future king." Her eyebrows lifted. "Join me in the bedchamber, and I'll remind you how crazy I can be."

Fuck no.

"Or take me right here, like you did in Oslo." Her smile grew. "And after we fuck, you can tell me again you didn't miss me."

"Go back to Borinkia. Talk to Alek. Tell him we will work toward peace."

Her expression sobered. "The queen," Inessa said, "she wants your son born here in Molave."

"We both know that's not my child."

Shock and sadness replaced her confident air. The metamorphosis was like watching a balloon pop. "Roman. I told you, in Oslo."

"You did. I wasn't with it then. I've had time to think. I don't believe it's mine."

"Of course he is yours. A child was part of the plan. You did your part. I'm doing mine. Alek is waiting, but he won't wait forever."

"Is it money you want?" I asked.

"A kingdom." Her voice grew louder. "I want a kingdom, more than Borinkia and bigger than Molave. I want to be welcomed around the world as the queen of Molavinkia."

Molavinkia.

She grinned. "I made that up. But I like it. You can call the country whatever you want when you're king."

"No."

She walked to the bookshelves and began pulling books from the shelves. Such as the roll of thunder, one by one the books fell to the floor, the covers opening and pages creasing.

Again, I followed her. "Inessa, stop."

When she spun toward me, she lunged forward, bringing her lips to mine.

Reaching for her shoulders, I pushed her away. "Get a test. If the baby is mine, I'll pay support. Either way, you need to go back to Borinkia. If you don't, I promise Mum isn't going to be the supportive babushka you expect."

"I can't have a test until the baby is born."

"Yes, you can. There are other options, including amniocentesis."

Her eyes opened wide. "No one is sticking a needle into my uterus."

Shaking my head, I walked toward the door. "I'm leaving."

"Roman, please, I need you."

When I turned, she was untying the side of her dress, slowly turning, showing me the nudity she hid beneath.

Inhaling, I closed and opened my eyes. I took a step toward her. Noah may not have prepared me for this, but if she was to believe I was the same man, I couldn't run away.

I seized her chin and painfully pulled it higher until her gaze was on mine. "You want to be fucked?"

"Yes. I need it."

I shook my head. "You're beautiful, Inessa," I lied. I could act. I'd done it most of my life. "I could take your ass against that wall."

She nodded.

"And pound your cunt until you can't come again."

"Yes." Her one word was filled with longing.

"It's not going to happen."

"Roman."

Releasing her chin, I walked toward the door. The sound of my name followed by another object crashing against the wall filled my ears as I opened the door and slammed it in my wake. I didn't take a breath until I was twenty meters away from the apartments. My mind was swirling as I turned the corner and nearly ran into a more frequent Inessa visitor. "Isabella," I said, surprised.

"Your Highness." My sister's smile grew as she tilted her head. "She said you were finally going to see her." Isabella took a step closer, her attention on my face. "Did you get into a spat with a cat, brother?" She tugged the handkerchief from my breast pocket and handed it to me. "You might want to wipe that lipstick off before Lucille sees you."

CHAPTER 13

Lucille

Lady Larsen sat at my side as she discussed the plans for our United States tour. My recently consumed lunch settled as we spoke. Word had gotten out about our tour faster than we anticipated, in part due to the article by Betsy Scholl in *Rolling Stone*. Unlike the critiques she was famous for writing, the article was a positive observation of the recommitment of the Prince and Princess of Molave.

Our tour would begin on the first of February. Lady Larsen coined it the Love Tour.

As we discussed locations, accommodations, formal and informal appearances, I pushed away thoughts of previous tours. This one would be different. Of course it would; my Roman was different.

The door to my private office opened, garnering the attention of both of us.

Quickly, we both stood. "Your Highness."

My heart rate doubled as I took in the expression on my Roman's handsome face.

"Lady Larsen, leave us," Roman commanded.

Her gaze met mine and I nodded.

Still standing, I remained silent until the door closed, leaving Roman and me alone. "My prince?"

His eyes slowly closed as he exhaled.

I took a step closer.

As his eyes opened, they were clearer than seconds before.

I scanned from his dark hair to his loafers. There was a scratch on his left cheek, but the splint on his hand reassured me that my Roman hadn't been replaced. A few more steps, and I reached for his other hand. "What's wrong?"

Roman lowered his forehead to mine. "My princess."

The rumble of his baritone timbre settled the onset of nerves brought on by his arrival. "What happened to your cheek?" Gently palming his cheeks, I lifted his face. "Talk to me."

His Adam's apple bobbed.

A faint, foreign, sweet aroma came to my senses. Pregnancy had unnaturally increased my sense of smell. I took a step back. "Is that perfume?"

He shook his head. "It is, it's not..."

"Roman?"

"I went to her. I'd put it off for as long as I could."

My neck straightened and the small hairs on my arms stood to attention. "Her. The princess?" I wasn't sure why I refused to use her name, but nevertheless, he knew who I meant.

"Yes." He reached for my hand and led me to the sofa.

As we sat, our knees touched. It had become second nature to touch one another when we were close as if we were incomplete without the other.

"What happened?"

Roman exhaled and stood. Running his hand through his hair, he paced back and forth. "I thought I was prepared. Noah told me things..."

My heart skipped a beat. "Oh no. Did she know you weren't...him?"

"I don't know." His dark orbs focused on me. "She's...not what I expected."

"What does that mean?"

He fell to one knee before me and again reached for my hand. "I've said it before and I'll say it again: Noah was a fool not to see you for the amazing woman you are, for not loving you, or even being kind."

I swallowed as tears blurred my vision. "Do you now want her too?"

"God, no," he said loudly.

A tear trailed down my cheek as I smiled. "Is she

beautiful?"

"Not even close to you, my princess." He closed his eyes and inhaled, his nostrils flaring. "I can't come up with words to describe her other than crazy."

"You don't need to tell me anything as long as I still have your heart."

"Lucille, you have more than my heart. You have my soul, my entire being is in your hands." He lifted my hands and peppered my knuckles with kisses. "I expected..." He stood.

"Roman, as long as she hasn't figured out that you're...different, it will be all right."

"I imagined going to her, telling her it was over between us, and her accepting the fate and agreeing to return to Borinkia. Hell, she thinks Mum is supportive. She has no idea that Mum's plan is to keep the child here in Molave."

"You must tell her. I can't be a part of stealing another woman's child."

He shook his head. "You can't understand her behavior. I don't understand it. One minute she was a seductress and the next an impudent child."

I couldn't picture what he was saying. "She is young. Queen Anne mentioned as much."

"No, not as in age. Noah described her as feisty, interesting... He said she liked things rough."

Wrapping my arms around my midsection, I tried

not to internalize that those words were from a man who was supposed to love me. "Isabella once told me I should try to be more like the princess, to keep my husband."

"Oh fuck no."

His response brought back my smile. "Seductress?"

He nodded. "One of her first sentences was saying I visited to fuck."

"She's straight to the point."

He pulled the handkerchief from his breast pocket and handed it to me.

My forehead furrowed as I took the white cloth. My stomach roiled at the smudge of red lipstick. I looked up at my Roman. "It's not a good shade for you."

For the first time since he'd entered my office, the prince smiled. "I love only you."

"I know that. I trust you. I also don't want her to be the reason we lose what we have."

Roman returned to one knee. "I would never leave you."

"We both know that isn't one hundred percent your choice." My mind filled with scenarios where the Borinkian princess told the world that Roman wasn't really Roman. She'd already brought on a scandal, with Noah's help. Would she fight to defend my Roman if she knew he was an impostor?

The answer was no.

"You must convince her," I said. "Talk to Noah. Tell him what occurred. She must leave Molave believing your relationship is over and without suspicion that you're different."

Roman stood. "You want me to go back to her?"

"No." I rose to my feet, meeting him, pressing against him. "But I think it's for the best."

"As I was leaving, Isabella was going to see her."

I inhaled. "I've been told that your sister visits regularly."

Roman's gaze narrowed. "Who is giving you information?"

"Did you forget, my prince, you unshielded me."

"You never mentioned it."

Lifting my hands to his broad shoulders, I brushed the material of his suit coat. "That's because when the two of us are alone, discussing your sister or the princess is not a priority."

His left hand came to my cheek. "For the first time since coming to Molave, I feel like I'm failing."

"You, Your Highness, may not fail. My heart won't survive."

Roman's lips came to my forehead.

"We are a team," I said. "Talk to me. Why is she different than other interactions?"

The prince sat back on the sofa, unbuttoned his

suit coat, and lifted one arm to the top of the cushions. After a moment, he turned to me. "In my career, it helped me to analyze my character, to talk about him, his motivation, and his shortcomings."

"You are without shortcomings."

His lips curled. "No, my princess, I'm not. After meeting with her, I didn't want to report to Papa or Mrs. Drake. Hell, I didn't even want to visit Noah. I needed to see you. You, Lucille, are my shortcoming."

While his confession caused my heart to swell, I too was able to see the problem. "Forget me when you're with her."

"Forgetting you is impossible."

"Then put thoughts of me aside. I used to do it when we were together—not you. I'd think about the man who proposed, not the man I was with. I replayed good memories to make it through the difficult times."

"I have no memories with her." He exhaled. "As I left her apartments, she unfastened her dress and stood before me practically naked."

"Were you aroused?"

"Appalled would be a better description."

"Do you not find pregnant women attractive," I asked with a grin. "I should hear the truth now."

"The pregnancy wasn't the appalling part. I don't find her attractive. She's too thin and while her appearance isn't horrible, her personality is." He closed his eyes and slowly shook his head. "She threw crystal objects from the mantel into the fireplace and tossed books from their shelves. She was a child throwing a temper tantrum."

My thoughts went back to my five years in hell. "She was pushing you, wanting you to punish her." I inhaled and sat at my husband's side, leaning into his arm, his warmth, and his aura. "She knows how to push your buttons—Noah's—and she apparently enjoys it. It's not the way I'm wired. Therefore, I'd do anything and everything not to upset you. With her, you could indulge in that behavior."

"I'm not wired that way, Lucille. But you're not wrong. At one point, I seized her wrist after she scratched me. I squeezed..." His dark orbs were filled with remorse. "Hell, I may have bruised her."

"Good."

"My princess?"

I tried to explain. "Not good that she's marred. I don't wish that on anyone. Good that you showed that kind of emotion. It will help convince her that you are truly Roman." I thought back on all he'd said. "What do you imagine she shared with Isabella after you left?"

"I don't know." He looked down at the handkerchief now on the sofa cushion. "Isabella was the one who saw the lipstick. I'd pushed the princess away. I didn't realize she'd marked me."

"There are only two people who know what they discuss—the princess and Isabella. I will visit your sister later. You must return to the princess. If not today, then soon. Tell her that now that you've seen her, you can't stay away."

"Lucille, that isn't true."

"Then act, my prince. Did you learn anything about the new king?"

"She didn't deny that her brother could be responsible for regicide. She also commented that Mum should live. She's sure she has Queen Anne in her corner. I denied the child is mine."

I opened my eyes wide. "Why would you do that?"

"Because Noah said something that made sense. He said he took the steroids to intentionally lower his sperm count."

"It only takes one."

"He said if you didn't conceive, he finds it hard to believe Inessa did—from him."

My pulse kicked up a notch. "Why would she claim to be carrying your child if she wasn't?"

"She said it was part of the plan...to unite Borinkia and Molave."

"Does she know we're expecting?" I asked.

"I didn't tell her. I said we were working on our marriage."

Standing, I moved in front of Roman, stepping

between his knees, laying my hands on his shoulders, and leaning forward. "I trust you with my heart, body, and soul."

His dark stare was not focused on my face, but instead, on the neckline of my blouse.

"Roman?"

His smile returned. "I like this view. I think they're getting bigger."

"Is it a better view than of the princess losing her dress?"

Pulling me to his lap with his left arm, he nodded. "Undeniably better. Infinitely better."

I lifted my palm to his cheek. "This is why I trust you. I'm not suggesting you sleep with her. I'm suggesting you work to earn back her confidence. Whether she realizes it or not, Molave is not a safe place for her and her child."

"Did you know she was granted political asylum?"

That was news to me. "I didn't."

"I learned this morning from Mrs. Drake."

Sighing, I laid my head on Roman's shoulder. "How did I live in this family for five years and not see the deceptions and limitless depravity?"

"Because, my princess, you are inherently kind and good. It is who you are so it's what you see in others."

"I see it in you."

Roman sighed as we connected in a kiss.

CHAPTER
14

Roman

B efore reporting to King Theodore, I decided to make a trip to the infirmary. Francis's new room on the main level was large, away from the examination rooms, and with a view of the gardens. He had all the comforts of a royal hospital.

I didn't intend to visit my brother-in-law. My attention was set on the guard at the end of the corridor.

"Your Highness," he said with a neck bow.

I nodded.

Unlocking the door to the descending staircase, the guard allowed me entry without question.

Sight.

That was all it took.

I was capable of appearing as Roman Godfrey in all situations.

Therefore, why was I concerned that Inessa wouldn't believe me?

At the first room, I checked in with the medical staff. Two male nurses were in attendance, both enthralled with whatever was on their computer screens. I cleared my throat.

Both men stood and bowed their necks. "Your Highness."

"I'm visiting the patient. Is there anything I should know?"

They looked at one another and back to me. The man with the dark skin and tight braids spoke. "He became agitated last night."

"I wasn't informed."

"Mr. Davies made adjustments to his medication."

"And?" I questioned.

"He's lethargic today."

The other nurse spoke. "He didn't eat much of his morning meal. He ate more of the midday meal. Do you want one of us to accompany you, sir?"

"No. I'll be fine."

Despite their warning about having a guard present, I'd not accepted their help. The conversations between Noah and me were not for the ears of the medical personnel. Since the time Noah was given the ability to move about, a camera had been set up in his cell. There wasn't audio. The nurses would see if there was a struggle even if they didn't hear it.

I inserted the key and pushed open the door. Instead of sitting up in his chair, Noah was lying in bed, his eyes closed. He barely stirred at the onslaught of light, yet the glare made his pale complexion visible. Calling his name, I walked closer. His eyelids fluttered as he squinted my direction.

"Not today," Noah mumbled.

"I have questions."

He shook his head. "I'm done talking."

"Then you'll be of no use."

Closing his eyes, he turned away.

I pulled the chair near the bed and took a seat. "Don't do this, Noah. You know if you stop talking, you have nothing to barter. I won't be able to hold off King Theodore."

Groaning, he rolled my direction. "What's the use? I'm going to die here. I guess I always knew that, just like you know you will too."

"In my sleep as an old man."

He scoffed. "Nice dream." He pulled the blankets up around him. "Why is it so cold?"

It wasn't cold. The temperature was pleasant; if anything it was warm.

Standing, I went closer and reached for his forehead. Although Noah flinched at my touch, he didn't complain. "Fuck, you're burning up."

"I don't know what it is."

"I'll talk to the nurses. First, I have a few questions."

"Not today," he replied.

I went to the sink and filled the cup with water from the faucet. "Here, drink." I offered him the cup.

Noah shook his head, but then reached for the button, lifting the head of his bed. "Were you a nurse in your old life? Or a doctor?"

I shook my head. "I just remember my mom telling me to drink plenty of water when I was sick."

Noah took the cup in his trembling grasp. "Mine said the same thing." He took a drink and began to cough, sloshing the water on the blankets.

"Let me take that."

Sighing, he laid his head back. "What do you want to ask me?"

"I visited Inessa this afternoon."

His lips twitched. "Did she jump you at the door?"

"Fuck, almost. You didn't warn me."

"I wasn't sure she would after so much time has passed, but it's her MO. I told you, she's interesting."

"She said there is a plan to combine the two countries and rule as my...your...a queen."

Noah closed his eyes. "That one is...she's fucking dangerous. Hell, she'd take out her brother to get what she wants. Watch out."

"You didn't think to tell me that before?"

"I'm helping you. There's no way to be prepared for Inessa. Go with your gut. Don't hold back."

"I'm not you."

His dark stare scanned from my waist up. "Once upon a time, I was you."

"What can I say to convince her to go back to Borinkia?"

"Nothing. Get ahold of Alek. Tell him she's here and you want her gone. He'll take care of her."

"What does that mean? I can't tell him. He'll accuse Molave of harboring his sister against her will."

Noah relaxed against the bed and closed his eyes. "She's lying. Everyone lies."

"What is she lying about?"

"Everything. We didn't have a plan, not like she said. I promised Alek that as king I'd open trade, taking down the sanctions against Borinkia. I even said I'd speak to NATO on Borinkia's behalf. He wants to be a player on the world stage. He needs support. As far as he's concerned, Inessa is only a means to his endgame."

"You promised him that you'd do that?"

"When I became king." He huffed. "Obviously, it didn't work."

"You told me before that the US was involved?"

"There's a coalition of senators who recognize the power and resources in Borinkia. If Molave took the first step to bring Borinkia to the world stage, they would vote to give US support."

"And Senator Sutton?"

"He's a crook. Hell, he'd sell off his daughter...oh yeah, he did that."

"How do I get in touch with Alek?"

"Francis was my go-between." His dark stare shimmered. "I suppose he's still dealing with the aftereffects of that car crash."

I flexed my fingers of my right hand. "Yeah, something like that. What about the phone back at Annabella?"

"I used it to call Inessa and Francis, not Alek. We always met in person. Francis would arrange it."

"Why did you trust him?" I asked.

"I don't trust anyone." He narrowed his gaze. "Alek or Francis?"

"I was thinking Francis."

"He was one of the few who could tell I hated this life...your life. I guess I wanted to trust someone." Noah's body convulsed as he coughed. Shaking his head, he lay back. "I never told Inessa that I was an impostor. I often wondered if I had if she would have cared."

"What do you mean?"

"I mean, she doesn't care who I am or you are, as long as we can help her rise in power."

"Are you suggesting I be honest with her?"

"Hell, I don't know. I fucked it all up."

Another round of coughs had Noah sitting forward and holding his side.

"I'm going to talk to the nurses."

"Listen," he managed to say, "I don't have any more fight left. I don't care what you do with your life. Just remember, you're not the first person to take this job, and there's a fucking good chance that you won't be the last. Don't do what I did. When you see the opportunity to leave, run. I should have."

CHAPTER
15

Lucille

Taking a deep breath, I knocked on the outer door to Isabella and Francis's apartments in Molave Palace. I'd been less than receptive to my sister-in-law during the last few weeks. In all honesty, it was the knowledge that she'd taken the princess to my home that had me upset.

My home.

Our home.

She'd called and asked for refuge for herself and her children. That I willingly gave. The princess was another story.

Lady Nora opened the door. "Your Highness."

"I'm here to visit the children and duchess. May I come in?"

Lady Nora took a step back and gestured with her arm. "Yes, of course. The children will be excited to see you. I'll alert Lady Sherry that you're here."

"The duchess?" I asked.

"I'm afraid she's away from the apartments. I

expect her back shortly."

Feigning a smile, I nodded.

In no time, Lady Sherry appeared with Alice in her arms and Rothy at her heels. "Your Highness."

"Aunt Lucille," Rothy squealed in his child-speak.

Crouching down, I lifted my arms seconds before I was nearly tackled by the two-year-old. "Goodness," I said with a giggle.

Rothy laughed as he reached for my hand. "We made decorations. Come see."

My gaze went to Lady Sherry's, who nodded.

Once in the children's nursery, Lady Sherry put Alice down. In the last few months, she'd gone from crawling to running. I was certain she totally skipped over walking. Rothy was giving me a step-by-step tutorial on the making of ornaments with Styrofoam balls, ribbon, and glitter when Isabella arrived.

Her smile was for the benefit of her children. "Lucille, it's nice of you to visit. The children are always happy to see you."

I stood taller, returning her smile. "I adore them. Even seeing them at dinner, I hadn't realized how mobile Alice has become." When she didn't respond, I added, "The queen has reminded me to watch and learn."

"Hmm."

"How is Francis?" I asked.

"I believe you're on the approved list of visitors. You could see for yourself."

"Yes, I must do that. Truth be told, I lose morning hours to nausea and afternoon to naps." I grinned. "I hear it gets better."

"Yes, it does." Isabella turned to the children. "Mommy and Aunt Lucille are going to talk grown-up things."

"I'm grown up," Rothy replied.

"Yes, you are."

"But maybe you'd enjoy some cakes before naptime," Lady Sherry said.

Of course, both children followed her from the room.

"Shall we," Isabella said, opening the door and leading me back to the main parlor. "Tea?"

"No, thank you." I sat on the edge of a velvet chair. "I owe you an apology."

Isabella's head tilted and she pursed her lips. "I'm sure that's not true."

"It is. I've been angry at you because you took the princess to my home without confiding in me that she would be with you."

"If I had confided, would you have said yes?"

I shook my head. "I don't know. I would have been uncomfortable. Why were you afraid to keep her at Forthwith?"

"It's no longer a matter. The guards found her. Now she's staying here of her own free will."

"Political asylum."

Isabella took a seat to my side. "I was worried what would happen when they found her. With Papa's sanctions on Borinkia, the guards could have claimed she was in Molave illegally." She shook her head. "I couldn't let her be imprisoned in her condition."

"When you asked to go to Annabella, the evening you called" —I tried to recall her words— "you said you were concerned that Francis had done something. What was that?"

Shaking her head, Isabella scoffed. "I don't recall. I guess I was letting the ambush darken my thoughts. I began to worry that if our husbands were targets that my children may also be. It's all moot. The attacker is no longer. No official statement has been made by any other entity taking credit. Francis and Roman are on the mend. Papa and Mum want everyone in Molave City, and I'm okay with that."

Wringing my hands in my lap, I sighed. "I asked Queen Anne to see the princess."

Isabella's eyes opened wide. "You did?"

"Yes, I want to talk to her. You talk to her, right?"

She nodded.

"Is she truly frightened to return to Borinkia?"

"That's why she was granted asylum."

"Do you think King Aleksander II is capable of harming his sister or his niece or nephew?"

"I'm afraid I'm no expert on Alek. I only know what I know from Francis."

"Has she said anything since she arrived here?"

"She finally was granted an audience with Roman."

Swallowing, I nodded. "I am aware."

"Hmm."

"Isabella, what do you think I don't know?"

Isabella stood and walked to the fireplace. "I don't know what you know, Lucille. I don't even know what I know. I've reached out to Inessa because in recent weeks I've experienced the isolation that comes when even your family turns their back on you." She lifted one eyebrow. "I thought it would be best if she had a friend."

"Very magnanimous of you."

"Or selfish. I too could use a friend."

Her words were a knife twisting in my chest. "I thought we were friends."

Inhaling, she nodded. "I thought so too."

"I've been wrong," I admitted. "I also know what it's like to feel excluded. How can I help?"

Isabella pursed her lips as she came closer and retook her seat. "I feel like Francis is withholding the truth from me."

"What truth?"

"I don't know. Papa and Roman reprimanded me about Inessa. After she asked for asylum, Papa started talking to me again. Mum is just Mum. She is oblivious to everything."

"I think she knows more than she lets on. Why would Inessa seek asylum?"

"She's afraid of what her brother will do when he learns she's expecting Roman's child. As I said, I'm not expert on Alek, but think about this from her perspective." Isabella lowered her volume. "Alek could use the child as a pawn, a bargaining chip. Especially since the world thinks you're incapable of conceiving."

I laid my hand over my stomach. "Have you told her, about me?" As I waited for her response, I wondered why in this world of secrets, the only ones spoken aloud were mine.

Isabella reached over and covered my hand with hers. "I wouldn't do that. Not until you're ready to announce it."

I felt my cheeks rise in a real smile. "I am sorry, Isabella. I too know what it's like to feel as though you're on the outside looking in. If I'm part of the reason you felt that way, I apologize."

We leaned closer in an embrace.

"Did the princess mention her visit with Roman?"

"She was..." Isabella inhaled. "It didn't go the way

she wanted. I guess that's good for you."

"Could you convince her to leave Molave?" I asked.

"And go where? If Borinkia isn't safe and she's considered illegal in other countries, where do you think she should go?"

Sighing, I leaned back against the cushions. "I hadn't thought of that."

"As you know, I'm not my brother's biggest fan, but from all Inessa said, he seems to have stuck to his story about wanting to make your marriage work." She shrugged. "I didn't think he had it in him."

"Roman is trying. He wasn't the only one to make mistakes. Maybe I should visit the princess to thank her for causing our troubles to be brought into the light."

"I'm afraid she might not take that as a compliment."

It wasn't meant as one.

I stood and brushed the front of my slacks. "I should go."

Isabella stood and reached for my hand. "You're always welcome. The children adore you."

"You can always visit me."

She inhaled. "I'd rather avoid running into Roman."

"Isabella, we are a family. We all care about one another."

CHAPTER 16

Queen of Molave
In the past

With a shaking hand, Theo reached for mine. The sadness in his eyes overflowed onto his cheeks. His strong body sagged with the weight of our loss. "Anne, I'm sorry."

"No. We won't do it. We're not losing another heir." Every cell in my body ached with a void that would never fill. Everything hurt from my temples to what remained of my crumbling heart. It wasn't only my grief, but that of my husband's. His emotions fed into mine, making the night unbearable and the dawn too far away. "They're wrong," I said, new determination in my tone. "The doctors are wrong. He will survive."

As if my proclamation would make it so.

Theo's body shook with the depth of his sobs, sounds no wife wants to hear and no father should express. Cradling his face, I held him close. His tears dampened my nightgown as mine rained down, falling to his greying hair. Neither a quarter century of marriage nor being the king and queen of Molave made us invincible.

In this moment, our titles meant nothing.

Our renewed devotion felt lacking.

Our world was crumbling without a hope for recovery.

As we held one another, I faced the reality that losing Roman was different than losing Teddy. We were younger. I never forced Roman to replace our firstborn; nevertheless, his presence within me gave me the strength to go on. In my dark bedchamber, I feared in the depth of my soul that without our son, I couldn't continue. I never would.

Holding the broken man in my arms, my fright deepened at the thought of losing him. One son was unbearable. Two was unfathomable. Theodore wasn't just any man but a king, a monarch with a throne to fill. He'd accomplished that twice, and somehow each one was taken from us.

Theodore lifted his face to mine. "We need to tell Isabella and Mother."

Our beautiful daughter, barely a teenager. She was at Annabella with her granny, the queen mother. Isabella had so much life ahead, so much potential, and now it would be over. She'd be damned to rule. Her goals and her loves would no longer be at her discretion. Everything would change.

Theodore sat back, his eyes bloodshot and his lips quivering. "She will be the first Godfrey female to rule."

"If she does, I'll lose both of my children—all of them."

"No, Anne." He reached for my hands. "We won't lose Isabella."

"If the country of Molave is placed on her shoulders, her life is over. The world has seen the toll it took on Elizabeth."

Queen Elizabeth II was crowned queen before her twenty-sixth birthday.

How long would Theodore live?

Isabella was but a teenager.

"I have ruled," Theo said. "Roman was going to do it."

Roman.

I imagined our son's face—handsome like his father. Dark hair. Regal eyes. Gentle hands. The knowledge of a ruler. The wisdom of an heir. Even his service to Molave's armed forces was a demonstration of his sense of duty for our country. It was never a question, but his destiny.

Standing, I shook my head. "No. We can't announce this news yet," I said. "Please, Theodore. If we don't make a statement, it's like he's still here."

"It will only prolong—"

Falling to my knees at his feet, I interrupted, "Please, Theodore. You're the king. You don't have to do anything you don't want to do."

"I don't want to bury another child."

Late into the night, my husband's words ran on repeat as I stared up at the ceiling of my bedchamber. My mind drifted back to Teddy's death. The sinking hole of mourning that almost swallowed us whole. I recalled the darkness, the impenetrable loneliness. I'd turned away from my husband because I blamed myself. If only I'd been with Teddy.

Does Theodore blame himself for Roman's passing?

Roman had followed his father into the skies, both pilots, both honored soldiers.

I sat up and peered around my bedchamber.

No.

I wouldn't allow my husband to sink into the quicksand of despair that I had. I'd been unreachable, the only one keeping me alive was Roman, and now he was nearly gone—being kept alive by machines.

From the time of Teddy's birth, I'd battled with postpartum depression. I wasn't myself. I pushed

Theodore away from what he needed—a wife. After Teddy's passing, it was worse.

There were rumors. At the time, I'd hadn't cared that he sought companionship where he could. The women didn't matter to me. I was his wife, his queen. They never would be. They were unimportant.

Did I hate him for what he did?

At the time, I was too busy hating myself.

A new thought came to me—one I'd never dared entertain. One whose answer didn't matter—until it did, until now.

Were there other children?

Other sons?

Other Godfreys?

Would Theodore even know?

Wrapping myself in my dressing gown and forgoing my slippers, I hurried through my apartment and into the connecting parlor. Not stopping to knock, I burst inside Theodore's apartment. My eyes scanned each room leading back to his bedchamber.

Is he asleep?

I pushed the final doors open.

"Anne?" he said, his voice coming from a dark corner of the room.

"Are there others?"

"Others?" He stood. "What are you talking about?"

"Do you even know?"

In the shadows, I watched as he stood. His movements suddenly seemed an old man's, not my husband. The loss of each son was a blow to his vitality. It seemed as if Theo had aged years in the hours since we received the news of Roman on life support.

I rushed toward him. "Bastards," I said. "I'm not upset. They have your blood, Theodore. Does one exist?"

"Anne." He shook his head. "I was wrong. We've agreed not to revisit that. We had our marriage blessed. I haven't strayed since."

The blessing was around Roman's fifth birthday.

My hands trembled with the possibility. "Have you kept track? Should we ask the Firm to investigate?"

"The Firm knows. I haven't kept track." He exhaled. "I was told of a few."

"What do they look like? Are there boys? How old are they? Do they resemble our son?"

His dark eyes widened. "You can't be serious. You'd accept another woman's child as your own?"

Taking a deep breath, I straightened my shoulders. "My king, I will accept your child as mine."

"Is it possible?"

"I don't want Isabella to rule." Tears came to my eyes. "Not because I believe she'd be incapable, but because it would dominate her life. I want her to love. I want her to know the joy of motherhood. I want her to follow her dreams. I want her future to be what she wants, not what is expected of her."

"Do you think this is even possible?" Theodore asked.

"You, my love, are king. Anything is possible."

CHAPTER
17

Lucille

Present day

The beating of my heart thumped like drums in my ears as I walked alone, passing doors and long hallways. While I wasn't as familiar with this area of Molave Palace as I had been, I wasn't lost. Five years ago, I knew every turn of these hallways. This wing of the castle was purposely meant to be secluded from the rest. Intended as residential, it required navigating a maze of corridors to find your way from here to the royal housing or even the business offices and apartments. Tours of Molave Palace never mentioned the second floor of this far wing.

Centuries ago, the catacomb of rooms was constructed to house visitors to Molave Palace. Years and years ago, reaching Molave required traveling by horse-drawn carriages on mountainous roads or via ships through the North Sea, creating a long and tiresome journey.

Unlike today, when visitors may travel via plane

and stay for only a day or two, when King Theodore's grandfather, Theodore I, or his great-grandfather, Archibald III, ruled Molave, it was customary to accommodate guests for weeks or months at a time.

During my study of Molavian history, I read stories of guests who remained for the entire winter season, unable to travel due to weather. This secluded wing offered lodging without daily interaction with the royals. I imagined it as a palace hotel for VIP travelers. Truly, while staying here in years gone by, guests may only have had one or two audiences with the king or queen. Nevertheless, their needs were met.

The accommodations varied. Some of the apartments consisted of many rooms, expansive enough to house large families or royal visitors with their own entourage of staff. Truly, the stories sounded like a page or an episode out of historical fiction, the kind of series people watch on streaming services.

It was funny that as much as times had changed—travel had improved, and the palace rarely kept long-term guests—these apartments were still in use. This was the wing where I was housed upon my initial arrival to Molave.

It wouldn't have been proper for me to stay where the royals did, not until Roman's and my marriage was complete. As an American female in a foreign land, it would also not have been acceptable for me to live on my own.

Never mind the fact I had lived on my own in New York for years.

This rarely used configuration of apartments allotted me the space to live and rooms to learn. Months of classes as well as direction from Lady Buckingham were spent here. This setting was my introduction to life as a royal. My escape was the gardens. I'd always loved the outside but as a future royal, my safety was paramount. I couldn't walk the sidewalks of Molave. Therefore, the paths that I strolled filled with flowers and trees within the security of the palace walls were my oasis.

It wasn't a stretch to assume that this was also where the palace would house the princess of Borinkia. I didn't know which apartment until Isabella told me. Similar to my adventure down below the infirmary, I was again solo.

I wouldn't say I was going against any of the royals. No one had forbidden me from visiting the princess. Other than mentioning the possibility to the queen, I hadn't asked.

It had been two days since Roman visited her.

While I thought he should visit again, the last we'd spoken, he'd said he hadn't returned. In his defense, his schedule was increasingly full. The next few days would be the last of the parliament's session before the holiday. King Theodore had Roman scheduled to make multiple speeches in committees as well as to the entire parliament.

Despite not going back to see her, I could tell the presence of the Borinkian princess was a concern for my prince. I saw it in his eyes whenever she was mentioned. While King Theo was increasingly confident in Roman's ability—both in relaying his message and not being questioned as to his identity, Roman's confidence had waned since his one meeting with the princess.

When I couldn't get a feel for Inessa's reaction from Isabella, I made myself a deal. If Roman didn't go back to her, I would. She deserved to know what the plan was for her child.

I couldn't imagine that she'd want to stay in Molave or at the palace if she knew the queen's intentions. My hope was to appeal to her, mother-to-be to mother-to-be.

Outside the double doors to the apartment where Inessa was staying, I stopped, took a deep breath, and lifting my chin, knocked on the door. My visit was unannounced. There was no reason to believe the princess would be away from her apartments.

An older woman answered, pulling the door

inward. Her eyes opened wide before she curtsied. "Your Highness."

"I've come to speak with the princess."

The woman took a step back, unwilling and unable to forbid my entrance. However, her expression was not one that said welcome. "Ma'am, the princess doesn't have you on her schedule."

"Is she not here?" I asked, looking around the front parlor.

"I will inform her of your arrival."

"Thank you," I said with all the graciousness I could muster.

"Would you like some tea?"

"No. I'll wait for the princess."

"Please, Your Highness," the woman said, gesturing toward the arrangement of chairs and loveseats. "You may rest. I'll inform Princess Inessa."

Truth be told, the nerves that had been twisting tighter during my walk to these apartments disappeared the moment I stepped through the door. Queen Anne was right. Inessa wasn't my concern. I was and am Roman's wife, his princess and his future queen. If he was uneasy about confronting her, I would do it.

My high-heeled boots clipped along the marble and sunk into the thick rugs as I walked around the room. There was nothing about my appearance to suggest I was expecting a child. The waist on my tweed slacks still fit without a problem—if anything I'd lost weight. Roman had been accurate, my breasts were larger, but not noticeably—to anyone but him. I had my long hair secured in a low ponytail and my long-sleeved blouse was fitted with tight cuffs and flowing arms.

Flames radiated heat from the fireplace.

I peered into the ashes, wondering if the shards from the princess's temper tantrum were buried beneath or if some poor butler had been tasked with cleaning the hearth.

With each passing minute, my ire grew.

"Privet."

My ability to speak other languages was minimal, but I recognized the Russian greeting. Spinning around, my gaze met Inessa Volkov's.

"Hello, Inessa," I replied with a smile.

The color of her eyes was strikingly light, barely containing blue pigment. Her blond hair was in a topknot, and I'd apparently caught her before she had a chance to change. Her clothes were soft, comfortable, and baggy. Yet I could assess evidence of a baby in her petite form. As far as her clothes, I wasn't certain if they were pajamas or lounging apparel. Her feet were covered in only socks.

The princess's forehead furrowed as she opened her eyes wider, her blond eyebrows almost invisible. "Lucille?"

I nodded. "I believe we saw one another at Forth-with a few weeks ago."

"I don't recall." She lifted a throw pillow and held it in front of her as she settled on the couch with one leg beneath her.

Taking her cue, I sat across from her, on the edge of the seat, my ankles crossed beneath the chair, and my hands in my lap. "Since you're staying in my husband's family's home, I thought I should welcome you."

She lifted her chin.

I'd come to her with good intentions; however, each second in her presence hit me wrong. I would do what I could for her child. That didn't mean I was here to make a new friend. "Queen Anne has spoken about you."

Inessa moved the pillow and ran her hand over her larger midsection. "Mum is sweet. She's happy about a grandchild." She lifted her hand. "She gave me this beautiful bracelet."

Mum.

I nodded. "She is happy about a grandchild. Roman and I are expecting. The heir to the Molave throne will be born next summer."

From the clenching of Inessa's jaw, I assessed that Isabella had been honest about not sharing my condition with the princess.

"My baby," she said, "he's coming sooner."

"Oh, do you know that you're having a boy?"

Inessa nodded. "The royal physician here in Molave, he did an ultrasound." Her smile grew. "Boy." Her faint eyebrow quirked. "Yours?"

"We don't know yet."

"Why are you here?"

I shrugged. "I wanted to see you, speak to you."

"You don't like me," she said, her expression adding that the feeling was mutual.

"I don't know you, Inessa." Saying her name still left a sour taste. "I feel bad for you. Your brother is upset because you have brought shame on your country, sleeping with a married man. My husband is over you. Honestly, you're pathetic."

Okay, that wasn't what I planned to say, but as the words came forward, I couldn't or wouldn't stop them.

"Me?" She sneered. "Roman doesn't want to be married to you. Yet you get pregnant to save a broken marriage. I think you should look in the mirror if you want to see pathetic."

Smiling, I clasped my hands. "Inessa, I'm going to be as brutally honest with you as I can. Queen Anne is interested in your child, so much so, she doesn't want him to be raised in Borinkia. Should you choose to raise your child elsewhere, she will keep tabs on you and him. Regardless of the savage origin of his mother, that boy is believed to be a Godfrey."

"Savage?"

"Your father's treatment of the good people of Letanonia."

She shook her head. "I wasn't even born. My child and I don't deserve to suffer for what was done long ago."

"You're right. You don't. Leave Molave. Go anywhere but Borinkia, and the queen and I will see that you're taken care of, well taken care of. Your son will have the best education, and you will both live in comfort and safety."

She lowered her feet to the rug. "The queen doesn't want me to leave Molave."

"It would be better if you did."

Her smile quirked. "It isn't my problem if you can't keep your husband happy, Princess. I won't be the one to leave Molave—it will be you and your child. Go back to the States. Cry to the press. It won't matter. When Roman and I marry, we will unite Borinkia and Molave."

I sucked in a deep breath.

Delusional.

She is crazy.

"Inessa, I know you have no reason to believe me, but let me make this as clear as possible. Prince Roman and I are married. We've both made mistakes, but that doesn't define our future—our future together. I am his wife, his princess, and one day will be his queen. My child will be our heir."

Inessa brought the pillow back in front of her. "Something isn't right."

"You, you're not right."

"No, Roman. He's different."

"Correct," I said, "he's different. He's decided to stay committed to me. Leave Molave while you can."

She shook her head. "You can't threaten me."

"I'm not," I answered, keeping my smile intact. "I'm giving you the best advice I can. For the sake of your child, leave. As long as that destination isn't Borinkia, you will be fully supported."

Inessa stood. "I'm not a mistress to be dismissed. I am to be queen."

"You're right. You're not his mistress. You're nobody." It was my turn to shake my head. "He lied to you." I stood. "I promise you, the next queen of Molave will be the daughter of Baroness Polina Astid, not a Borinkian whore."

Her lips opened. I took the opportunity of her speechlessness to excuse myself.

As I reached for the doorknob, I heard her response.

"You will not win."

Craning my neck over my shoulder, I broadened my smile. "I already have."

CHAPTER
18

Lucille

Beyond the windowpanes, a light flurry of snow swirled in the cold wind, reflecting like small crystals in the light of the streetlamps. The clock read close to eleven by the time Roman finally arrived back to our apartments. As soon as I heard him enter, I made my way to his side. Lord Martin stepped away as I entered, leaving us with a bow and wishes for a restful night.

Despite the late hour, as I scanned from his head to his shoes, I was struck with how incredibly handsome my husband was, still dressed in his shirt and suit pants from dinner. The sleeves on his shirt were rolled to his elbows, showing off his muscular forearms, and the splint on his right hand was smaller than he'd had this morning. The top button of his shirt was undone, and his tie in his hand, recently pulled from his collar.

Wearing my dressing gown over my nightgown, I unceremoniously made my announcement. It was the one I'd been rehearsing since I left the Borinkian princess; nonetheless, it came out rather bluntly. "I visited Inessa today."

Roman spun toward me, an incredulous expression on his face. Dropping the tie on the floor, his hand went to his head, and his long fingers raked through his dark hair. "Fuck, Lucille. You could have said good evening before dropping that bomb."

I stood tall, straightening my shoulders. "Good evening, Your Highness. You weren't going back to her, so I did."

"It has only been two days." Inhaling, the prince paced back and forth.

His Adam's apple bobbed as his dark stare intensified, darkening the brown irises or dilating the pupils. In the fire's light, they looked like black holes pulling me in.

"Roman, listen to me." I walked toward him. When I stood in the way of his trek, he stopped. Laying my hands against his shoulders, I met his gaze. "Think about it. My husband's mistress is under the same roof as us—all of us. She has claimed to be carrying your child. Who would expect me to *not* talk to her?"

"Noah."

His answer took the wind from my sails. My hands dropped to my sides.

Furrowing his forehead, Roman narrowed his gaze. "If I were Noah, would you have gone to her?"

I shook my head. "I can't answer that."

"Or you don't want to answer."

In my bare feet, I stood decimeters shorter than my husband. It wasn't only that my Roman towered over me. His shoulders were twice as wide as my own. He outweighed me by over forty kilograms. If the man before me hadn't shown me that I could trust him at every turn, I could and would be frightened.

If he were Noah...

"Fine," I said, stepping away. "You're right. If you were...not you, I probably wouldn't have done something that I knew would upset you." Slapping my hands against my robe-covered thighs, I sighed. "Or I might have done it to garner your attention."

"You have my attention, Lucille. You're admitting that you knew this would upset me."

Tucking my chin down, I looked up through veiled lashes. "I hoped it wouldn't."

"Does Mum know?"

"I don't know. I went to the princess earlier this morning. I didn't tell Queen Anne or Isabella. I didn't mention it to anyone until now."

"Because..." He prompted.

"Because if I would have mentioned it to you earlier, we would have had to table the subject until after dinner" —I looked around— "until now, and I knew you'd want to discuss it."

Clenching his jaw, Roman shook his head. "Damn it, Lucille. The princess is a liability."

"I agree."

"What did you say to her?" he asked.

"I told her to leave Molave. I told her if she went anywhere except Borinkia, the queen and I would make sure she's well taken care of."

"But you didn't talk to Mum first?"

"No. Queen Anne wants the princess here until the baby is born. I don't agree. If you're nervous about Inessa suspecting you're different, then I say we get her out of here."

"Anything else?" he asked.

"I told her we were expecting a child next summer."

Roman's eyes widened as he shook his head.

Scrunching my face and speaking fast, I added, "I said she shamed her country, was pathetic, and I might have added something about her being a nobody. But" —I opened my eyes wide— "I did reassure her that she would be well cared for—if the child is a Godfrey. Which we both know it isn't."

The prince exhaled. "Answer me, Princess, how will antagonizing Inessa help?"

"She will leave."

"Or she will dig in her heels." He shook his head. "I fucking hate having to think like him." Roman turned toward me. "For months I've worked to make Roman me, the man I am. I can't be me with her. I have to be him."

"Could *he* be him?" I asked. "Noah?"

"No," Roman answered quickly. "For one, we don't resemble one another as much anymore, and two, allowing Noah and Inessa to communicate seems like a very bad idea."

I again stepped closer, inhaling the aroma of Roman's cologne mixed with his unique scent. Leaning into his chest, I smiled up at him as his heart thumped beneath my breasts, and I wrapped my arms around his torso. "She must leave. Queen Anne said if she lived anywhere but Borinkia she would only be watched."

"I spoke with Mrs. Drake about her yesterday."

"You didn't tell me."

Roman shook his head and reached for my shoulders with both hands. "I wish I could remember every word I think of telling you throughout the day."

Leaning my face toward his right hand, I smiled. "I feel your grip."

He nodded. "It's getting better each day."

"You think of me throughout the day?" I asked.

"Only every second." He sighed. "No more visits to Inessa."

At arm's length, I could see the exhaustion on his

face, the lines around his eyes and darkness below his eyes. "You're tired."

"I am. Tonight after dinner I was informed that Papa delegated another meeting with the parliamentary committee on defense to me. I've spent the last few hours reading about Molave's military."

"Another reason, my prince, why you shouldn't be dealing with her. Let me."

"Papa wants to know what she knows."

"About what?" I asked as I picked up Roman's tie from the floor and began to undo the buttons on his shirt.

"I don't know. I've quizzed Noah a hundred times. He swears he didn't tell her that he was an impostor."

"Do you believe him?"

"I do. He's been...ill."

I took a step back. "Noah's ill? With what?"

Roman shook his head. "Mr. Davies said it's a virus. I don't know how he could have gotten it. He's isolated from almost everyone."

"Maybe one of the medical staff?" I suggested.

"Mr. Davies suggested I stay away until he's better." Roman sighed and sat on the bench near the end of his bed. "I shouldn't care. There's so much happening; he should be the least of my concerns."

Going toward him, I shook my head. "You're right. You shouldn't." I sat at his side. "But you do."

Roman reached for my hand. "Lucille, some days I worry that I can't do this."

My eyes opened and my mouth grew dry.

He closed his eyes with a sigh. His attention went to our hands, turning mine in his. "I love you." He lifted my hand and kissed my knuckles. "I already love our child."

Palming his cheek, I swallowed. "I can't lose you." Tears prickled the back of my eyes.

"Do you remember asking me if I truly believed King Theo to be ruthless?"

I nodded.

"He has made ruthless decisions. Mrs. Drake presented me with one."

"What decision does she want you to make?"

"She suggested that if I'm concerned about Inessa, there is an alternative."

"An alternative to keeping her here? Good. What is it?" As soon as the question left my lips, I knew the answer. I could read it in Roman's expression. "No." I stood and walked back and forth. "No, absolutely not."

"Logic clearly states that the needs of the many outweigh the needs of the few or the one."

I scoffed. "Are you quoting *Star Trek*?"

Roman nodded. "It was a powerful scene. Have you seen it?"

"Yes. My father is a big *Star Trek* fan. He has all

the movies." I felt my forehead furrow as I recalled the dramatic exchange. "In that scene, Spock sacrifices himself for his shipmates. You are not sacrificing yourself for Molave."

"No, Mrs. Drake's suggestion wasn't nearly as altruistic."

"Killing Inessa isn't an option," I said. "Harboring her is dangerous enough. King Aleksander would consider the death of his sister an act of aggression."

"That was my first reaction too. I'm not a murderer. However, as time has passed, I've come to realize how silencing her could help us—you and me."

"But Noah said he didn't tell her."

Roman looked up at me. "She made odd comments. What if someone else told her?"

I considered his question. "Who else knows?"

"More than we ever assumed. It's one person in particular who I'm concerned about." When I didn't answer, Roman went on, "Francis."

My bare feet padded over the soft rug. "Isabella said Inessa was at Forthwith before we arrived, after the speech in Odnessa. She hasn't mentioned Noah."

"I'm confident Inessa and Noah didn't cross paths. It's Francis I'm concerned about. If Inessa knows about the impostors, it's because of him."

"Inessa went to Isabella not Francis. They were each harboring guests unbeknownst to one another."

Roman took a deep breath and stood. "Noah is certain that Isabella and Inessa dislike one another. When I told Francis that Isabella hid Inessa at Forthwith, he indicated she was covering for him. What if Inessa didn't go to Isabella but to Francis?"

I spun toward my husband. "Does this mean Francis is close to both Alek and Inessa?"

He shrugged.

"Isabella said that Francis and Alek have known one another since childhood. She didn't act like she and the princess were close until she was caught hiding her. Now she visits her almost every day." I had a new thought. "Oh my God."

"What?"

"Could Francis be the father of Inessa's child?"

"Well, shit. I'm authorizing the amniocentesis."

"Didn't you say she said no?"

Roman's smile grew. "Too fucking bad. I'm the prince of Molave. She's in my country. I make the rules."

"Maybe you can be ruthless?"

CHAPTER
19

Roman

I n three steps, I was standing before Lucille. The possibility of her suggestion refueled my tired body with fresh strength. If the child wasn't Noah's, we could be rid of Inessa Volkov for good.

Snaking my left arm around Lucille's waist, I pulled her close as I grasped her chin with the fingers of my right hand. A smile, brought on by the realization my hand was healing, combined with the vision of the blue orbs staring up at me, cracked my sober expression.

"You're tired, my prince."

"Not as tired as I was a few minutes ago." Leaning down, I captured her pink lips, drinking her in, her sweet taste, and the soft mews coming from deep in her throat. With little persuasion, her lips parted, offering my tongue access. As our kiss deepened, Lucille's body melded with mine. With each second, the tension from her earlier announcement faded, lost in the backdrop of the crackling fire.

The long day filled with study and meetings regarding the upcoming Parliament sessions was temporarily forgotten. Concerns over Noah's health and Inessa's motives evaporated as my body came to life.

Earlier, when I was walking toward the apartments, I felt as if I were Frankenstein's creation. Lying on a slab, the fabrication of a man being made from the parts of multiple people. The Oliver side of me waned as Romans past were becoming second nature. Trudging forward through the quagmire of unknowns had me ready to surrender. Making life-and-death decisions, questioning my own ethics, as well as the imaginary boundary between right and wrong wore on me.

I hadn't recognized the growing void within myself until this moment—until Lucille refilled and refueled me, the connection we shared making me whole. Releasing her chin, I palmed her cheek and stared into the burning embers of her orbs. "I'm never leaving you, Princess."

Her lips curled. "I told you the first night we met that royal life wasn't what Americans thought it was. There's more to this way of living than crowns and castles."

"I've never been offered a crown."

"Only on your coronation, Your Highness."

"Assuming I'm not discovered or replaced—"

Lucille's finger came to my lips. "Please don't mention such things."

"They're real possibilities. We need to be wary."

She dropped her forehead to my t-shirt-covered chest, my button-down shirt hanging agape from where Lucille had unfastened the buttons.

I cradled her face against me. "Assuming all those things," I repeated, "I wish King Theodore a long life."

My princess looked up. "You do?"

"I do. He is knowledgeable beyond my comprehension. I need more than six months or six years to fully understand the complexities that steer everyday decisions."

"That's what advisors are for."

I nodded. "True, but I don't know who to trust."

"You trust the king?"

My answer didn't require intense scrutiny. "I do. When it comes to Molave and his family, the man is steadfast." I took a step back and while holding Lucille's hand, swept my gaze from her freshly brushed hair and naturally exquisite complexion, over her dressing gown, and down to her toes. "It's late, my princess. You're readied for slumber."

"I'm ready for bed," she replied with a smirk. "Slumber will come."

Unlike her, I wasn't prepared for night. Lord

Martin had generously made himself scarce upon Lucille's arrival. I longed for a shower, the feel of water beading down as steam filled the stall. Alas, a bath would be in my future. "Give me ten minutes."

"I can assist you."

Placing a kiss on her forehead, I smiled. "That royal life you described."

She nodded.

"To continue quoting Spock, he said, "After a time, you may find that having is not so pleasing a thing after all as wanting. It's not logical, but it's often true." I think that's the American illusion of royal life. From the time many are young, they hear stories and dream of the crowns and castles, they think they want it, but having it isn't as pleasing as one would imagine."

"You aren't pleased?"

"I'm grateful every day that I'm standing here with you, my princess. It's the simplicities I miss." I lifted my cheeks. "A shower."

"Ahh," she sighed. "And a solitary stroll through Central Park."

"That doesn't seem safe."

Her expression was wistful. "When I was at Columbia and I had a break from classes, I would go to the park. Sometimes I'd walk the trails. Other times, I'd simply sit in the grass and read or watch people."

"Do you miss that?"

She nodded. "At times. When I was speaking with Lady Larsen about our upcoming tour, I found myself reminiscing about the city." Her expression saddened. "It won't matter where we go. It won't be the same."

"Where do you want to go?" I asked. "A carriage ride through the park?"

Lucille inhaled as her stunning smile returned. "No carriage ride. I always felt bad for the horses. I was thinking about the Met and maybe a show." Her eyes opened wide. "Or should we stay away from Broadway?"

"People see what they want to see."

"Is that another Spock quote?"

I shrugged. "I believe he said something similar, but the truth remains. All contextual clues tell the observer that I am Roman Godfrey. There are enough uncertainties in this world for the average person not to invent more. Therefore, they will believe what they see with their eyes and hear with their ears, regardless if it's accurate. Broadway would not be a problem, but I must share that I'm a critical theatergoer."

"Will you share all the secrets of what occurs backstage?"

"If only your ears will hear, I'll tell you whatever you want to know." Lucille tilted her head. "What are you thinking?"

"It's about Noah. He went to his hometown and learned of his demise. He saw his headstone."

Her face scrunched. "Where would you be buried?"

"I don't know," I replied honestly. "I was born on an air force base in Germany. We moved around multiple countries. I didn't live in the US until I was a young teenager. At first, we resided in Virginia. My mother and stepfather were both employed as independent military contractors. Later, they were transferred to California. After high school I left. I never really went back." While I hadn't disliked my youth, saying the history aloud sounded sad. "In other words, no hometown."

"You were in California when you were approached by the Firm?"

"Yes, Hollywood. I had a nice apartment."

Lucille reached for my hand. "None of this is fair to you. At least I had a choice to marry."

That wasn't what Noah said.

Looking into Lucille's blue stare, I couldn't tell her that, the things Noah said about her father. No matter what he'd done in the past, I was here for the future— or I planned to be.

There it was.

My resolution.

My reason for continuing this life.

Lucille—and now, our child.

"Ten minutes," I said, offering her a chaste kiss.

Vapor hung heavily as the tub filled with steaming water. A look in the mirror confirmed everything I'd said. Since late last summer, the world saw this face as Roman Godfrey.

Unbuckling my belt and my pants, I let them fall to my ankles. A Velcro strap and I removed the splint, flexing my fingers. Soon, my clothing was in a pile on the tile, and I stepped into the hot water, wishing the liquid could wash away the drudgery of the day. It wasn't until I was settled with my head against the end of the tub that the door opened inward.

"Your Highness?"

My smile returned as Lucille entered, a crystal tumbler with amber liquid in her hand. Her hair was piled on top of her head. Her dressing gown was missing, leaving her covered by a light-pink nightgown. The bright light of the vanity allowed me to see her curves beneath the material.

"You're a vision."

She came to a stop next to the tub, her gaze peering beneath the clear water as her smile grew and the bathroom lights reflected in her eyes. "I'm happy with what I see as well." Kneeling at the side of the tub, she handed me the drink.

Swirling the liquid within, I asked, "How did you know I liked bourbon?"

"I am your wife."

"You are."

"I've tasted it on you, and I found the small cabinet in the connecting parlor."

Taking a sip, I closed my eyes as my throat constricted at the familiar burn. Before my eyes opened, the water splashed. Lucille submerged a cloth and after coating it with bodywash brought it to my shoulders. Her fingers massaged my slick, soap-covered skin. Gently, she washed around the remaining bandage on my arm, down my back, and over my torso.

I reached for her hand as she went lower.

Her gaze met mine.

"If you want to sleep, you'll let me do the rest myself."

"Your Highness, if I wanted to sleep, I would be in your bed, not at your side."

CHAPTER
20

Lucille

If I were to choose what type of intimate experience I enjoyed most with my Roman, I would be hard-pressed to pick only one. The nights of unbridled passion, my body sandwiched between him and the wall, bent over a table with my breasts pressed flat, or over the end of a sofa with my behind lifted in the air, were exhilarating. The switch from royal protocol to savage desire took my breath away. Roman's devotion to my pleasure centered my world in a way that focused my thoughts, consuming them with the here and now and taking away the outside world. The spark we shared was unlike anything I'd experienced.

Somehow, we'd jumped from introduction to the familiarity of five years married in a matter of weeks. Now after months, we'd developed an ease that in hindsight I realized Noah and I never shared. I don't believe the first Roman—the man I wed—and I did either. Our relationship was too new.

As Roman stepped from the bathtub, his skin glistening with water droplets and his penis semi-erect, the passion we'd shared and would share was present—a sensual cloud engulfing us.

Yet we both knew without speaking that tonight's union would be different.

Softer.

Gentler.

Quieter.

After Roman dried himself with a plush towel, we walked hand in hand to his bedchamber. There was no need for him to clothe himself. We weren't unaware that the night would culminate in a sexual union.

As we both settled beneath the blankets of his large bed, there was no rush. The dichotomy of this from what we knew possible was refreshing and comforting. We didn't need the exuberance of starved lovers to find pleasure. There was an indescribable luxury in holding one another. The sense of the other's touch as our fingers skirted one another's skin. The arousal that came with deepening kisses as well as the shivers from those that fluttered over my flesh like butterfly wings.

The two of us came together in a way that was more than physical.

Time had played with our minds. The minutes we'd shared were days. The days were months and the months years. Our lovemaking superseded the simple act that had been repeated throughout time. We relished the closeness, the beat of the other's heart against our chest, the sound of the other's breathing and intimacy of the noises we vocalized as well as the sounds of our bodies joining over and over as one.

The pleasure was less intense, yet no less gratifying.

Nerve endings crackled as endorphins gushed throughout my circulation. My core spasmed as I held tight to Roman's shoulders. My lips parted as I rode out my orgasm. The world was right as I watched the change in my prince's countenance, as his thrusts grew more exaggerated, and his neck stretched. There was something truly magical as his handsome face morphed into an expression of sheer bliss.

I'd once said that I sensed his desire the first time he'd taken me over a table. With his body slack over mine, his breaths in my ear, and the beat of his heart against mine, I felt equally desired.

True love and partnership wasn't limited to erotic exchanges that left one speechless, but also in slow and steady interactions that brought each other closer. My heart swelled with the realization that what we'd come to share was exactly what we'd promised.

A partnership.

Roman lifted his head from my shoulder, bringing his nose to mine. "You're the best part of my day."

Nodding, I smiled. "You're the best part of my life."

Slowly rolling, Roman disconnected our union and tugged me to his side. "I don't like the sense of insecurity Inessa brings."

While speaking of his mistress after sex wasn't a great segue, I appreciated his candor and honesty. The two of us had little time during the day that was only ours to share. We could skirt around difficult subjects, or we could face them head-on.

I lifted my chin to meet his gaze. "What are you willing to do about her?"

He shook his head. "I didn't like the idea, but I think you're onto something."

Pushing myself up over his chest, I looked down at him. "Truly, Your Highness? What am I onto?"

"I'm done with her. I was thinking." He cupped my cheek. "What would Noah do, and how is it different than how I would respond?"

"Would you like an alphabetical list?"

Smiling, he shook his head. "Noah would react. I respond. I also have a greater sense of empathy. It's why I'm currently lamenting over his health and future. I'm not sure if I can ever be as ruthless as Papa, but I do know how to deal with Inessa."

"How?"

"I won't." He stretched his neck and lips, reaching

up and kissing my nose. "My princess, she is yours to deal with. I will tell Papa and Mrs. Drake I'm done. I'm committed to our marriage. Inessa can't claim I'm not me if she has no more contact."

I inhaled. "You went from being upset I visited her to handing her to me?"

"Yes. I trust you. I'm here. Speak to me about her, confide, ask my opinion, or simply make your own decisions. With all that Theo keeps adding to my schedule, I need to delegate."

Lying back, I looked up at the ceiling. "When I first told you I wanted to do more, this was about as far from what I was thinking as possible."

"Talk to Mum. The princess's future is in your hands. I recommend you share the responsibility with the queen."

"I will." I rolled to my side. "Good night, my prince."

"Good night, my princess."

Opening my eyes, sunlight spilled around the edges of drapes in Roman's bedchamber. My eyelids fluttered as Lady Buckingham's silhouette registered. Reaching to my side, I felt the coolness of the sheets.

"Your Highness."

"Roman?"

"It's after ten, ma'am. He said for you to be allowed to sleep. However" —she looked down at her wrist— "I was concerned. Would you like your toast?"

Letting out a breath, I looked up at the ceiling and assessed my well-being, laying my hand over my midsection. At the same moment, I became overtly aware of my nudity. It wasn't as if Lady Buckingham hadn't seen me without clothes. It was that when it occurred, it was usually under different circumstances. With a turn of my head, I grinned. "I think we may have found the cure for my morning sickness."

"I'll alert Lady Larsen to make accommodations to your schedule. You have an audience with her this afternoon."

"Mary, please bring me my dressing gown." I tried to recall where I'd left it. Thoughts of the night brought back memories of Roman. Before I could come up with the location of my robe, my mistress had it in her hand and was bringing it forward. Feigning a lack of modesty, I pushed back the blankets and swung my legs over the side of the bed. As I stood, Lady Buckingham brought the robe to my shoulders. Slipping my arms inside, I tied the sash.

"I've had your morning meal sent back. A new one should arrive shortly."

Looking around Roman's bedchamber, I grinned. The scenario shouldn't be unusual, but it was, and at the same time reassuring. I reached for Lady Bucking-ham's hand. "I'm happy."

Swallowing, she nodded. "I can see that, ma'am. Would you like to eat...here?"

"No, we will go to the other side. After all, my clothes are there."

Lady Buckingham nodded.

My bliss evaporated as I looked down at the bed. Gasping, I turned to my mistress.

The bright red spot caused my knees to grow weak.

"Lucille, are you all right?"

With tears filling my eyes, I shook my head and reached for my midsection. There wasn't any discom-fort or cramping. I met Mary's eyes. "Call Mr. Davies and Roman. I feel well, but I'm scared."

"Right away."

CHAPTER
21

Roman

Lady Buckingham's voice was calm, yet her words sent my mind into a tailspin. Looking around the conference room, my gaze met King Theodore's. "It's Lucille. I need to go to the infirmary."

Placing his hands on the table, the king stood. "Is she all right?"

I was too distraught to think much about the way his left hand trembled. Emotions choked my response. "I don't know."

"The baby?"

I shook my head. "I don't know."

"Hurry, son. Let her know we're praying."

The additional eyes and ears in the room didn't register. Whether I'd received the king's permission or not, I planned to bolt from the room. With his permission, as the guard opened the door, I took off as if my life depended upon it. It wasn't my life I was concerned about. With so much at stake, it was too easy to lose sight of the biggest concern—the health and well-being of Lucille's and my child.

"Your Highness," Lord Martin called as I fled the maze of offices and meeting rooms.

Heads bowed and respectful greetings were given as I literally broke into a jog. With each step, each clip of my shoes on the marble tiles, I prepared myself for the worst, for news of a miscarriage.

In the minutes it took to navigate the palace corridors, I went through the five stages of grief.

Denial.

Anger.

Bargaining.

Depression.

Acceptance.

There was another one, one that overcast all the others.

Guilt.

This was my fault.

I was to blame.

If only we hadn't made love last night.

That final unrecognized stage caused me to double over, my breathing heavy, as I approached the infirmary. Moving to the wall, I listened to the buzz as a cyclone of thoughts nearly brought me to my knees.

Regroup, Roman.

Yes, I was referring to myself by that name. I

couldn't pinpoint the moment it happened, but it had happened. Now I needed to remember who I was.

No matter what I'd find beyond the doors, I would be strong for Lucille.

An unimaginable thought came to mind.

Lucille.

We could survive the loss of the pregnancy and try for more.

I couldn't and wouldn't survive the loss of my princess.

Molave meant nothing without her.

"Your Highness," Lord Martin said, panting. "What is happening?"

Standing tall, I met my assistant's gaze. "Lucille."

"The baby?"

With a stiff upper lip and clenched jaw, I nodded. "I don't know more." I looked toward the doors. "The answer is in there."

"If I may...?"

I had neither the energy nor the inclination to listen to my assistant's advice regarding Lucille.

However, before I could gather my thoughts into words, Lord Martin clasped his hands in front of him and spoke softly. "You care for her. No matter what you learn, make certain she knows that."

Swallowing, I nodded, straightened my shoulders, and entered the infirmary.

If I'd expected chaos behind the doors, I was pleasantly disappointed. There weren't medical personnel rushing through the hallways pushing Lucille on a stretcher or wheeling monitors from here to there. No one was shouting orders and no alarms were blaring as was common on medical dramas.

The nurse behind the desk stood and bowed her head. "Your Highness."

"Princess Lucille," I forced myself to speak without emotion and kept my expression stoic.

"This way," she said, leaving her station and leading me down one corridor to another.

I recognized the area we'd entered. It was the restricted area for royals. It was where Francis was still being housed. She led me away from the duke's room. Knocking on the door, she opened it.

"Prince Roman is here."

Calling on all my acting experience, I worked to keep the turmoil within me from showing on the outside. Unlike walking onto a stage in front of hundreds of onlookers, I was stepping into a room, ready to meet my most important audience ever.

Lucille.

I inhaled. The clean, antiseptic scent infiltrated my nostrils as a strange, swishing sound registered in my ears.

The nurse opened the door wider.

Ignoring Mr. Davies and the other nurses, my gaze went to the only person who mattered, the stunning woman lying on the table. I held my breath as her blue orbs glistened. "Lucille."

She lifted her hand, "Roman, come see."

"Your Highness," the others said with a round of neck bows.

Grasping her petite hand was like holding a tether —a lifeline. With her touch, the angst since Lady Buckingham's call calmed, my heart rate slowed, and the room around us began to make sense. I leaned down, dropping a kiss to her forehead. "Everything will be all right."

"Look," she said again.

I followed her gaze to the screen. The image was fuzzy and all in shades of black, white, and grey. It took a moment for my mind to recognize what I was seeing. The small peanut-shaped object surrounded by a larger dark bubble was the focus. Moisture came to my eyes as I stared. "Is everything...?"

"The fetus is strong," Mr. Davies said. "Heart rate is 127 beats per minute."

One hundred twenty-seven?

"Is that...too fast?" I asked.

"No, sir. That is normal for six weeks and two days."

Exhaling, I squeezed Lucille's hand and asked Mr.

Davies, "What about the blood?" It was the message Lady Buckingham had relayed to me.

"Spotting is normal in the first trimester," the royal physician said. "The princess was right to call and make sure everything is well." He grinned. "It's always good for mothers-to-be to rest. Within a day or two, as long as no more bleeding occurs, you, Princess Lucille, may resume your normal schedule."

"You're saying that Lucille is all right?" I asked, needing the verbal confirmation.

"Yes, sir. She is well."

My smile grew as I looked down at Lucille's beautiful face. "You're better than well. You're perfect."

"I'm sorry I scared you. I didn't mean to interrupt your meetings."

I shook my head, my gaze again going to the screen. "I told you I wanted to be here for all future ultrasounds." I looked at Mr. Davies. "Be certain my office is notified in the future."

"Yes, Your Highness."

The screen went black.

The nurses adjusted the drape over Lucille's lower half before stepping from the room. Mr. Davies remained, moving things around to the side.

Once it was only the three of us, he spoke. "Princess Lucille confided that there was intercourse last night."

The statement didn't need affirmation.

The physician nodded slowly. "Assuming there is no more spotting, you may resume that activity in a few days. In general, intercourse isn't a problem during pregnancy. As a matter of fact, some studies suggest it is beneficial for mother and baby. Who doesn't enjoy some endorphins."

Swallowing, I nodded. "Thank you, Doctor."

"Princess, you may dress." He bowed his neck. "I'll give you two a moment."

"Thank you," Lucille said.

When the door shut, I leaned down and kissed her lips. "I was so worried."

"I'm sorry."

"No," I said, shaking my head. "Never be sorry."

She reached again for my hand. "It means the world to me that you dropped everything to come here."

"You are my world, Lucille. On the way here, I played out the awful scenario of facing the loss of this pregnancy. It was horrible to imagine, but then I thought about you. We can spend our next forty years trying to make children, but my life means nothing without you."

Gripping my hand, Lucille sat up and smiled. "Forty years is a long time."

"You heard Mr. Davies; you're to rest for the next

few days. That means no visits to the other wings of the palace."

"I'd like to still talk to the queen about it."

"There's no rush. Mrs. Drake said the princess isn't going anywhere. I also learned her incoming information is vetted—shielded," I said with a grin.

"I know what that's like."

"And her outgoing communication is monitored. If the princess suspects anything about me, she hasn't communicated it to anyone outside the palace."

"What about inside—Isabella?" Lucille asked.

"One problem at a time." I removed my phone from my pocket and sent a text message:

"LUCILLE AND BABY ARE BOTH WELL."

"Who did you text?" Lucille asked.

"Papa. He said he would be praying."

She smiled. "Prayers from the head of the church are always welcome."

Lucille got down from the exam table and walked behind a small curtain. While I appreciated the room's setup for privacy, my emotions had run the gamut in a short time. I wasn't ready to let her out of my sight. Walking to the curtain, I tugged it back with a grin, taking in the beautiful woman dressing. "I'll walk you to our apartments."

She pulled the waistband of the soft slacks she'd worn to the infirmary up to her waist. "I'm fine, Roman. I can walk myself. Mary is waiting." Her blue gaze left mine as she looked down, slipping her feet into a pair of flat shoes.

Offering her my hand, I shook my head. "Today, you'll obey your prince."

Taking my hand, she came closer, leaning against me. "Yes, Your Highness." Moisture came to her eyes. "I was so frightened."

I stroked her long hair. "Me too, my princess. Me too."

"I thought about what Queen Anne said. For a moment in time, I even considered it."

I laid my hand over her lower stomach. "Lucille, a child isn't *our* child. Inessa's child will not be mine. I've never given children much thought." I kissed the top of her head. "Adoption isn't out as a possibility for us one day. Right now, you're well. The baby is well, and you will rest."

"I will."

Instead of walking through the infirmary the way I'd arrived, Lucille and I passed through a back exit, one that led out to the gardens. The door was usually locked. It was only present as a way to take patients out for fresh air. Once outside, we both stood, looking up at the blue sky.

"I know it's cool. I thought you might enjoy a stroll before you're restricted to our apartments."

Lucille hugged my arm and stayed close. "Thank you. I love the gardens, even in the winter."

We took a few paths before reaching a set of French doors off one of the residential parlors. Once inside, I wrapped my arm around her. "It's a fine line between fresh air and freezing you."

"You could have offered me your jacket again."

"I should have," I admitted. "I mostly wanted to avoid all the people in the other wing." I leaned down, kissing the top of her hair. "I like having you to myself."

CHAPTER
22

Lucille

Never before had I had as much difficulty sitting still. As Roman spent his daytime hours working toward the upcoming parliamentary meetings, I was left in our apartments. Despite the inactivity, I reminded myself this was nothing like my lonely days, weeks, and months at Annabella Castle. For five years, I'd wasted my time, doing anything to stay busy.

Now, because Roman had kept his promise, I had work to be done.

By day two, I was ready to climb the walls.

Since I couldn't go to her, I requested Lady Larsen visit our apartments. Together, we worked to further refine the itinerary for the United States tour. In the name of delegation, Roman's office gave me and my staff the ability to complete the planning. The only stipulation was that once the schedule was complete, it would go to the prince's office who would arrange security.

With our recent domestic tour postponed, Lady Larsen suggested daily social media posts as an alternative way of staying in contact with the Molavian subjects. The public relations tactic was working well for other royalty throughout the world. She explained pictures were a visual means of communicating with the younger people of Molave, Europe, and the world.

Together, my secretary and I spent hours reviewing photographs, deciding which ones and what information would be posted. As she brought out older photos, I couldn't help but stare at myself.

At the time—when they were taken—I'd thought I'd done a sufficient job hiding my unhappiness, but now, removed and looking back, I wondered how everyone hadn't seen my melancholy mood.

My Roman had seen it. He'd commented to me early on in our relationship that he wanted to reach through the films and shake Roman for not giving me any attention or recognition I sought.

Could it be that when walking through the bleakest times of our lives, we are so busy looking for the light at the end of the tunnel that we miss the darkness in the mirror?

"Look at this one," Lady Larsen said, turning the screen of her laptop toward me.

My lips curled with the fond memory. "Rothy's second birthday."

"We can't use that one. Look at your expression."

The royal photographer had been on-site. While the Firm had released a family picture of everyone present, the photo now on Lady Larsen's screen was candid, taken as Roman and I walked into the gathering. His fingers were splayed in the small of my back and I was looking up at him. We'd just shared a kiss in the dining room.

Lady Larsen shook her head. "You're looking at the prince as if you'd never seen him before."

I nodded. "I agree. I can't imagine what I was thinking."

She brought up another photo. "This one of you and the duchess is great with the children playing on the floor," she said. "Oh look, the duke is on the floor too."

Looking closer at the picture, I spotted Roman in the background. His customary scowl seemed perfect at the time. Now, months later, it was out of place. I also saw the difference in his shape and greyness of his hair.

"You know," Lady Larsen said, "Prince Roman seems to be getting younger not older."

"And me?" I asked, changing the subject.

She scrolled through some more photos before looking up at me and grinning. "Happier."

"Is it that noticeable?"

"In person, day in and day out, the transformation isn't as stark as looking back at these photos." She turned the screen to me. "This is a year ago."

My stomach turned.

It was a holiday Godfrey family photo. I recalled that Roman and I had a row only minutes earlier before leaving our apartments. The red jumper covering my dress wasn't because I was cold. I'd hurriedly added it to my attire to cover the red handprint on my upper arm.

I looked closer, seeing what at the time I'd thought well hidden. Not only were my eyes dim, but my cheeks were gaunt and hollow. The constant stress of my husband's ever-changing moods had my stomach in a constant state of nausea.

Even now, I'd take the morning sickness over that crushing sense of despair.

"It's not the best photo," I said.

"Ma'am, it's as if you and Prince Roman are new people. If you'll allow me to say something personal?"

"Go on."

"I am pleased that things have improved. The marriage blessing shows on both of you."

I nodded. "Thank you. Maybe we should concentrate on more recent photos."

Despite my assessment that I felt well and confirming that there hadn't been any more spotting, the night of the scare and the following night Roman sent his regrets to Queen Anne, telling the monarchs that we would dine in our apartments.

The third night, I was dressed for dinner in the dining room when he arrived.

He entered my parlor without a knock. His dark stare intensified as he scanned from my hair to my shoes.

I stood. "Your Highness."

His smile broadened as he came closer. "You're breathtaking, Lucille." He gently reached for my hips and pulled me closer.

The spicy aroma of his cologne mixed with the floral scent of my perfume. I craned my chin upward, keeping my gaze on his.

"I've told you before," Roman said, "you don't need to dress up for me. I quite prefer you without clothes."

"I'd obey, my prince; however, if I did, I'd be concerned that such attire would threaten Mr. Davies's orders." Reaching upward and straightening my neck, our lips united. Once the kiss was done, I tilted my head to the side. "I haven't seen the king or queen for over two days. I thought we could join them."

Roman shook his head. "No, Princess. We're following Mr. Davies's orders. Tonight, I get you all to myself."

"Do the monarchs know that I've been kidnapped?" I asked in jest.

He snaked his arm around me and lifted my chin. "They should. I'm world-renowned for my tendency to kidnap princesses."

The lightheartedness of our bubble burst. I took a step back. "Oh no. Is there new publicity about Inessa?"

"The Firm made a public statement asserting that Inessa Volkov requested and has been granted political asylum by Molave."

"Has Alek responded?"

Roman nodded. "He's claiming that his sister would be safe in Borinkia and must return immediately."

Walking around the parlor, I stopped at the large windows, looking out to the streets of Molave. Spinning, I faced my husband. "I need to speak to her."

"I've ordered the amniocentesis."

"Has she agreed?"

"I don't care," he said resolutely. "We're not waiting months to learn the paternity of her child."

"There are less invasive ways to determine paternity."

"I want to know more. If Noah isn't the father, who is?"

"Can you force her?"

Roman went to the sideboard and poured himself a shot of bourbon. His eyes met mine. "Sadly, yes. This is another of the 'don't think like an American' situations according to Mrs. Drake. The only one who can stop it is King Theo." He shrugged as he lifted the shot. "And he has no reason to do that."

"What do you think she will say when she's told the baby isn't a Godfrey?" My mind cycled through scenarios. "I mean, what if she didn't sleep with anyone else? She'll learn that you aren't a Godfrey."

Roman scoffed. "I don't know her, but I'd bet the Crown that monogamy isn't Inessa Volkov's strength."

I looked down at my left hand, seeing my engagement ring and wedding band.

"Princess, why are you sad?"

When I looked up, Roman was in front of me.

"I never thought I'd be someone who wasn't monogamous."

He lifted my chin. "For every day forward."

Forcing a smile, I nodded. "Yes, my prince, from this day forward."

CHAPTER
23

Roman

"I don't understand," I said, staring incredulously across the conference table at King Theodore. Our first presentation before Parliament prior to the holiday break was scheduled to begin in two hours.

"What's not to understand. You've been briefed and are capable. I believe in you."

"The parliamentarians are expecting the king, not the prince."

He shook his head. "Son, I'm nearing eighty years old. I intend to reign for many more years. I also need to know, to have the peace of mind in knowing, that when the day comes that I can't reign that you can."

I lowered my voice. "I haven't had enough time."

King Theodore sat forward, lifting his clasped hands to the table. "I wish I could turn back the years. Alas, some things are impossible even for a king."

My attention went to his hands, the age spots, pale

skin, and especially the slight tremors. I met his gaze. "Are you ill?"

He shrugged. "Mr. Davies is running a battery of tests." He separated his hands and lifted one. The trembling was noticeable. "I don't want to be seen like this."

"Papa." For some reason, the endearment felt right. "You can still sit in the congress."

"I'd planned to, but today..." He groaned. "Some days are better than others. Today is not a good one."

My chest ached at the sight of such a strong man admitting a deficiency. "Is this because of Noah?"

The king's lips pressed together. "The physician isn't certain. The long-term effects of the poison could be accelerating what may simply be brought on by age."

"King Arthur VI," I said, trying to recall the history of King Theo's father. "He was younger when he passed on."

Papa nodded. "Too young. Today we know about the markers for the cancer that took him. Back then, it was all too unknown."

"Do you have the markers?"

"Yes."

My skin grew cold. "Is this cancer?"

"No. The physician believes the origin is neurological. The progression is unknown. He has hypothesized that the poison caused damage to cells at an exponential rate, greater than what would have occurred naturally. The regenerated cells are, for lack of a better word, faulty."

"You haven't mentioned this." I sat back against the chair.

"Don't tell me you've gotten cold feet."

I shook my head. "Right now, I'm sad."

"Don't be sad. Go across the city and look every one of those fuckers in the eye. Show them you're the prince of Molave. Earn their respect as much as their trust." He cleared his throat. "Before you leave, we should discuss something Elizabeth said."

I waited.

"She said you're concerned about the Borinkian princess."

I nodded. "Mrs. Drake is correct. I don't know why, but I have a gut feeling she knows."

"If that's the case, Noah told her."

"I have given it a lot of thought. Noah has denied coming clean with her. He has no reason to lie to me."

"Then she doesn't know," King Theo said.

"Francis knows."

The king's nostrils flared as he fidgeted in his chair. "His jaw is almost healed. Soon, he'll be able to speak clearly."

"He's been monitored and hasn't gone against our wishes."

"Not yet, but what if he speaks to King Aleksander II?"

"We can't allow that to happen."

The king's eyes opened wider. "If the Borinkian princess knows?"

If she knows, she's a liability. The needs of the many outweigh the needs of the few or one. The meaning behind that quote was growing clearer by the day: the needs of Molave outweigh the needs of Francis and Inessa.

I met his stare. "Same consequences, if necessary."

The king nodded. "Tell me how you came to this conclusion."

"The scare with Lucille and the baby," I began, "it put everything into perspective. I love her. I can't allow anyone with knowledge of my identity to threaten our way of life, to take this life away from me—from us. I won't."

"That is why you, Roman Godfrey, must address Parliament. You must stand before those people with the confidence of a prince—of a man who was born and has been raised for this occasion." When I started to talk, the king shook his head. "Don't doubt me. You were born to be here. The raising...we know that part isn't true. Never let on. If at any time you're questioned, deny. Tell me, how is Princess Lucille?"

"She's well. The scare was only that—a scare. Mr. Davies called for her rest. Today, she's resumed a lighter schedule."

"Does that mean that we'll see you both at dinner?"

"Yes," I answered.

"The tour in the States? Tell me it's still on the agenda."

"Yes. Lucille's office is working on the final details and then my office will coordinate with the royal guards for security."

The king gripped the arms of his chair, trying to stop the trembling that had resumed in his left hand. The left seemed to be worse than his right. "It's important that the two of you are seen. Make yourself the face of the Godfrey monarchy, and if anyone presumes to question, call them out as fake news."

"If anyone called for my DNA..."

"No one would dare."

I wished I were as confident as the king. My gaze went to his hands. "Does Mr. Davies believe your condition will improve?"

"I've begun a natural regimen of vitamins and supplements, as well as a detox protocol, all designed for cell regeneration. Though I've felt better in general, the decline has steadily increased over the last few months. Now that Mr. Davies knows about the poison, he's working on a few new ideas."

"Queen Anne?" I asked. "Is she aware?"

"The one person in my life who has always received the truth is the queen. I wasn't always punctual about giving it, but in the end, I did. I do my best to shield her, but that damn woman is usually a step ahead of me." He smiled. "She researched cures before I even told her what was happening."

"It sounds like you're in good hands. What will I tell Parliament as to why you're not present?"

"Elizabeth has a statement."

I sighed. "Of course she does."

"She's a brilliant woman and a better chief of the ministry than those before her. I say that with the utmost respect. Her guidance has been appreciated. She's been with us for over twenty years and is trustworthy beyond compare."

That was good to know.

I gripped the arms of the chair as I was about to stand.

"One more thing, Roman."

My knees bent as I lowered myself again to the chair. "Yes?"

"There won't be an amniocentesis for the Borinkian princess."

"Why? I've already ordered it."

"And I've put a stop to it. The girl told Anne that she's frightened to have the test. It's invasive. It's not worth risking the life of the child."

"It isn't my child."

"Nonetheless, there are less invasive means to determining paternity."

That was what Lucille said. Gritting my teeth, I contemplated my response. "I don't believe Noah is the father."

"What makes you say that?"

I told the king the same thing Noah told me about the steroids, low sperm count, and Lucille. I ended with the one definitive statement, "He doesn't believe he can father children."

The king hummed as he leaned back again. "Do you have a possible candidate?"

"Not from the princess. It's sheer speculation."

"Okay, son. Tell me what your prince's intuition is telling you."

I shook my head. "Again, sir, no proof. That's why I want the test. I want to know more than that Noah isn't the father. I want to know all we can about that kid."

His dark stare remained focused on me.

"Francis," I said.

"I'll reconsider the test."

Standing, I nodded. "Thank you. I wish you were going with me."

He lifted his left hand. The trembling increased the higher he raised it. "If I went with you, this nonsense would be the news story." He lowered his hand. "Without me, I'll be a byline, but you, Prince Roman, will be the headline."

CHAPTER 24

Lucille

"I'm glad you're feeling better," Queen Anne said. "You look lovely." Her bright stare was upon me. She looked striking in her bright blue pantsuit. Her customary string of pearls was in place, and a pair of reading spectacles sat perched on the end of her nose.

Smiling, I thanked her. There were still few outwardly signs that I was with child. The soreness of my breasts, increased libido, and periodic bouts of nausea let me know that all was well. "The spotting was a scare. Not uncommon, according to Mr. Davies."

Taking the glasses from her eyes, she hummed as she folded them and placed them on a nearby table by her tablet. "I recall. Sadly, Theo and I lost multiple pregnancies along the way. I don't wish that on anyone."

With my hand over my midsection, I smiled. "Thank you for seeing me."

"Anytime, Lucille. You know that."

Looking around, I lowered my voice. "I want to speak to you about Inessa Volkov."

"Dear, she isn't your concern."

"She is," I replied. "Roman has made her my concern."

"I'm certain he's regretful—"

"He's made her my concern," I said, interrupting, "by asking me to deal with her. He would rather not."

The queen squared her shoulders. "I would expect more from him. What he's asking isn't very princely."

I sat taller, the need to defend my husband fueling my strength. "Roman is increasingly busy. King Theodore has bestowed many responsibilities upon him of late. You're right. He regrets his affair and sees no reason to continue a relationship beyond what is his responsibility."

Queen Anne pursed her lips, exhaled, and leaned back against the sofa cushion. Her gaze never left mine until she looked down to her lap, studying her hands.

While the silence continued, my urge to speak was outweighed by my desire to wait. The queen was considering her words, and I hoped that for once, she would be completely truthful with me.

Her gaze met mine with a steady smile. "And what do you want to do with this newfound responsibility?"

"The answer is why I'm here. I went to you first about the princess. After I told Roman I'd visited her, he was" —I sighed— "...less than pleased. However, once he truly thought about it, he asked me, or commanded me to take her off his list of responsibilities. He and I both agreed that you should be a part of whatever I do. Inessa trusts you."

She smirked. "They always do." She tilted her head. "You went to visit her? When?"

"The day before my mandatory rest. Isabella gave me enough information for me to figure out where the princess was being held. I spent months in those apartments. I'm ashamed to say that my visit didn't go well."

Queen Anne's cheeks rose as her smile broadened. "Do tell."

"I went to her with good intentions. I'm sorry, Your Majesty, but I'm not in favor of taking another woman's child. I went to her to speak mother-to-be to mother-to-be."

"You were to warn her about me."

"Yes, but not you...the plan."

"And did you?" she asked.

It was my turn to look down at my hands, clasped in my lap. Images of Inessa's smug expression, the casual way she was dressed, and the unrefined way she sat all came back. I could almost hear her superior tone. I looked up. "No, ma'am. I didn't."

"Why?"

"Because...May I stand?" It was customary to sit

when the sovereign sat, but my skin was tight and my nerves taut.

"Yes, my dear. Whatever makes you comfortable."

Standing, I tried to rein in my emotions. Somehow when face-to-face with Inessa, it no longer mattered that she hadn't slept with *my* Roman. She thought she had. Or she knew she'd slept with a man who at the time she believed to be the Prince of Molave. I walked behind the chair where I'd been sitting and gripped the ornate wood frame. "When I saw her, I hated her." I let out a breath. "That isn't who I am. I've never experienced anything quite like it. The disgust surprised me. I said things I shouldn't have said."

"Such as?"

Shameful, disgrace, mistress, nobody. I confessed it all.

My skin prickled beneath my blouse as I waited for Queen Anne's response.

"Sit, child."

Child.

I am thirty-three years old and a mother-to-be.

I sat.

"You weren't wrong," Queen Anne said. "You're rightfully entitled to your emotions."

Swallowing, I nodded again.

"Now that the first encounter is over, what is your plan?"

"I want to find out the paternity of her child. I also want her gone. Roman wants her gone. The Firm can house her anywhere but here in the palace or at Annabella," I added.

"Inessa said she was afraid of having an invasive test prior to the birth of her son."

Son.

I'd forgotten she knew the gender.

"There are less invasive tests," the queen suggested.

"Roman wants her to have it," I said. "If the child isn't a Godfrey, we can put this nightmare behind us."

"And if he is a Godfrey?"

"The Firm pays child support."

"Either way, news will get out that Roman has another son."

"If it is his." I knew it wasn't. "I don't trust her."

"Well, I suppose you have that right. Are you doubting she had a sexual relationship with Roman?"

Quirking an eyebrow, I shook my head. "I'm doubting that her only relationship was with Roman."

"Oh. Why would you question that?"

Again, I stood, popping up before thinking to seek permission. "It's a bit difficult to have confidence in the morality of a woman who would knowingly sleep with a married man." I met the queen's stare.

"Morality is something I've learned not to judge.

You're young, and I don't fault you for doing so. With time, I've learned that life isn't black and white. The greys are where we flourish or falter. When we look back, we can see that it is those times that are the most relevant. The thing about the grey is that until you're in the middle of it, you can't predict your response.

"Viewed from the outside, some may see your response as wrong and others as right. None of those opinions matter." She lifted her palm to her chest. "It's in our hearts, Lucille, that we find the answers. Life has presented me with greys that as a woman your age, I could never have imagined. It's astounding how we humans are quick to judge yet equally capable of justifying behavior in ourselves." She tilted her head. "Have you ever been faced with the grey—a decision regarding something you may have considered morally corrupt at one point, but when it presented itself, your circumstances had changed, and you saw your choice from a different view?"

Accepting an impostor as my husband.

To those who knew, my grey was more of a neon sign.

Sitting back on the edge of the chair, I nodded.

Queen Anne exhaled. "So you understand?"

"My grey wasn't the same as Inessa's. I didn't set out to ruin a marriage and unite countries."

"It's easy to judge when her greys are laid out for

us to view. If she could see your greys, would she judge?"

Taking a breath, I met the queen's gaze. "That is why she must go."

"You believe the princess from Borinkia will expose your grey?"

"I am."

"And you worry for your reputation?"

"No." I raised my voice. "God, no. I worry because I love my husband. I'm willing to sacrifice the princess and her child to keep him safe."

"You perceive her as a threat?"

"Without a doubt."

The air around us crackled with the static electricity of our shrouded secrets. The truth was right in front of both of us, yet neither was ready to take the next step. Before I could gather the courage, there was a knock on the door.

We both exhaled, each aware of how close we'd been.

"Come in," Queen Anne said.

"Your Majesty," Lady Kornhall said with a curtsy. "The prince's speech to Parliament is on the telly. You asked me to remind you."

"Roman's speech?" I asked, unaware that his speech would be televised.

"Yes, thank you. Turn it on," the queen said.

Shifting her attention to me, she patted the sofa to her side and asked, "Please, stay and watch with me."

"Yes." I nodded. "Of course."

I moved to the sofa as the queen's mistress opened a large cupboard, revealing a television. Reaching for the remote, she turned on the telly and found the proper channel. There in all his glory was my Roman.

After Lady Kornhall left us, we both remained silent, staring at the picture on the screen and listening to Roman's oration.

A sense of pride bubbled within me. My Roman was a much better speaker than his predecessor. His baritone voice garnered attention. His pronunciation and Molavian accent were perfect in every way. Multiple times, he was interrupted by applause. On a few occasions—such as when he spoke about the commission he'd instituted with citizens from all the various regions—members of Parliament stood in a standing ovation.

My lips quirked as I watched his manufactured impatience with the thunderous approval. It was exactly as he'd learned to behave. I had to wonder how differently he would have reacted if instead of Parliament, he was on Broadway.

When the live coverage ended and two talking heads began to dissect and analyze every word Roman uttered, the queen reached for the remote and turned off the television.

Her gaze focused on me. "He's his father's son, through and through."

My mind stuttered.

"Roman is a Godfrey, King Theo's son?" I asked incredulously.

"Of course, Lucille. You know that. You're his wife."

As I stared, no longer did I believe Queen Anne was a feeble-minded woman unaware of her surroundings. No, in that moment I was struck with what I should have seen from the beginning. Queen Anne was ruthless, a mother determined to keep what she held dear.

"Lucille?" she questioned. "Do you believe that Inessa could jeopardize the future of my son?"

"Your son?"

"The process of giving birth is a miracle enjoyed by many, yet not all. Mothering is not birthing. Mothering is loving and guiding. One need not have the first to be committed to the second."

There were too many questions in my thoughts. A cyclone of unknowns. While I wanted to sit at the queen's side and ask each one, instinctively, I knew that I'd learn what she wanted me to know in time. Instead of asking for more, I reached out and laid my hand at her side. "I love him. I didn't ask for him." I smiled, warmth filling my cheeks. "I think I wished him into being. Now that he's here, I want to love your son and support him for the rest of my life, staying true to the commitment I made five years ago and again recently. I knew what I was doing. Please help to ensure that his life, our life, the future of the monarchy, isn't sabotaged by the other woman."

She reached out and covered my hand with hers. "You have my word."

As I walked back to the apartments I shared with my husband, I wondered if I'd interpreted the queen's statements correctly or if my mind was so flustered with the Borinkian princess that I was making assumptions.

While I longed to share my thoughts with Roman, I recalled his image on the telly. He'd made the queen and his wife proud. The reception was far better than I even imagined.

No. For now, I'd ruminate on the possibilities my mind conjured.

CHAPTER
25

Roman

The holiday came. Unlike the parliamentary address, Papa made his annual holiday address himself. As it had been in years past, the address was a televised event, broadcasting beyond the Molavian borders. Reminding me of the old fireside chats of past US Presidents, Papa appeared stately, regal, and aging. The multiple cameras and expert editing kept his growing tremors from the screen. Through it all, his voice remained boisterous and commanding.

The address was the perfect diversion for those skeptical of the king's health after my solitary appearance during Parliament. Many of the country's pundits as well as international news media personnel spoke of his vitality and strength.

The reviews of my performance were also positive, comparing it to my performance in the dreadful summer Eurasia tour. While Lucille hadn't made any planned public appearances since her speech in Forthwith, her new social media presence was trending. She'd also made private appearances throughout Molave City. Her presence was never leaked to the media until after the event.

While the appearances were more of what Lucille considered fluff, she was going out as a spokesperson for the Crown. It was more than she'd done in the past. The patients at the children's hospitals and people at other venues were excited and honored to speak with the princess.

Beyond those assignments, I wasn't ready to risk her safety.

Lucille wasn't privy to the specifics of Queen Anne's plan; nevertheless, she was reassured that the queen would do everything within her power to lessen the threat of the Borinkian princess.

Noah's health had improved while deteriorating at the same time. The virus was gone, but it seemed that at each visit, he was more lethargic than the time before. Truly it was sad to watch his body deteriorate before my eyes. If anything, he'd lost his fight. Whether it was to live or to die, the will had faded.

Francis's treatment took a turn when his knee refused to heal. In the coming weeks, he will be receiving a titanium replacement. He'd kept his word, to the best of our knowledge, in maintaining the story Mrs. Drake had concocted. With his jaw now functioning, once his physical therapy deemed him fit, the Duke and Duchess would return to Forthwith.

There was one variable. Things were heating up at the Borinkian border.

While it had taken the royal engineers some time, they were ready for my excursion. I would travel to Brynad, only thirty minutes from the palace, and publicly meet with the newly assigned commissioner from the province.

Lord Rowlings and I would travel in cars with hidden GPS beacons. The transmitters were a few the guards pretended not to find—the ones placed at Forthwith. The plan was that with the knowledge the royal engineers had gathered from other transmitters, they would be able to track the signal as I traveled as bait.

Before the new year, the Firm made the official announcement: The Prince and Princess of Molave would travel to Brynad for a ceremonial meeting to signify the beginning of increased royal-civilian communication and relations. The announcement was bogus regarding Lucille. She wouldn't travel.

"I'm nervous," Lucille said, straightening my tie the morning of my excursion. The blue of her orbs was filled with the clouds of an impending storm.

Grasping her shoulders, I tried to reassure her. "I'll stay safe, my princess."

"If you're safe, why can't I be at your side?"

Framing her cheeks, I stared into her blue orbs, brought her luscious lips to mine, and grinned. "Because there is no place safer than the palace." I lifted my left arm and flexed the fingers on my right hand. "Since my arrival, I've been shot and broken my hand. Through it all, I'm still here." I reached out, laying my palm on her midsection. "You aren't allowed to risk your health or that of our child."

Lucille sighed. "They could say it is the two of us, but when the doors open, it's Mrs. Drake in our stead."

"The guards will be close, and the foreign minister and I will be in an armored car."

"What about our upcoming tour in the US?" she asked.

"If all goes well today, this will flush out the person or people who sent the drone. Once they're known, we can take the necessary precautions. And the ministry has been working with US law enforcement. We will be well guarded."

"We're supposed to appear casual, not surrounded by royal guards."

"Appearances" —I grinned— "can deceive." When she didn't respond, I added, "Trust me."

"Be honest with me," Lucille asked, "what is the risk assessment for today in Brynad?"

"Low. Nothing has happened since the one drone.

There's probably a better chance that nothing will happen than that something will."

"Please call me," she said, stretching her toes and bringing her lips to mine. "I'm going to Inessa today. Queen Anne invited me. We're going together."

The final statement made me feel better. "Do you know what Mum has planned?"

"If I were to guess, she's going to try to talk Inessa into the test."

I shook my head. "It would be wonderful to have her gone, back to Borinkia, and out of the royal gossip."

Lucille nodded. "I agree, my prince."

Turning, I took in my reflection in the full-length mirror. "No one notices."

Lucille met my gaze in the glass. "Notices what?"

"When I look at Noah, I see how different we appear. When I look at myself, I realize the extent to the change over the last four months."

"It seems like years," she said with a grin.

"I saw you on the telly in early August."

"And now look where we are." She took a step back and scanned from my hair to my shoes. "Your Highness, you appear healthier and happier than on our tour last summer. It was well known that you were summoned to the palace for rest." Her smile grew. "It appears as though that rest has been beneficial. No one will question a positive transformation."

"Shall I escort you to the queen's offices?" I asked.

Lucille's arms came up, her fingers intertwined behind my neck. "I want every minute with you." The blue of her orbs swirled. "I also am frightened, so I'd rather part from you without the eyes of others."

My smile quirked. "I'm dressed, but I'm game for a quickie."

Her laugh was a melody echoing through the bedchamber. "No, Your Highness. I will leave you with a kiss. Tonight, return to me, and I'll be yours to command."

Damn.

That gave me some ideas.

Lucille pressed toward me, her lips taking mine and stoking the remnants of last night's blaze. My fingers splayed behind her head as I sought what she was offering. Our tongues mingled as moans reverberated from her to me. "There," she said, pulling back. "Come back for more."

"Nothing will stop me."

Beyond the door of my private parlor, Lord Martin was waiting. "Your Highness."

"I'll be gone for the better part of the morning. You should take time for yourself," I suggested.

"Sir, I'd like to join you."

My gaze narrowed as we exited Lucille's and my

apartments. "Don't tell me you have a feeling, like the one at Forthwith."

He nodded. "A feeling. Not the same."

"I'm a decoy, man. Lord Rowlings will be at my side. At best, the technicians will be able to follow the transmitters, find out who is watching." Glancing sideways, I took in my assistant's expression. "Talk to me."

"Chatter, sir. I can't pinpoint it, but something feels—" Lord Martin stopped, pulling his phone from his breast pocket and reading a text message. "Mrs. Drake is in your office, sir."

I looked down at my watch. "Our arrival time was set for eleven. I need to speak with Lord Rowlings."

"Mrs. Drake says it's urgent."

CHAPTER
26

Lucille

The walk to the far wing of the palace was less solitary with the queen of Molave at my side. Together, we led a small parade through the corridors. The queen's guard and mistress were never far from her side. Today's journey required two guards, making me question why I'd visited earlier all by myself.

As we neared the apartments housing the princess, the queen slowed, motioned for those following to give us space, and reached for my hand.

"Ma'am?"

"I invited you today because you deserve to be present. However, I won't be responsible for making you uncomfortable. If you'd prefer to wait for me, it's completely acceptable. Inessa was told only of my visit."

She wasn't warned I'd be there?

As soon as the question came to me, I remembered. I was supposed to be with Roman on the outing to

Brynad. The thought brought back my concerns for him.

Focusing on the queen, I took a deep breath. My growing breasts pushed against the bodice of my blue dress. It was long, flowing, and casual. My shoes were ballet flats, and my hair was tied back in a low side ponytail. While my attire was perfectly acceptable, I considered it only one step up from loungewear. Of course, Inessa had been informed of the impending visit. I assumed she'd be better prepared, especially for the queen.

"It never occurred to me," I said, "to decline your invitation. Thank you for including me." My lips curled. "I wouldn't say that I'm comfortable with our guest" —I used the word in the broadest of terms— "but I'm also not uncomfortable."

Queen Anne's gaze focused on mine as if she were reading my thoughts and seeing my insecurities. Her grip of my hand intensified. "You, Lucille, are Roman's princess. You will be queen. I understand how emotions affected you during your first visit with the princess, but now that is done."

Swallowing, I nodded.

She lowered her voice. "Being queen isn't a thankless job, child. There are plenty of recognitions and many reasons for gratitude. Nevertheless, it is a job. When I married Theo, I accepted the lifelong position of being his defender, his supporter, and his partner. I've not always made the right choices. And I've recognized my mistakes. You, Princess Lucille, must keep Roman and Molave first in your thoughts. The time for snide remarks is over."

I looked down.

Queen Anne lifted my chin. "That wasn't a reprimand. I admire your fiery resolve. I believe your behavior set the tone. Now, your approach must be as more than Roman's princess; it must be as his future queen."

Warmth filled my cheeks as I stared at the strong monarch before me. I'd been wrong about her over the years. She was infinitely more important to Molave than planning state dinners. Had I not seen the woman she was capable of being, or was I simply not looking, too lost in my own despair?

"You told me that you love Roman," she said.

Although she hadn't asked a question, I answered, "I do, Your Majesty."

"Do you believe you have his love in return?"

"Without a doubt. I know I do."

"That is your shield, Lucille. There is nothing that Inessa can say or do to take that from you. Keep it close, use it to protect your heart, and at the same time, never lose track of your job."

"To defend and support my husband."

She nodded. "It's not as archaic as it might sound. The reality is that while our husbands fill the sovereign duties of their positions, in many ways, they're an island, isolated from others. The heavy weight of their titles is their burden they must bear. While they have to learn to delegate, there are few people they can truly trust. Having that solidarity in their partner is more important than the world gives credit. Theo and Roman are the men who they're capable of being because of us."

Inhaling, I stood taller. "Thank you."

"No, thank you, for not giving up on Roman."

"He's been worth the wait."

"Very well." She inhaled. "Are we ready to announce our arrival?"

"Yes."

Queen Anne nodded to Lady Kornhall. The queen's mistress knocked on the apartment door. The princess's mistress answered, welcomed us, and bid us entry. Her eyes widened as I followed a step behind the queen.

"I invited Princess Lucille," Queen Anne said to the princess's lady.

She bowed her neck. "Your Majesty. I'll inform the princess of our additional guest."

Lady Kornhall and the two guards remained in the hallway as Queen Anne and I entered. As the princess's lady left us, we sat on the same sofa where Inessa had sat during our meeting. The room buzzed with an electric silence, the crackling of particles—electrons and protons—bouncing in anticipation of a change in motion.

The queen's clasped hands rested properly in her lap. Her ankles were daintily crossed below the sofa and her posture was straight. It was the elevation of her chin that differed from other conversations. Despite coming on friendly terms, she demonstrated an air of authority that displayed a sense of mission in her stance.

My posture mirrored the monarch's, without the raised chin.

As we remained silent, I found it within myself to also emulate the rest of her demeanor, to nonverbally assert myself as Roman's princess, the future queen, and the daughter-in-law to the monarch present. Slowly, my chin jutted forward.

"Princess Inessa of Borinkia," the lady-in-waiting announced.

Inessa appeared, her expression unreadable. Unlike during my visit, the princess appeared ready for guests. Her white dress did little to hide her baby bump. It had grown quite a bit since I'd last seen her. With her pale complexion and light-yellow hair, I would recommend that she wear another color. The white wasn't flattering.

Then again, Inessa and I were far from a relationship of offering one another style advice. Her long locks were pulled into a tight knot on the top of her head, making her appear stark. Remembering the queen's advice, I settled on Inessa's cheekbones.

Yes. She had prominent cheekbones.

Inessa curtsied to Queen Anne and took a seat in the chair across from us. "Your Majesty, I didn't realize we wouldn't be alone to speak."

The queen smiled. "I invited Princess Lucille. It seems that my son has delegated your care to his wife."

Her light blue stare came my way. "You? Why you?"

"Roman knows very little about the needs of an expectant mother." I laid my hand over my stomach. "He's learning. As for you, he wants what is best for you and your child."

"His child," she said under her breath.

"That is to be determined," I replied.

Sniffing, Inessa turned her attention to the queen. "What does this mean?"

"You have asked for political asylum, and King Theodore granted your request. The royal council to the king is looking into a different location for your stay."

"What is wrong with here?"

I had the answer on the tip of my tongue. However, it was my reverence for the queen, not the Borinkian princess, that kept me silent.

"You are a princess," the queen said. "You should have more space." Before Inessa could respond, the queen continued, "I've been told your child is due in May of this year."

Inessa nodded.

"You will be well cared for until that time."

"And after?" she asked, a twinge of panic in her voice. "My brother won't allow me to enter Borinkia with Prince Roman's child. Neither of us will be safe."

"The king and his council will evaluate the situation at that time." The queen squared her shoulders. "Child, it would behoove you to be honest with me. Is there any possibility that the child you're carrying isn't my son's?"

Inessa laid her arm protectively over her baby bump. "I swear."

"Mr. Davies has informed me that at this stage of a pregnancy, the risk with amniocentesis is small, less than one percent. I took your concerns to King Theodore; however, he has discussed it with Roman, and they have decided you will undergo the test."

"Het."

The hairs on the back of my neck stood to attention

as I moderated my tone. "Princess, I don't know much about Borinkia. I do know Molave. In Molave, you do not say no to the queen."

Her volume rose. "No one can make me have a test."

"That is where you're mistaken," I replied. "In Molave, King Theodore and Prince Roman have final word in all matters. As Queen Anne stated, Roman has asked me to be the one to personally deal with you. I agree with the king and prince. The paternity of your child must be ensured." I decided to use a different tactic. "Once it is proven that the baby is of Godfrey descent, we will make more permanent arrangements for you and the child."

She shook her head. "I will make my own decisions."

"Not in Molave," the queen said definitively. "Mr. Davies is expecting you tomorrow morning at nine."

I forced a smile. "Would you like me to accompany you?"

Her invisible eyebrows knitted together. "You? No."

"If, for whatever reason, you miss your appointment," Queen Anne said, "guards will arrive and escort you."

"This isn't right."

I inhaled. "You are always free to revoke your petition for asylum and leave Molave."

The princess's gaze went to Queen Anne. "You would be okay with me taking your grandchild?"

"No, Inessa, I would not. I suggest you do as you've been told."

She stood. "I want to speak to Roman."

Since the queen was still sitting, I too remained seated. "I am your communication with Roman, Inessa. I will ensure that your mistress has my mistress's number. If you have any concerns or unmet needs from this time forward, you will bring them to me."

"I won't have the test."

"Then I don't believe that is Roman's child."

"Son," Inessa said louder. "His son. Do you not believe that he would make love to me?"

Noah.

Make love.

I almost laughed. "We can resume this conversation after we have the results."

The door to the hallway opened without a knock. The two guards and Lady Kornhall entered. After a quick curtsy, she spoke to Queen Anne. "Your Majesty, you are needed with the king." She looked at me. "And you, Princess."

A cold chill scattered over my flesh as my fingers flew to my lips. "Something is wrong."

"Please come with me," Lady Kornhall said.

My heart galloped in my chest as I thought about Roman's meeting in Brynad.

"Lucille," the queen said. She was already standing. Somehow, I'd missed the last few seconds.

Nodding, I stood, my head in a fog and my knees suddenly weak.

The queen was a few paces ahead of me. My gaze went to the princess. "I will ensure your lady has my lady's number."

Her next comment was spoken so softly, I could have missed it. Maybe I imagined it. As looming concern enveloped me, I was uncertain.

"You were supposed to be with him."

Similar to a slap on the cheek, her words pulled me from my trance. "What did you say?"

She lifted her chin and kept her volume low. "American. Daughter of a Letanonian cunt."

Ignoring my desire to cause bodily harm, I squared my shoulders. "Perhaps you have not heard the saying 'don't bite the hand that feeds you.'" With that, I stepped away, catching the queen just outside the apartments.

CHAPTER 27

Roman

A few hours ago

With Lord Martin at my side, I hurried through the palace corridors. As we approached my offices, an echo of voices came into range, speeding our steps.

"Your Highness," the staff said, standing with a bow as I entered.

My attention was divided between Dame Williamson and the voices coming from beyond the closed door of a conference room. "What's happening?"

"Sir, the chief minister is inside with the minister of the interior, as well as General Dickerson, members of the royal cyber-security team—"

"What the hell?" I interrupted.

"Yes, sir." My secretary's expression reflected the tension at whatever was happening.

Inhaling, I took a quick look at Lord Martin before

heading toward the closed door. The royal guard manning the entry offered a neck bow before opening the door. The loud voices immediately ceased, as all sets of eyes turned to me. "What is the meaning of this?"

"Your Highness," the group said in unison as they stood to their feet.

A quick turn and a nod to the guard at the door and he closed the barrier.

With my pulse thumping in my ears, I motioned to the chairs around the table. "Sit and explain."

The exchange of glances and murmurs didn't go unnoticed as we all took seats, me at the head of the conference table. My gaze moved around the table, finally settling on the person who ranked highest below me. "Mrs. Drake?"

She exhaled. "Sir, the Royal Ministry cyber-security team has been listening to increased chatter since the announcement of your and the princess's visit to Brynad."

"The trip was announced before the first of the year."

Lord Rowlings spoke. "Sir, the threat level has gone up since then."

I felt my forehead furrow. "Borinkia?"

"Not entirely, sir," Mrs. Drake said. "The main

threat seems to be coming from an extremist group out of Norway."

"What is the group called?"

"Unofficially," Lord Rowlings said, "they're a European branch of the Lads' Guild."

"The Lads' Guild," Mrs. Drake said, "was founded in Australia. Their movement has recently started to make their presence known in Europe."

"Why would they target the Godfreys?"

The room grew eerily quiet.

Finally, Lord Rowlings replied, "Their motive is unknown."

My gaze settled on Mrs. Drake. "What aren't you telling me?"

Her jaw clenched, tightening the muscles along the sides of her face.

"Mrs. Drake," I said louder. "I will not ask again."

Her gaze darted to Lord Rowlings and back to me before she exhaled and pressed her lips into a straight line. "Sir, the members of this extremist group are considered to be purists."

Purists?

"How does that factor into this?"

"It seems that they were first noticed by the Royal Ministry cyber-security team after you and Princess Lucille visited Odnessa."

I shook my head. "That was last November."

"Your Highness," one of the unnamed security members at the table said.

"Your name, sir." I demanded.

"Hastings, Oscar Hastings, I oversee the royal cyber-security team."

"Hastings," I said, "tell me what you know."

He shook his head. "We don't know with certainty, Your Highness. We are only able to collect the clues and make assumptions."

"And your assumptions say that there is an increased risk of danger with today's trip to Brynad?"

He nodded.

"Don't be shy, Hastings."

His Adam's apple bobbed. "In Odnessa you made an announcement. It hadn't been cleared by the ministry."

"Announcement," I said, remembering. "Yes, about the marriage blessing. I did."

"From what we can assess, your announcement was not welcomed by those who consider themselves purists. As you recall, when Princess Lucille first came to Molave there were rumors of unhappy citizens."

There was no way for me to remember that. At that time, I was blissfully unaware that Molave existed. My eyebrows knitted together. "The princess has always had a high approval rating."

"Yes," Mrs. Drake interjected. "Amongst the vast

majority of Molavian citizens and abroad. It was incels who weren't happy about the monarchy marrying an American."

"Are you saying that this group is targeting Lucille?"

Hastings nodded. "Before your announcement in Odnessa, this group seemed pacified with your marriage woes. They consider the Borinkian princess to be of like lineage."

"Lucille's heritage goes back to Letanonia."

Mrs. Drake spoke, "Most members of these groups are young. Borinkia has been in existence for nearly four decades. They don't remember Letanonia."

Hastings met my gaze. "They're not happy that it appears you and Princess Lucille are working out your problems."

Closing my eyes, I exhaled as I gritted my teeth. With a shove, I pushed my chair from the table and stood; all occupants around the table followed suit. "Who the hell are these people that they think they have a right to even have an opinion?"

"Your Highness," Mrs. Drake said, her tone pacifying. "You're correct. They have no right. They are also dangerous and tied to other factions." She looked across the table at Lord Rowlings.

"Sir," he said, "we recently discovered that the

Lads' Guild may be funded by citizens in Norway. These people have been around for decades. They were rumored to have been instrumental in Borinkia's success against Letanonia."

Francis.

Placing both hands on the table, I leaned forward, meeting Lord Rowling's stare. "Tell me if that group has a connection to the Duke of Wilmington."

"It is believed so, sir."

"Believed." I repeated the word, each time louder. "I need more than belief. If I'm going to accuse my sister's husband, I need proof."

A rather thin man lifted his hand.

"Yes? Name?"

"Meade, Your Highness. We met awhile back about the drone. I'm one of the engineers who dissected it and inspected the transmitters."

"Right," I said, "I remember now. What are you able to add?"

"We have refined our ability to track the signals from the transmitters. If a car is driven to Brynad as planned, we could possibly determine where the transmissions are being sent and who is receiving them."

Mrs. Drake shook her head. "Your Highness, it isn't worth risking your life."

Standing tall, I ran one hand over my hair. "And

then what? Lucille and I spend the next fifty years hiding from these people?"

"There are other ways," she said.

I looked at Mr. Meade. "You think you can track the transmission?"

"Yes, sir."

My focus went to the one man who had remained quiet. His royal uniform was decorated with his obvious accomplishments. "General Dickerson, I assume you're involved in this planning. Are you prepared with the means and personnel to apprehend the culprits?"

"If the perpetrators are in Molave, yes, sir. If they are in Norway or Borinkia, by chance, we do not have jurisdiction."

"Have you contacted the Norwegian authorities?"

"No, sir. Not without your approval or that of King Theodore."

"The car is armored, right?" I asked the room.

"Yes," Hastings answered.

I peered around, sensing there was more. My gaze returned to General Dickerson.

He inhaled. "The car can withstand bullets. The concern is explosives. Particularly, shrapnel in the case of an explosion. The royal armored fleet was upgraded. The cars have a second layer of protection, the first to absorb the energy of a blast and a second to protect the occupants. In theory."

My heart skipped a beat. "In theory."

"The extra layer has done very well in tests. Fortunately, we have never had to learn if it works. I suggest we don't do so today."

"And what?" I asked, shaking my head. "Would this group risk harming citizens in Brynad or is the greater risk on the more isolated roads?"

"There's no way to know for sure," Mrs. Drake said. "Taking out the Godfrey line of succession would have a more powerful effect if it was done without harming innocent people."

"I don't want to purposely put the citizens of Brynad in danger."

"Your Highness," Mrs. Drake said, "please don't consider putting yourself in danger."

"If I don't, they win."

The chief minister squared her shoulders. "Prince Roman, may we speak privately?"

A quick glance at my watch told me our time was limited. "Excuse us," I said to the rest of the table. Once the room was cleared, I retook my seat at the head of the table. "Mrs. Drake?"

"Sir, you were planning on being a decoy. That's what you said. You wouldn't allow the princess to be the target."

Leaning back, I sighed. "I can't believe she is the target. Just because she's an American. Hell, if they only—"

"No," she interrupted. "Never utter those words."

"I want this danger under control before the States tour. I want these lunatics found."

"Would you please consider an alternative?"

CHAPTER
28

Roman

I didn't know that there was a situation room in Molave Palace. Of course, I couldn't let on that I was unaware.

Lord Martin took me up the stairs Lucille had described. Once in the queen's parlor, we went to the king's side of the apartments. Through another hidden staircase, we made it to the king's offices. The safe room was located through a series of locked doors, in a bunker below the king's offices. There was only one entrance, hidden and guarded. The room itself required a recognition sensor, scanning the eyeball of the guard. According to Mrs. Drake, the room hadn't been used in over five years, and yet the technology was new with improved Wi-Fi speed. With one wall filled with screens, we were able to watch the royal fleet from various angles, including from the windshield of the car I was supposed to be in.

General Dickerson, Mrs. Drake, Hastings, and I had only been in the room for less than fifteen minutes when King Theodore entered. Everyone within stood, bowed their neck, and offered his majesty our greeting.

When I looked up, his dark stare was on me. I felt his eyes in a way I never knew possible. In a matter of seconds, they assessed and judged. In that moment, I wasn't certain I'd made the right decision. It wasn't until the edge of his lips moved and he nodded that I dismissed the idea that I'd somehow failed Molave and failed him.

"Roman," he said with a quirk of his neck.

I followed King Theo into the hallway. A guard opened a second door, and together we stepped inside a private room. It took a moment, but King Theo pulled back a chair and sat with a 'humph.'

"Are you confident?" he asked.

I shook my head. I was about to admit that I wasn't when I stopped, inhaled, and straightened my neck. "Yes, sir, I am. I'm also worried."

"Why?"

"The threat is real. In the other room, we are able to see a barrage of numbers, coordinates, and pinpoints on the map. The transmitter on the car is doing its job, sending a signal. The cyber security tells me that they know it's being ricocheted off various points to camouflage the receiver. Nevertheless, the car is being tracked.

"He could use this opportunity to destroy us."

King Theodore's statement took me back to the cell below the infirmary where Noah made the same statement.

Turning the key, I entered Noah's room. Maybe it was my expression or the pace of my steps. I may never know what caused him to expect the worst, but he did.

"I'm going to die today," he said.

I shook my head. "I hope not."

Noah stood. The pajamas he wore hung from his shrinking frame. "How?"

"You're not sentenced to die, Noah. There's a situation." *For the next few minutes, I did my best to lay out what was happening. The Firm didn't want to bow to the pressure of the extremists—I didn't. If we did bow, we would never recover. I needed to go to Brynad, to face the commissioner and address the crowd. The bulk of the meeting was meant to be in private, between Lord Rowlings, the newly appointed commissioner, and me. Addressing the crowd was only important in making an appearance.*

He met my gaze. "You want me to be you."

"You can do it. You know what to say."

Noah looked down at his body and back up. "I'm not you any longer. The people will see the change."

"The Firm has an answer for that. They can make you appear as me. The question is will you do what you're asked?"

He scoffed. "Is the sun shining?"

"No," I said with a chuckle. "It's January in Molave."

Noah nodded. "I want to feel fresh air. I haven't felt it since...since Forthwith."

"There's a risk."

"What can you promise me if I do this?"

"You once said I was powerless. All the power resides with the king."

His thin lips came together. "I was wrong about you. If I make it out of this alive, I want to leave, to disappear. I could ruin everything for Molave in the meeting or in front of the crowd. When I don't, when I show my sincerity to the Firm, I need you to convince the king I will never be heard from again."

"Do you know anything about the Lads' Guild?"

His forehead furrowed. "In Australia?"

"Started there. There's a relatively new faction in the region. They don't want the Godfrey line to continue with an American. It seems your affair with the Borinkian princess was their preferred union."

"Fuck, it always goes back to Lucille."

Clenching my teeth, I stood taller. "I love her."

With a snicker he shook his head. "If they don't want you to be blown up, they must have run out of Romans."

"I want to keep this position, this world—all of it. Lucille is pregnant."

"Oh fuck. Has that been announced?"

"No. It would only make these people more upset. We need to find them. The engineers believe they will be able to track the transmissions from the devices on the cars. Even if you're being tracked, it doesn't mean you're a target."

"Who put the transmitters on the cars?" Noah asked.

I could lie or pretend I didn't know. However, since I was asking Noah for a favor, I chose to be truthful. "Inessa. The royal guards uncovered footage from Forthwith. It had been recorded over, but they found it."

"Is she dead?"

I shook my head. "The queen wants her baby if it's yours."

"It's not."

"That is still to be determined. If it is, do you want a nice cottage with the princess?"

"Fuck no. The love of my life is gone." He turned, peering around the small room. "This place has made me realize I don't want to die."

"Noah, we don't have a lot of time. This is my life on the line. Can I trust you?"

"Yes, Your Highness."

The flood of relief from his answer washed through me. I reached out and grasped his arm. "Thank you, Prince Roman." I hurried to the door. Lord Martin and Lady Caroline rushed in, carrying a suit, much like the one I was wearing, along with a shirt, shoes, tie, and the padded shirt.

"Is this thing bulletproof?" Noah asked as Lord Martin helped him dress.

"It's damn heavy," I said. "It might as well be."

Once he was wearing the suit pants and shirt, Mrs. Drake joined us in the cramped room. "Your Highnesses," she said, bowing to both of us.

"Tell her," Noah said.

"Noah will do this," I said, "show the Firm that he can be trusted. Once it is done, he wants his freedom."

She inhaled, standing taller.

I went on, "I've agreed to help him accomplish his goal."

"Prince Roman," she said to Noah.

"No, don't call me that. My name is Noah. Fucking say it."

"Noah," Mrs. Drake said, "are you capable of staying in character?"

"I did it for five long fucking years."

"There," Lord Martin said as he took a step back.

As he'd worked on the clothing, Lady Caroline sprayed color in Noah's greying hair and shaved his cheeks. *Last, she added makeup, giving his complexion a healthy glow.*

Noah took a step back and looked at his reflection in the two-way window. He lifted his chin and turned one direction and the other. His dark gaze met mine. "Promise me this is the last time. I won't be kept a prisoner only to be your body double."

I couldn't help thinking of the UDARVIS comic universe.

This was the same, yet this risk was greater than occurred with a stuntman on the set. While those situations can be dangerous, SAG had precautions. For example, live explosives were not allowed. In other words, on a set, the chance of death was low.

Offering him my hand, I spoke as we shook. "You have my word." I paused. "Thank you, Noah." I looked to Mrs. Drake. "What about Lord Rowlings?"

"He has been told that a body double will step in. He has no idea that it's happened before." Mrs. Drake turned to Noah. "And he won't know."

"I'll never tell another soul if I can get out of this hole forever."

"We must go," Mrs. Drake said. She turned to me. "You need to wait. We can't have two Romans leaving together." She looked at Lord Martin. "In five minutes, escort the prince to the situation room. I will be there shortly."

"Noah," I said.

He turned back.

"Was she someone you left in Norway, your love? Did you learn she was gone when you went back?"

He shook his head. "No."

"I'm sorry that she's gone."

"Thank you. I will forever be in his debt."

Prince Roman walked beside the chief of the ministry. I watched them exit with an aching sense of how fragile the world truly was as I turned to Lord Martin. "His?"

He nodded. "It was rumored but known by a few."

"Lord Avery?"

Fuck.

Noah wasn't so unlike me. This ruthless world had given him a soulmate. And his was taken. I couldn't allow that to happen to me.

King Theodore's question returned me to the present. "The man tried to kill me, and you put the future of Molave in his hands?"

"No, sir. I made the decision to not risk the future of Molave." I inhaled. "I am the future."

"I hope to God you're right."

"I hope we're wrong, and Noah and Lord Rowlings return safely. When they do, I will further advocate for Noah. When he proves himself faithful, he deserves his freedom." The king's eyes narrowed, but he remained silent. "You told me that I would need to make difficult decisions. That's what happened today. I chose to stay here, learning from you, and loving Lucille."

The king lifted his trembling left hand and grasped my forearm. "Time is the only determination of our choices."

"Shall we?" I asked, motioning toward the door.

"The last time I was in that room..." King Theo shook his head. "It was before Roman—Noah —arrived."

"After Lucille's wedding?"

The king nodded.

"What happened?"

"I think you can figure that out." He lifted his chin. "We need to be over there."

I opened the door from within and followed the king toward the situation room. As the guard opened the door, the people within stood. Tension crackled through the air as King Theo and I joined the rest of the viewers. My gaze went over the various screens. "What have we missed? Has anything happened?"

CHAPTER
29

Lucille

Once we were in the corridor, Queen Anne reached for my hand. "Lucille, stay calm. Everything will be all right."

"You don't know that."

"I do," she said with conviction.

There were a million questions spiraling through my thoughts, yet none were spoken. Uttering them aloud would give them energy. I refused to do that. I wouldn't entertain the idea that something had happened to Roman, not *my* Roman.

If something had happened, and Noah was under the infirmary, would they bring him back?

My stomach churned with the summoning of that thought.

They couldn't.

I couldn't.

My palms grew clammy. Having that Roman back was more than I could bear.

Now that I'd experienced unconditional love, I couldn't go back.

Those thoughts and more came and went, a tornado threatening not only our lives but my mental health, as the royal guards ushered us through the maze of hallways. While I stayed in step with the queen, my mind returned to what Inessa had said as we were leaving. 'You were supposed to be with him.'

Occasionally, Queen Anne's gaze met mine, an expression of concern seeping through her usual mask. She was a master at staying indifferent. It was why many thought her to be unaware. However, the more we walked, it seemed that the prospect of something happening to Roman clearly also had her worried.

Once to the first floor, we turned toward the king's apartments of offices.

"Where are we going?" I asked.

The queen took my elbow. "Stay with me, Lucille."

Swallowing, I nodded.

The guards outside the king's office bowed before opening the doors. Inside, the guards who had been with us led the queen, her mistress, and me down a series of hallways I'd never before seen. At each doorway, more armed guards were present, allowing us entry through locked doors. Finally, we came to a staircase, reminding me of the descent to the cells below the infirmary.

My fearful gaze met the queen's.

"They're taking us where we'll be safe," she reassured.

"From what?"

"We must trust them."

My grandmother's stories of my family's escape from Letanonia came back to me. The hiding and running. The people who risked everything to help the once-powerful family.

More locks were present at the base of the staircase. It was as if we were entering a prison. The sounds of locks echoed through the concrete stairwell.

What if we weren't being protected but instead imprisoned?

I was on the verge of fainting by the time we were brought to another door. The guard outside this door placed his face before a recognition pad. Instead of feeling relieved at the increase in technological security, I experienced a greater level of fear.

What is happening?

As the inside of the room became visible, the dam I'd tried to keep strong broke, smashed to smithereens. I gasped for breath. Tears flooded my eyes, cascading down my cheeks. It wasn't the room; it was the dark stare of the man I'd feared I'd lost.

In two strides, he was with me, wrapping me in his arms. Within his embrace, I momentarily forgot the room around us. Holding tight to the front of his suit, I took comfort in the beat of his heart against my ear, the sense of his reassuring embrace, and the spicy scent of his cologne. I had no doubt as to his identity. This was *my* Roman.

My prince stroked my hair as my tears dampened his tie.

Finally, I pulled away and looked up at him. "You're safe. I was so frightened. Did you go to Brynad?"

"What have you been told?"

"Nothing."

As if a camera's lens sharpened, the room around us came into view, especially the other occupants. "Oh," I said with a curtsy to the king, "Your Majesty. I'm sorry. I didn't see you."

King Theo smiled. "I can't complain that your first instinct is to go to my son."

His son.

My mind was too disoriented to give that more thought. Instead, sniffing and taking comfort in Roman's presence, I nodded.

"Lucille," King Theo said, "have a seat next to Anne. We need to talk."

I started to sit as the other occupants of the room began to file out. Stopping, I stood straight as my gaze met Mrs. Drake's. "Before you go," I said, turning to the king and my husband. "As we were called away from the Borinkian princess's apartments, she said something. Something I think all of you should hear."

The king lifted his hand, signaling for the chief minister to wait.

Once the others were gone, he coaxed, "Go on."

"She said that I was supposed to be with him." I looked up at Roman. "She meant you. I was supposed to be with you."

The king's gaze narrowed. "She said that?"

"Yes, sir. She said something else, something that was offensive."

"What?" Roman asked.

"She called me an American—that's not offensive," I quickly added. "It was the next part...the daughter of a Letanonian cunt."

Queen Anne gasped.

As Roman spoke with the tone and command of a sovereign, I did as the king bided and sat.

"Mrs. Drake," Roman began, "I want Inessa's apartments guarded. She's not to be allowed to wander the palace. I also want the premises thoroughly searched. Somehow, unbeknownst to our security, she's been communicating with someone. It's the only way she would know what occurred."

"Her apartments are restricted," the chief minister

said. "Electronically monitored. She can't communicate without our knowledge."

"I'm not satisfied."

"Yes, Your Highness." She turned to King Theodore. "Sir?"

"You heard the prince."

"Yes, Your Majesty."

There was something I couldn't pinpoint in the nonverbal exchange happening between the king and my husband.

"Wait," Roman said to Mrs. Drake. "On second thought, have the princess removed and placed in a new secure location. The ministry guards will do a more thorough search if she's not present, and I want the amniocentesis completed today."

"I told her," Queen Anne said, "she had an appointment tomorrow."

"I'm not waiting, Mum," the prince said.

I lifted my hand to his, intertwining our fingers and staring up at him with a renewed admiration. In these tense times, he truly was regal. Not only that, but there was a connection—a partnership—with the king. They were working in tandem, something I'd never witnessed.

After Mrs. Drake left, I looked up at Roman. "Where are we? What happened?"

"This is our safe room," the queen said. "No one can get to us here."

My fear returned. "Are we in danger?"

King Theo sat in the chair beside the queen and took her hand in his.

On occasions during our evening meals, I'd seen the way the king's hands trembled, especially when he reached for his glass. Watching the way the queen secured his hand in hers, brought back things she'd said. She was his supporter, his partner, and his defender. It was her job, and she committed to it for life.

"There is an extremist group called the Lads' Guild," King Theodore began. He went on to tell us about the purist views. He said there'd been some similar static when Roman and I announced our engagement, although at the time they'd kept that from me. This new group was more radicalized, dangerous, and funded.

"Our security believes the Lads' Guild," Roman went on, "is connected to the underground Borinkian supporters in Norway."

"Francis?" Queen Anne asked.

The king sighed. Lifting his wife's hand to his lips, he kissed her knuckles. "Anne, I'm sorry you have to know this."

"Theodore, I think we have been through enough

to know that we will always be here for one another. If Isabella's husband is a threat..."

"We're confirming, Mum," Roman said. "There is a possibility."

"But not Isabella?" the queen questioned.

"We won't make any moves until we know exactly what's happening and who is involved," the king reassured.

"Why are we down here?" I asked. "Has the group made a move?"

Roman answered, "I was notified of the increased risk this morning. Remember how I was concerned about transmitters found on the royal cars?"

"Yes."

"Our security purposely left some beacons in place, hoping to track where the signals were sent. The cyber-security team felt they had perfected the technology. That was why our trip to Brynad was announced."

"You knew you were a target?" I asked, recalling conversations where Roman forbade me from joining him.

"We both were."

"Especially you, Lucille," King Theodore said. "The Lads' Guild isn't happy about Roman's marriage. It seems they were pushing for the rumors of divorce, wanting Roman with Inessa, believing it a purer union."

I opened my eyes wide as my heart beat in double time. "I'm sorry."

"No, Lucille," Queen Anne said. "You are loved by the people. Whoever these individuals are, their opinions don't matter."

"They do," Roman said, "if they put your life at risk."

"You canceled your trip to Brynad?" I asked.

CHAPTER 30

Roman

My gaze met King Theodore's. If this was my chosen life, it was time that the four of us in this room came clean with one another. It was now or never. If the Firm decided to get rid of me, today's news would make it plausible. Every ounce of conviction flowing through my circulation reinforced my determination. I wouldn't go without a fight, and I'd never leave without Lucille.

"Roman didn't go to Brynad," King Theo answered. His dark stare met mine.

"Noah did," I said.

"What?" Lucille's eyes widened.

The queen's gaze went down to her lap.

Obviously, everyone in the room was aware of the multiple Romans. How it all began was still a mystery to Lucille and me. Nevertheless, the present was where we were.

"The time for secrets is done," I said. "I'm committed to this family and Molave—if you'll still have me." I inhaled, clenched my jaw, and looked down at Lucille. "However, I won't go without my wife."

"Roman," the king said, "no one wants you to go. You said it earlier today; you are the future of Molave."

"Is Noah okay?" Lucille asked.

I shook my head. "Once the threat was explained to me, I made the decision not to cancel the meeting. I was determined to go. Chances were favorable that the transmissions from the beacons would be followed. I didn't want to miss the opportunity." I crouched down and laid my hand on Lucille's knee. "Then I was reminded of what I would sacrifice." Shades of blue swirled in her orbs. "I couldn't stand the thought of leaving you. I went to Noah and asked him to step in for me. It's my fault he's gone."

"Gone?" the queen asked. "What happened? Where is he?"

Standing, I exhaled. "In a nutshell, the beacon began transmitting the location of the royal car as soon as they began the drive to Brynad. Our cyber security was able to follow the signals. They were being picked up in Norway."

"That means we can't apprehend them," the queen said.

"I called the prime minister," King Theo said.

"They're cooperating with us. We are waiting to hear what they found."

"Noah?" Lucille asked.

I replied, "He kept his word. He and Lord Rowlings met with the newly appointed commissioner. The meeting went well. Of course, the commissioner doesn't know me well enough to know it wasn't me."

"He helped us?" Lucille asked.

"I'd promised him his freedom."

"You can't," the queen said. "The risk is too great." She turned to the king. "Theo."

"Anne, he's gone," King Theo said. "Another drone dropped an explosive device." He backtracked. "After the meeting in Brynad, Lord Rowlings stayed behind to work with the commissioner. On the prince's return to Molave City, Noah's car was bombed. The explosive missed the car, but the blast caused the driver to lose control. Apparently, Noah wasn't wearing a seatbelt. The car rolled. He suffered head and neck trauma." The king shook his head. "Tragic."

Tears slid down Lucille's cheeks as her chin fell forward.

Again, I crouched near her feet. "I'm sorry."

Looking up, her gaze met mine and she forced a smile. "I think I'm happy he tried to help, and that he thought his freedom was near."

I nodded.

"How long have you known?" King Theo asked Lucille.

Her eyes met mine as I stood. Her smile grew. "The night of Rothy's party. I met *my* Roman in the gardens. I thought I'd wished him into being."

"You weren't upset?" Queen Anne asked. "How did you justify your grey?"

While I didn't understand the queen's question, Lucille did. She turned to the queen, her straight posture emphasizing her determination. "I told you my grey is different. Changing my husband wasn't my doing. I didn't set out to find another man. We fought our attraction for as long as possible. I'd been incredibly lonely with Noah, not understanding why he hated me so."

"He wasn't happy," I said. "That wasn't your fault."

"Since we're being honest," Lucille began, "did I marry the real Roman?"

Queen Anne took a deep breath. "Each one has been real, child."

"The one you birthed, if you did."

The queen shook her head. "I did. We lost him while he was at university. It was an accident. After losing Teddy, we couldn't bear to lose another child. Finding Theodore's children was my idea."

Theodore's children.

"What?" I staggered with the sensation of a gut

punch. "We...I'm..." I shook my head. "No. That isn't true."

"It is, son," Papa said. "I remember your mother. She was a remarkable woman." He turned to the queen. "I'm sorry, Anne."

She smiled. "I'm not. I am your queen." She turned to me. "I didn't know your mother, but she raised an honorable son. I'm proud to call you my own."

Childhood memories were spinning in fast-forward through my thoughts. "My father was an officer in the air force." As I said the words, I recalled my mother's final hours, how she tried to tell me something about my father.

King Theo shook his head. "No, he wasn't. Mr. Davies confirmed your paternity. It was confirmed years ago."

Lucille reached for my hand. "You're a Godfrey. That means our child is a Godfrey."

I shook my head. "It also means Noah was my brother?" Taking a step back, I collapsed against the wall. "I sent my own brother to his death."

Lucille stood and came to me. "Are you all right?"

I met Papa's gaze, suddenly recalling the way he'd watched Noah through the window of the basement cells. "You were willing to kill your own son?"

Queen Anne stood. "Noah had gotten out of control. I made the decision."

"Are there more?" I asked.

"Not that would pass. A girl and another boy. Different coloring." Papa shook his head. "Only three who shared the same traits." He laid his hand on the queen's shoulder. "We had the pleasure of parenting all of you. Five with Teddy and Roman."

"Who did I marry?" Lucille asked. "And what happened to him?"

"We don't need to rehash—" the queen said.

"No more secrets." Lucille stood, crossing her arms resolutely over her chest. "I'm committed to this marriage, to this country. I've been steadfast. Tell me the truth."

"Lucille," King Theo said. "You shouldn't be upset, in your condition."

"Who did I marry?" the princess repeated.

The king spoke. "In my mind, they all have the same name." A slight smile spread over his lips. "That boy was adventurous. He had the skills of a pilot, like our son." He looked at Anne. When he turned back, his smile was gone. "Accidents. After your honeymoon, he traveled to Indonesia."

"I remember," Lucille said, taking her seat. "He wanted to hike." Her eyes opened wide. "And he was delayed in his return."

"Mount Ijen," the queen said, "is thought to be one of the most inhospitable landscapes. He'd been with us for almost two decades. He'd truly become royal. And unfortunately, some royals believe themselves to be indestructible—immortal."

"He liked to push the line—a brazen, wild side. He was addicted to adrenaline, and that's what took him from us," King Theo said. "That was why we then chose...Noah. He was much more reserved and down to earth."

"How didn't I know?" Lucille said.

The queen replied, "I prayed you never would need to know. You were so young and in love. I prayed your rose-colored glasses would help with the transition."

My heart hurt, knowing all that Lucille had suffered, the loss of the man she fell in love with and the pain at the hands of another. "Who knows all of this?" I asked.

Papa cleared his throat. "Only those who must. Mr. Davies, Mrs. Drake, your assistants."

"Lady Buckingham?" Lucille questioned.

"No," the king said. "Roman's assistants. Lady Buckingham was never informed."

"What happened to Lord Avery?" I asked.

The king shook his head. "Tragic. He'd been with two Romans. We always hoped each one would be the last. I'm not sure of the details. Noah was out of control and needed to be stopped. I didn't order his demise."

He turned to the queen. "And neither did Anne. He was to be imprisoned."

A conversation with Lord Martin came to mind. *"No, sir, we don't put people to death. We imprison."*

The king was still talking. "Lord Avery got wind and took it upon himself to help Noah escape. His death was unintentional."

I wanted to believe what the king was saying to be true. I didn't want to think that Lord Avery was sentenced to death because he and Noah shared more than a platonic relationship. That relationship was undoubtedly why Lord Avery risked his own life to help Noah escape.

"Does Isabella know?" Lucille asked.

"No," the queen replied. "Every person who knows is a liability. I wouldn't do that to our daughter."

"She should rule," I said.

Queen Anne took a step toward me. "I didn't give birth to you, son, but I wish I had. Theo is right. You are Molave's future. You possess all your father's good qualities." She smiled at Lucille. "You have his capacity to love. I've watched the change in Lucille. You also have the ability to make difficult decisions. It seems you proved that today." She turned to the king. "What is the story on the royal car accident?"

"We've kept it quiet."

The queen turned to me. "Now that the truth is

known by the four of us, I'm asking for the two of you to make another difficult decision."

Swallowing, I reached for Lucille's hand.

"Fulfill your destiny, Prince Roman," Queen Anne said. "The two of you are exactly what Molave needs to move forward. Or take this rare opportunity to flee. We have no more options."

I blinked my eyes, wondering if I'd heard her correctly.

Flee.

Lucille and I could leave.

Noah's advice came back to me, telling me to run.

"Roman?" Lucille said.

We turned to one another, neither of us speaking. Our fingers intertwined as our bodies melded together. Time stood still as the monarchs awaited our reply. "My princess," I said softly.

Lucille lifted her palm to my cheek. "My prince."

My vision blurred as I blinked away the moisture. "Remember what you told me in the gazebo that cold, rainy night? You spoke about your commitment to Molave."

Lucille nodded, and her smile grew.

"I didn't understand it then."

"Now you do."

"I do."

She nodded.

We turned back to the king and queen. Holding tight to Lucille's hand, I renewed my commitment—our commitment—to Molave, the Firm, and my father.

My father.

The queen smiled. "It is forbidden to discuss this again. We will all take the truth to our graves. The world must never know. Don't burden your children or your grandchildren with this knowledge. This is what is right, just, and meant to be. I have no doubt that when the time comes, Molave will flourish under your leadership." She turned to Papa. "Isabella and Francis should be brought down here until the threat is neutralized."

"Francis knows," Papa said.

The queen's expression soured. "We will talk. For now, our daughter and grandchildren should be safe."

"Francis?" he asked.

"There would be too many questions if he were left out."

King Theo went to the door and opened it. Speaking to the guard, he said, "Send for the Duke and Duchess of Wilmington and the young prince and princess. We will all remain here until we are assured all is well."

"Yes, Your Majesty."

CHAPTER
31

Lucille

I t was nearly five in the afternoon when word finally arrived. King Theodore received news that three people had been apprehended and taken into custody by Politi, Norway's national police force. All I knew was that the signals transmitted from the beacons placed on the car led law enforcement to an isolated cottage in Loen, a village in the inner part of the Nordfjord region. Roman later told me the members of the extremist group had a very sophisticated setup including state-of-the-art technology and a large stockpile of weapons, including the same explosives used on the royal vehicle. A storage hangar was also found with additional drones.

Arresting the three men was only the beginning. Soon, they were to be extradited to Molave and charged with crimes against the Crown. Those were very serious charges on their own. The assailants were also to be charged with murder and the attempted assassination of a prince. Despite the Firm's efforts to keep the accident a secret, word got out. The details weren't accurate, creating a lot of speculation.

The Crown released a statement: a body double had been killed, a brave man who gave his life for Molave. Noah's real name wasn't used; nevertheless, he died with a name and the distinction of a true Molavian patriot.

Two days after the scare, Roman and I made an appearance in Molave City to show the world that rumors of his demise were greatly exaggerated.

We were on our way back to the palace when Roman received a call from Mr. Davies. The results of the amniocentesis were in. Roman reached for my hand as I listened to his end of the conversation. When he disconnected the call, I asked, "What did he say?"

Roman let out a long breath. "He wants to go over the results in person." Concern swirled in his dark brown orbs.

"Has he shared the results with the princess?"

Roman shook his head. "He isn't sharing it with anyone until he speaks with me." Roman tilted his head toward me. "Us."

"Us?"

"Yes, Lucille. The information is important to more than me—it will affect us." He swallowed, his Adam's apple bobbing. "What if the boy is Noah's?"

I shook my head. "If the baby is Noah's, that means

he is a Godfrey." I recalled what Queen Anne had said about how the capacity to love is infinite. I saw the meaning behind her wise and prophetic statement. "I didn't think it was possible, but the more I consider it, if the child is Noah's and therefore a Godfrey, I could love him, even raise him, if that's what you want."

Roman squeezed my hand. "I don't know what I want. I do know that I don't want Inessa in our lives. I also can't imagine taking a child away from its mother."

"Even when that mother is an awful person?"

Roman's cheeks rose as his smile grew. "Our baby is due the end of August."

I nodded.

"I was thinking. That is about the same time of year I saw you on the telly."

"And you thought we were crazy, playing make-believe."

"I've learned a lot since then, my princess." He leaned closer until our lips met.

The car slowed as we approached the palace gates. Beyond the windows, people waved and shouted our names. With a shy smile, I lifted my hand and waved. From the corner of my eye, I saw my husband's charming grin as he too waved.

While I hadn't allowed myself to think too much about Noah's passing, knowing that he too was King Theo's son put our five years of marriage into a new light. How naïve I'd been to simply accept Noah as the man I'd married. It was a lot for anyone to process. Yet sitting next to my Roman, I chose to concentrate on the present. I'd spent five years mulling over the past, wondering what I had done wrong and why my husband had stopped loving me. Now I realized he never loved me at all—Noah never did.

The queen never told me the real name of the man I'd married. To her and King Theodore, he was Roman. He was the first replacement, having been their son for nearly two decades.

The car came to a stop. After unfastening my seat-belt, I buttoned the front of my long wool coat and slid my hands into leather gloves. The afternoon sun did little to warm the January air.

Roman offered me his hand as I stepped from the car.

"I miss Annabella," I said, looking up at the exterior of Molave Palace.

He kissed my cheek. "I have so much to learn from Papa."

Smiling, I nodded. "He has a lot to teach you."

"I could send you to Annabella, if you want."

I met his gaze as our breaths crystalized in the winter breeze. "I would rather miss a house than my husband. Where you are is where I want to be."

Once inside, a butler helped us with our coats and gloves.

Roman again offered me his hand. "Shall we go to the infirmary?"

"He could come to us."

"Princess, I need to know what he found out. I don't want to wait."

"What if he's with a patient?"

"Unless that patient is the king, he will see us. I'm the prince."

Holding his hand, I leaned close to his arm. "Yes, you are."

We were seated at a round table in one of the small rooms in the infirmary. As I looked around, I recalled the number of times Mr. Davies would call me in, sit me down, and discuss my fertility. For years, I despised these rooms. It seemed there was never good news delivered in one of them.

Roman looked my direction and tilted his head. "Talk to me, Princess. What's bothering you?"

A smile curled my lips. "I love that you can do that."

"Do what?"

"See my feelings without me saying a word."

"What can I say, your eyes are a beautiful open book to your soul. The more I see, the more I read, the more I want. Now, why were you sad."

Inhaling, I looked around, up to the ceiling and around the four walls. One wall contained the door while the other three had pictures. They were all soothing photos of nature. One contained a spiderweb, glistening with water droplets. "This room," I said. "There are three that I know of in the infirmary. They're all the same, except for the pictures. The spiderweb always fascinated me."

"Unless it also made you sad, you're not telling me the truth."

"It's the truth. It's in these rooms where Mr. Davies would talk to me about conceiving." I swallowed. "Where he would confirm that I wasn't with child."

Roman laid his hand over my stomach. "Those days are over."

Covering his hand with mine, I sighed. "I was always alone. Just Mr. Davies and me."

"Roman didn't..." He didn't finish the sentence. "You're not alone now."

"Sometimes, I'm afraid if I blink, you'll be gone and Noah...I know that isn't possible. It's that even I didn't realize how miserable I was until now that I'm not." I looked around again. "I associate these rooms with bad news." My gaze met his. "I don't know what will be bad news today. Is it better if the child is a Godfrey? Is it better if it's not?"

"I don't have the answer. Whatever it is, we will face it together."

Roman moved his hand as the door to our side opened and Mr. Davies entered.

"Your Highnesses," he said with a neck bow. His gaze went to me. "I didn't realize you'd be with us, Princess."

"I asked her to come," Roman volunteered. "What you have to say affects both of us."

He took the seat across the table and laid a file in front of him. "Legally, Miss Volkov has agreed to my sharing her information only with you."

Roman smiled. "Sir, you're in Molave. My father and I make the laws. Lucille will hear what you have to say."

Mr. Davies's nostrils flared as he nodded. "Yes, Your Highness."

I sat forward, as if needing the closeness to hear all we were about to learn.

"I will get to the point," Mr. Davies said. "The DNA sample taken from the amniotic fluid found that the child has a condition called haemochromatosis. It results from two copies of HFEC282Y mutations."

"What is that?" I asked. "Is it serious?"

"The faulty gene mutation is one of the most common genetic disorders in northern Europe. That is why we test for it."

Northern Europe.

Roman told me that Noah was from Norway. Inessa was also from the region—from Borinkia.

Mr. Davies went on, "This condition is treatable. Actually, having this test now will help the child. The condition results in a build-up of iron in the body. That can damage vital organs. Now that it's discovered, treatment can begin shortly after birth."

"Will he be okay?" I asked.

"Yes, Princess, he can be. Common symptoms even with treatment include extreme fatigue and joint pain."

I turned to Roman as he spoke. "Is the child a Godfrey?"

"No."

"You are sure?" I asked.

"I'm positive."

Roman exhaled.

"To have two copies of the faulty mutation, it must be present in both parents. Inessa does have this mutation. No Godfrey does."

I exhaled and watched Roman's reaction.

"You're saying there is no chance this child is a Godfrey," Roman clarified.

"That is what I'm saying."

"Do you know who the father is?" I asked.

"I do not."

Roman sat taller. "Does the Duke of Wilmington have that mutation?"

Mr. Davies looked down and inhaled. "Your Highness. I'm not comfortable—"

Roman lifted his hand. "Your prince has asked you a direct question."

"The mutation is a recessive trait. If the duke had it and the duchess didn't, they could pass the recessive trait on to their children."

"Rothy and Alice," I said. "Should they be tested?"

"No. Neither of their parents possesses the mutation."

I turned to my husband. "The baby isn't yours and isn't Francis's. Who is the father?"

"If I'm understanding this correctly, it is someone with the same mutation?"

Mr. Davies nodded. "That doesn't narrow it down. As I said, the mutation is common in this region."

"When are you going to tell the princess?" Roman asked.

"That is up to you, sir. I didn't know if you wanted to be the one to inform her."

"No. You can inform her, and then she can leave Molave."

I reached out to Roman's arm. "Will she need anything special for the child's condition?"

"I'm certain they are capable in Borinkia," Mr.

Davies said. "I will be happy to send the results of the test with her. She can take them to another physician."

Roman looked at me. "We're done with her."

"I want to go to her."

"Why?"

"Because if I received news about our child, even if the condition is treatable, I wouldn't want to hear it alone." I turned to Mr. Davies. "Let me speak with the queen. One of our mistresses will get back to you. Until then, please don't inform the princess."

"Yes, Your Highness."

CHAPTER
32

Roman

Francis entered the king's office. With each step, he moved his cane. He'd received the new knee less than a week ago, and he was up and walking. Isabella entered a step behind. They briefly looked my direction before addressing the king.

There was no doubt this was about to be an uncomfortable discussion. Therefore, Papa chose to forgo the formality of his desk and utilize the less formal sofa and chairs near the windows.

Once we were all seated, the king began. His expression was as melancholy as I'd seen. The two of us had discussed what he was about to say, and I knew it wasn't easy. Isabella was the last remaining child of Theo and Anne. By all rights, she should have learned her place in the ascension to the throne when she was still young. The fact she should be next in line to reign would remain a secret. Currently, there were other issues.

King Theo stood.

The anguish was palpable.

"For once," he began in his boisterous tone, "I am without words."

Isabella's expression paled. "What is it, Papa? Is this about your health?"

His gaze snapped to his daughter. "My health is as well as can be expected. I believe you both know why I summoned you. Now would be the opportunity for confessions. What would you care to confess to your king?"

She shook her head. "I have nothing to confess." She turned to Francis. "What is he talking about?"

"Roman," the king said.

Taking a breath, I sat taller. "Do you know much about technology? The sending and receiving of transmissions?"

Isabella shook her head. It was Francis who had his eyes zeroed in on me.

"I'll take your silence as a no," I said. "Truth be told, I don't know a lot either. Thankfully, the Firm has within its ranks some incredibly intelligent individuals. Between the cyber-security team, General Dickerson, and the engineers...there were more people involved. Anyway, it was fascinating to watch as those people tracked transmissions. We never would have found the cottage in Loen without them."

"That's good, right?" Isabella asked.

My eyes were on Francis. "What do you think?"

"The same thing I thought when we were all stuffed in that bunker. I'm glad those fuckers were caught."

King Theodore took the seat to my side. "Those weren't the only transmissions they intercepted."

Francis lifted his hands. "Fill us in. If you haven't noticed, I've been in a damn hospital bed."

"You've been back to your apartments since the surgery," the king replied.

"I don't exactly have a lot of access here."

I asked, "Did you know that Inessa Volkov's apartments were monitored?"

Isabella's forehead furrowed. "You were spying on her?"

"I like the word monitoring. Mum gave her a bracelet."

"She showed it to me," Isabella responded.

"Yes, well, that bracelet had a GPS tracking device. The engineers were able to track her movement around the palace."

Isabella shook her head. "She didn't move around the palace."

"How familiar," Papa asked Isabella, "are you with the infirmary?"

"Too familiar," she said. "Francis was there for over a month."

I spoke up. "Were you aware of the door leading to the gardens?"

Isabella crinkled her face and shrugged. "I guess I forgot about it." She looked at me. "We used to sneak through that when we were young."

There was no way for me to remember that. "The door is locked from the inside, but there are keys."

Francis stood and faced Papa and me. "I have kept my word, but it's not too late. I can still tell the world."

King Theodore stood. "Tell them what? You have nothing to tell."

Francis looked from the king to me and back.

"What is it?" Isabella asked.

"It's Roman," Francis said.

I turned to Isabella. "On numerous occasions, your husband had a late-night visitor."

"Inessa is only a friend," Francis said.

"Inessa went to your room," my sister asked, "at night?"

"She was lonely. We've known one another for all her life."

"The amniocentesis came back," I interjected.

Isabella looked at me. "She swears it's yours. You've admitted—"

"I've admitted my mistakes. The child isn't mine."

"Noah's," Francis said.

"Who is Noah?" Isabella asked.

"No," Papa said. "The royal physician said with one hundred percent certainty that the child is not a Godfrey."

"Neither is he." Francis pointed my direction.

King Theo was chest to chest with Francis in three strides. "He is a Godfrey. He's my son, and if you dare say otherwise, you will be removed from the royal family."

"I don't understand what is happening," Isabella said.

I watched as Francis took a step back from the king and waited. I'd pummeled his face once. If he so much as clenched a fist, I was ready to do it again.

Francis turned to Isabella. "It's time for us to go back to Forthwith."

"Forthwith is property of the Crown," Papa said. "We aren't done. Sit down."

Clenching his jaw, Francis sat beside his wife.

King Theo looked to me.

I continued, "This is what we have. Please feel free to fill in the blanks."

King Theo sat.

I spoke to the duke and duchess. "My mistakes include colluding with the duke to poison the king."

Isabella gasped.

"Cherry pits," I said, "when ground, contain poison that the body converts to cyanide. The royal guards found jars of cherry pits at Forthwith."

"We have servants," Isabella said. "You can't prove they're Francis's."

"This isn't debatable," I said. "I was a part of it. I've confessed. Francis saw my stress and came up with a solution."

He narrowed his gaze. "What the hell are you saying? It wasn't you."

"Alek Volkov, King Aleksander II, was also part of the plan."

"You can't prove that," Francis said.

"No, but Inessa can. While she's been cozying up to my sister, she has been working with you behind the scenes. To be honest, I suspected that her baby was yours."

"No," Isabella said, her glare on her husband. "Is that possible?"

I waited a few seconds, wondering if the duke would confess. When he didn't, I threw him a lifeline. "No, sister, her child isn't Francis's either."

Francis's expression visibly relaxed.

"Did you sleep with her?"

"We're more concerned about the information you sent via your secret phone," Papa said. "Inessa knew about the plan to kill Roman and Lucille. She carelessly admitted it to Lucille."

I interjected, speaking to Francis. "She didn't have the means to communicate with the Lads' Guild, but you did. She visited you and the two of you came up with a plan. We have footage of her placing the transmitters on the cars at Forthwith."

"This isn't true," Isabella said.

"I'm sorry, dear," Papa said, "it is. We have proof of everything. The only thing we don't know is the paternity of Inessa's child."

We all turned to Francis.

"Fuck, I don't know."

"You slept with her?" Isabella repeated, incredulously.

Francis sat taller. "You can't go public with any of this. If you do, I'll tell everything. Hell, I'll write a book. It's been done before."

"No, you won't," Papa said. "The British have a constitutional monarchy. Molave has a true monarchy, the oldest form of government. As of this moment, you are under royal reprimand."

Isabella gasped. "Papa?"

He continued, "You, Francis Eriksen II, will forthwith no longer hold the title of duke. Your residence will forever remain Molave. You will not leave or write a book." He spoke to Isabella. "I can force you to divorce this man, but I won't. That will be your decision. In the meantime, he will be housed at Lilith Cottage outside of Deca."

Lilith Cottage was once King Arthur's hunting lodge. It hasn't been used in decades and is isolated at a high elevation. The perfect prison.

Tears fell from Isabella's eyes. "Papa."

Francis's gaze filled with hatred, yet he remained silent.

King Theo said, "He deserves death for attempted regicide."

"That was Roman," she said. "He admitted it."

The king placed his hand on my knee. "Roman is a new man, Isabella. No one will hear that confession. You will not repeat it. Francis is also guilty of plotting to kill the Prince and Princess of Molave. He's been working with adversaries from Borinkia."

"So fucked up," Francis mumbled. "If you would have just left Lucille. I told you that she'd never leave you, no matter how awful you were. We were so fucking close."

I considered correcting him, telling him that wasn't me. Yet to stay in this life with the woman I loved, I was willing to shoulder Noah's sins.

"What about me?" Isabella asked.

"Did you collude with the enemy?"

She shook her head. "I visited and talked to her. I felt badly for her. I thought she was all alone. I didn't know..." Her lips came together. Inhaling, Isabella sat taller. "If I may" —she was looking at the king and at me— "I'd like to take the children back to Forthwith."

"We can discuss visitations in Deca," Papa said.

Isabella stood. She glared at her husband and turned back to us. "That won't be necessary. I'll work with the Firm on a divorce."

"Isabella," Francis said. "You can't seriously believe what they've said."

"Thank you, Your Majesty," she said to Papa with a curtsy. "And to you, Your Highness." She curtsied again. "I hope my children and I are welcome in Molave."

I stood. "Always."

CHAPTER
33

Lucille

I waited in Mr. Davies's office while he consulted with Inessa Volkov. With each passing minute, I wondered what her reaction would be. Was she concerned about her son's health, or was she surprised by his paternity?

The condition Mr. Davies described was common in this region; nevertheless, it would be scary to learn of any condition that impacted your child. I laid my hand over my midsection. I was still wearing all my clothes. There hadn't been any changes in my waist size. While my morning sickness had lessened, I still had bouts of nausea. Everything I'd read or been told said that I should feel back to normal in the second trimester. Back to normal with a growing baby bump. At ten weeks, my baby was about the size of a prune. I had a fun app that weekly gave the fetus's size in comparison to fruits. The visualization worked, even if thinking of my child as a prune or a strawberry made me laugh.

There was a knock and the door opened inward.

"Your Highness," Mr. Davies said with a neck bow. "The princess has agreed to speak with you. She's in the room we were in the other day."

"How is she?" I asked as I stood.

"It's not my place to say, but I'm surprised you're concerned."

"Why would it surprise you? The haemochromatosis you mentioned yesterday, I looked it up last night." I laid my hand again over my stomach. "I'm sorry for her and her son."

"In most cases it is manageable. It's better for her to know now so they can monitor the boy."

"Could our child have the mutation? Could I? Should I have a test?"

"No, Princess. Your child will not. As for a test, that's up to you and the prince. No Godfrey has the necessary mutation. It takes two people with the mutation for the condition to occur. Even if you have it, which is less likely due to your nationality, the most you could do is pass on the mutation."

"My mother is from Letanonia."

"I can run a test on you if you'd wish. Again, the prince doesn't have it."

I let out a breath. "I think I'd like to know about me."

"Do you want to discuss it with the prince?"

"Is there any chance of harm to our child if I have a test?"

"No, I'll simply get a DNA sample from you."

"Then we will schedule it."

"Yes, Your Highness." He opened the door and took a step back. "She is distraught over all of it."

I nodded.

Outside the room, I reminded myself that I was present for support and as the conduit between her and the prince. Knocking first, I opened the door. Inessa's eyes were moist, glistening under the light. There was a bright white tissue in her hand.

"Your Highness," she said softly.

"Your Highness," I replied. "What can the Crown do for you? Are you still afraid to return to Borinkia?"

Her jaw clenched and a vein in her temple throbbed as she met my gaze. Finally, she dropped her chin to her chest. "Alek won't hurt me. He'll want something worse."

I took the seat across the table. "What do you mean?"

She closed her eyes and shook her head. "I'm sorry. I thought...we thought...Roman was supposed to be my escape."

"You wanted to unite the countries," I said, remembering what she had said when I went to the apartments where she'd been staying.

"Alek does. He told me to pursue..." She looked away.

"Inessa, your brother told you to seduce my husband?"

"It was his and Francis's idea. After a few meetings, they thought Roman would leave you if I was with child." She shrugged. "Everyone knows you can't —or couldn't..."

I sat tall. "Did you want...were you even interested in Roman?"

"Not at first, but I couldn't stop. Getting Roman on Alek's side was essential for his plan."

"For whose plan?" I asked.

"I don't know if it was Alek or Francis who came up with it. They both were involved."

My stomach twisted. "The plan is foiled. Francis has been banished."

Her eyes widened. "Where?"

"Why do you ask?"

"Isabella?" Inessa asked.

"She and the children will be safe."

"Divorce?"

"That hasn't been decided," I answered honestly.

The princess leaned back, placing her hand over

her midsection. "My son, he has a genetic abnormality. It is what the physician called it."

I nodded. "It is treatable. He will be healthy as long as he gets all the treatments he needs."

"Yes," she said, her tone melancholy.

"Did you know the child wasn't Roman's?"

More tears filled her eyes. "I didn't know. I hoped." She dabbed her eyes. "I wanted to do as Alek commanded, and in doing so, earn my freedom. I dreamt of one country, one where I could be queen."

My thoughts were stuck on the first part of her answer—she didn't know. I tried to keep my expression caring. "Do you know who the father could be?"

Closing her eyes, more tears slid down her pale cheeks. "I asked the physician." She sighed. "You must think I'm a slut."

Maybe.

I didn't say that. "I don't know your situation."

She shook her head. "Did you know that my mother was my father's sister—my aunt?"

"No," I said quickly. "From what I recall reading, your mother died many years after Aleksander I invaded Letanonia."

"Complications with her third pregnancy."

"Oh, I'm sorry. That's frightening."

"I barely had a mother." She looked down at her stomach. "I don't know if I can be one."

"Of course you can. Someone told me that love is infinite. Your son will know the love of his mother."

She met my gaze. "If I go back, he will force me to marry him."

"Who will force you?"

"Alek. The child is his."

I swear on all things holy, the floor fell out from under my feet as a newfound wash of compassion for the woman I should despise flooded my circulation. "I-I don't know what to say."

She smirked. "You could congratulate me on doing as I was told, keeping our bloodline clean. The Volkovs are pure."

Purists, that was what King Theo and Roman called the Lads' Guild.

"The mutation," I pointed out.

"I carry it and so does Alek, a recessive trait. We've known that it was a danger in maintaining our line. Despite that, I was told long ago what my future would hold."

"He can't force you to marry him," I said, the small hairs on the back of my neck standing to attention. Tiny soldiers ready to do battle for a woman I barely knew.

"He is now king." She dabbed her eyes again. "I will be queen."

"Aren't there laws or rules against siblings...?"

Inessa shook her head. "The king makes the laws."

I recalled something she'd said earlier. "You said Alek won't hurt you. Is that true or has he hurt you?"

"My brother loves me."

"He told you to seduce my husband."

"And I obeyed. Doing so is my job."

I shook my head. "No, Inessa, it isn't. I will help you. Queen Anne will help you."

"You want me gone."

"I did," I admitted. "But not like this, not sent back to be your brother's queen. Maybe you could go to Forthwith and stay with Isabella."

"Het. You said Francis was banished? Then they know I worked with him to hurt you."

"But you didn't succeed." I tilted my head. "Why?"

"The drone missed, and you lied. You weren't there."

"No. Why did you want to do Roman and me harm?"

"He chose you. My brother will take me back, but he will forever remind me of my failure and blame me. Without the two of you, there was hope."

"Hope? Isabella."

She nodded. "First, she would become queen. Then, she dies. I could raise her children and rule beside the duke."

"The duke wouldn't rule. He isn't a Godfrey."

"His son is. Francis and I would be the regent king and queen until Rothy was of age. By then, the countries would be united."

"Unbelievable," I mumbled. "Isabella needs to know."

"She won't believe you. I'll tell her you're lying."

I stood, brushing the front of my slacks. "I think I'm done with our conversation."

"What will happen to me?" she asked.

"You confessed a plan to harm the Prince and Princess of Molave. I would expect the royal guards to apprehend you soon. The rest is up to King Theodore."

"My brother will not allow me to be imprisoned."

"That will be between the two kings. It appears your only way to avoid prison here in Molave is to go back to the life sentence your family had planned out for you. Whatever happens, I wish your child health and happiness."

Stepping out of the room into the hallway, I called Roman's cellphone.

He answered on the second ring. "My princess."

"I just spoke to Inessa. She admitted to working with Francis to harm us."

"She admitted it?"

"She's in the infirmary."

"I'll send royal guards. Lucille, are you all right?"

I thought about it for a moment. In microseconds I

assessed my well-being. I recalled my years with Noah and even through that darkness, I couldn't comprehend what Inessa had suffered or would suffer.

Am I all right?

"Yes, my prince. I am."

CHAPTER 34

Lucille

"My princess."

Lady Buckingham and I both turned. I couldn't help that I scanned from Roman's shoes to his dark mane, with the wonder of a lovesick teenager. His tie and suit coat were missing. His shirt was unbuttoned, showing a hint of his dark chest hair. And his sleeves were rolled up to below his elbows, giving him a sexy, casual appearance.

With each passing day, week, and month, our attraction intensified. I rarely let myself ponder the actuality that I'd been married once and had three husbands—three Romans. The fact was astounding, even laughable.

Roman told me that before Francis was banished, he'd threatened to tell the world the truth of Noah and my Roman. He didn't know about the first Roman replacement or that my Roman was a literal actor from Hollywood. Francis would never tell our story, but even if he did, who would believe such an improbable tale?

If Inessa knew the truth, we would never know. King Theodore arranged Inessa's passage back to Borinkia. The two kings came to an agreement. The tension between the countries wasn't resolved, but it had quieted. I have been watching the news of a royal wedding in Borinkia. Nothing had yet come across the newsfeed.

It was easier for my mind to comprehend that I'd married once, and that marriage took unimaginable twists and turns. When we first met, I was awestruck and filled with lust. The daring, wild side of Roman Godfrey was intoxicating. When that element disappeared, our relationship took a nosedive, leaving me wallowing in the depths of despair and loneliness.

While the outward appearances of the men were shockingly similar, it wasn't only the handsome beauty of the man whose gaze was on me that I adored. It was the entire package, the caring individual who brought back to me not only love and passion but also honesty and partnership.

It could be said that with age comes wisdom, and I have aged since first meeting the Prince of Molave. Now as a happily married mother-to-be, I saw more than the dashing exterior—his handsome face, wide shoulders, trim torso. I saw the man inside.

The man who took a job and gained a family.

The man who pledged his life to a king and a country.

The man who has never let me down, keeping every promise he's made.

The man with whom I long to spend my days, my nights, and the remainder of my years.

That was why as my eyes met his, my heart fluttered in anticipation of whatever our evening would hold.

Lady Buckingham curtsied. "Your Highness." She laid down the hairbrush. Her hazel gaze met mine. "I will return in the morning."

"Thank you, Mary," I replied, feeling the warmth in my cheeks.

Once the door closed, Roman came closer and lifted my chin. "You're stunning when you blush."

My lips curled. "I'm not blushing."

"You are." He offered me his hand. "And it makes me curious."

"About what?" I asked as I stood, all the time keeping my eyes on his gleaming dark stare.

"You yourself have said that Lady Buckingham is aware of what married couples do in private."

I nodded.

"Then what could you be thinking that would

cause you to blush?" His eyebrows danced. "I'm ready for details."

Leaning closer, I pressed myself against his hard chest with my senses on overload. His arms surrounded me, caressing my back. The aroma of his rich cologne tickled my nostrils. Pushing myself to my toes, my lips met his. As our kiss deepened and the passion between us went from a flicker to a flame, I tasted a hint of bourbon.

"Hmm?" he asked as our kiss ended.

"My prince, I don't have details. That's why I'm blushing—if I am. It's anticipation of the unknown that leaves me longing to be with you." I took a step back, remembering that after dinner, Roman had gone to King Theo's apartments. "How is he?"

The king suffered a TIA—transient ischemic attack. While it was considered mild, the better news was that it hadn't left residual symptoms or lasting damage to his brain. The royal physician was watching him closely and adjusting medications.

"Better than yesterday," Roman replied, unbuttoning his shirt.

I went to the bed and sat on the side, curious about the king while taking in my husband's striptease. Okay, it was simple undressing, but in this world, doing it alone was a luxury. "Will he be back to attending dinner soon?" I asked, realizing I missed seeing him.

"He said he would have been there tonight, but Mr. Davies wanted him to continue to rest and Mum heard the instructions."

I laughed. "In other words, Queen Anne grounded the King of Molave to his apartments."

"That about sums it up."

Roman slipped his arms from the button-up shirt and dropped it to the floor. The muscles of his arms bulged as the undershirt came over his head. I scanned from his bare chest to his toned abdomen, lower to where he unbuckled his belt.

"We can postpone the States tour," I offered. We were scheduled to leave in two days.

Roman looked up at me. "Did you see Mr. Davies today?"

"I'm sure you know I did."

His lips quirked. "I was briefed. I wanted to hear it from you."

"I did see him." I laid my hand over my lower stomach. While still small enough to be hidden by clothing, there was now officially a bulge. "I listened to the heartbeat. I'm officially in the second trimester."

"What did your app say?" he asked with a grin.

"Lime." I smiled. "I got the seal of approval for traveling."

"That was what Papa wanted to talk about."

My heart sank. "I understand if we need to postpone."

Wearing only silk boxer shorts, Roman came my way and crouched near my legs. "Papa insists we go on with the schedule. The leak concerning Isabella's pending divorce and news of Francis's title being revoked will hopefully get lost with the news of our tour. Papa wants us to go."

Palming his scruffy cheek, I tilted my head. "What do you want?"

"I'm both excited and nervous about going back to the States."

I nodded. "I remember my first visit back after our wedding. I had conflicting feelings. Part of me thought it would feel like going home, as it always had, but it didn't. We will be followed by bodyguards and there is always someone taking our picture. I think in the States I feel like a fraud." I thought a moment. "Impostor syndrome."

Roman sighed. "I've been worried about that as well. I mean, I am an impos—"

My finger pressed on his lips. "You, sir, are the son of the King of Molave and the husband to the princess. You have sworn your commitment. Never think of yourself as less."

He nodded.

"Besides, the queen forbade you to speak those

words." I thought about something. "What happened to you?" I asked. "Did you just disappear?"

"Me, Oliver? I haven't asked. I don't want to learn of my own demise." Roman stood. "I'll be back." He placed a kiss on my hair.

Untying the sash of my dressing gown, I climbed between the sheets of the big bed and leaned back on the propped pillows. I was struck by how easily the two of us communicated. I'd never told anyone about that first visit back to the States. And yet with my Roman, it was natural to share.

When Roman reappeared, his hair was damp and his cheeks smooth.

From the end of the bed, he came closer, a lion on the prowl.

Hand.

Knee.

He moved with the stealthy determination of the king of the beasts. By the time his lips met mine and I tasted the fresh mint of toothpaste, I was content to be the prey in this upcoming scenario.

I supposed prey was an incorrect term.

As Roman's hands roamed and his lips skirted over my skin, I wasn't a victim to be overpowered. No, I was the winner, and his masterly choreographed moves were my reward. While our nights were often filled with discussions, ones we saved for one another, there was something cathartic and refreshing in lovemaking.

After a day with separate agendas and schedules, coming together was a physical reassurance of our commitment.

I wasn't certain of when my nightgown or bloomers fell to the floor. Yet I knew the second Roman's lips moved lower over my abdomen, reaching my core. Biting my lip, I stifled a scream as his tongue teased. My breathing labored and my hips bucked against his ironclad grip. Thoughts of conversational topics were quickly replaced with pure ecstasy coursing through my system brought on by his ministrations.

It wasn't until my legs straightened and my toes curled as I gasped for breath that Roman moved over me, his solid chest covering and his arms caging my body. My essence replaced the earlier toothpaste as our tongues tangoed and we became one.

Never in the history of time had two people fit as perfectly together. His length and girth filled me, stretched me, in a wonderful way. The rhythm of his heart beat in time with mine as the flames from our earlier kiss ignited into a raging wildfire.

In time I found myself on my hands and knees with Roman's commanding grasp of my hips. He was the director of the scene as the bedchamber filled with sounds only we could hear. Our bodies' connection, the moans of pleasure, and guttural praises were the melody of our soundtrack. Unsure if I could reach another precipice, I took pleasure in Roman's unbridled desire, his passion, and his vigor.

My orgasm hit like a train barreling through a dark tunnel. No warning bells or flashing lights until all at once my body detonated. Synapse after synapse fired as my nerve endings electrified. Fireworks to rival the king's jubilee flashed behind my eyelids. I wasn't alone as Roman's deep baritone curses came in time with the increased intensity of his hold and thrusts.

I collapsed to the pillow as Roman's body landed over me. Craning my neck, I smiled as his brown eyes radiated the love and desire we'd just exhibited.

"I love you," he said. Disconnecting our union, he rolled to his back and pulled me to his side. "I don't know what it will be like going back to the States, but as long as we're together, it will be fine."

Pushing myself over his chest, I smiled and palmed his cheek. "You don't have to shave before bed."

"I seem to recall you complaining about abrasions."

I shook my head. "It wasn't a complaint. It was an observation. And sometimes, it's...nice."

"Oh," he said with a laugh. "I was thrown off by your multiple orgasms tonight. I'll try to make it nicer next time."

I lowered my forehead to his chest. "It was nice tonight, too. I'm just saying."

Reaching for my cheeks, Roman rolled us until his face was over mine. "Being with you, my princess, isn't nice. It's amazing."

"I love you, too."

CHAPTER 35

Roman

Being in New York, I let my mind wander back to the life before the one I had now. They weren't bad memories. I loved what I did. Acting had always been second nature to me. I supposed it still was. While many facets of my current life were natural and the progression of all I'd learned, there was still an element of pretending. I was reminded of that as we entered the senator and baroness's apartment, in the heart of the Upper West Side.

This wasn't my first visit or at least I needed to act as if it wasn't.

Our staffs had arranged for one evening of privacy with Lucille's parents. The royal security thoroughly scoured the entire two floors and posted one bodyguard at the door. Other than that, we were like every other husband and wife joining the in-laws for dinner—a senator, baroness, princess, and prince.

Just like everyone else.

As Lucille and her mother caught up and discussed the baby, Edwin showed me to his den. The air smelled of rich tobacco, the walls were lined with bookcases from floor to ceiling, a fire glowed from a hearth, framed with a beautiful hand-carved mantel. The only wall without bookshelves contained large windows and a stunning window seat. The entire room—apartment—was accented with ornate wood-working. Standing near the window, I looked down on Central Park. Even in February, the park was beautiful, with glowing lampposts creating circles of light. I recalled Lucille saying that she loved spending time in the park.

My thoughts went to my friend Ricardo. The last time we spoke, he'd offered to let me sleep on his couch while I worked on my Broadway comeback. I never made that flight. I haven't spoken to him since.

"Here you go," Edwin said, handing me a tumbler of bourbon. "Blanton's Single Barrel. I should have gotten some Glenlivet. I recall you were more of a scotch man." He shrugged. "Then again, I recall you offering me bourbon in Molave."

Smiling, I lifted the glass, seeing the transparency in the amber liquid. "Tastes change. I enjoy a good bourbon."

"Lucille is Americanizing you."

"I don't think so," I said. "Molavian through and through."

"That child will be both."

Taking a sip, I enjoyed the way my throat contracted. "Yes, he or she will be. He or she will also be the second in line to the throne."

Edwin took a seat in a highbacked chair and pointed to the other. "After our last visit, I hoped we'd have a chance for a private talk."

I nodded.

"I was never keen on that plan of yours and the duke's. It seemed risky to me. Hell, I don't know if the new king—Aleksander II—is trustworthy or if he's as shady as his father. Brutal son of a bitch."

He was referring to Aleksander I's invasion of Letanonia.

"It's over," I said, referencing the plan. "Papa and Alek came to an understanding regarding Inessa."

"Does that mean you'll recommend Borinkia to join NATO?"

"No. Our stance hasn't changed. Molave will be fine for now. We're always willing to speak with our allies and work for the common good. Speaking of good, what is the status of our agreement?"

The senator took a drink of his bourbon. "The proposal we discussed is in the bill. Right now, it's still in committee. No balkers yet."

I nodded. Setting my glass tumbler on a marble-top table, I leaned forward. This was a stretch, an occasion to ad-lib—improvise. I couldn't pass up the opportunity. "Edwin, before we close the conversation on that plan, tell me what you know. See, I don't recall sharing the details with you."

"The duke..." He waved his hand. "Remember when he invited me to his house at Forthwith."

I lifted my brow. "No."

"Yes, yes. I met with you in Molave City and told you about the invitation."

"You didn't."

He hummed. "I thought. I suppose I could be mistaken. You were rather short with me—with everyone. Well, anyway, I took the side trip up to Forthwith. The duke took me in the cellar and showed me the jars of cherry pits. At first, I thought he was joking. Then he began talking about the untapped petroleum in Borinkia. Of course, I'm aware of the sanctions. I played dumb, as if I didn't know about Molave and Borinkia cooperating." He scoffed. "After the cherry pits, I watch my drinks carefully."

I recalled the way he inspected the drink I poured him at Molave Palace.

"Who have you shared this information with?"

He shrugged. "I haven't come out and said

anything. I've been feeling the temperature of the water. There is a growing thirst to get into places like Borinkia. Hell, if we don't, the damn Russians will."

"When did you last speak with the Duke of Wilmington?"

Edwin paused, seemingly thinking. "It's been since before that accident you two had. He took the brunt of that."

Yeah.

I replied, "I would remove him from your call list. Francis Eriksen II has been banished and relieved of his royal duties. I'm surprised you didn't know that. My sister has filed for divorce."

"Well, damn," the senator said with a grin. "I suppose you don't want good ole Dad to find out what the two of you had cooking."

My grin quirked. "Papa knows everything."

"Surely, you didn't tell him..."

"I did. We're good. I hope to have many more years to learn all his ruthless ways."

"I thought you wanted to bring Molave into the present, hell, beyond. You were talking making Molave City the new Dubai."

Lifting my glass to my lips, I took another sip. "The UAE can keep Dubai. It's beautiful but too untouchable for the serenity of Molave. And in many ways, I do want Molave to advance. I also don't want to lose the grandeur of our history."

The senator was quiet for a moment. When he looked up, he smiled. "Lucy seems genuinely happy."

"I hope she is."

"For her sake, I'll never speak of that trip to Forthwith. That girl means the world to her mother and to me."

"That woman means the world to me. There's nothing I wouldn't do to protect her."

Edwin did a double take. "That almost sounded like a threat."

Again, I brought my glass to my lips and lifted one eyebrow. "Did it?"

* * *

The next morning, Lucille and I met with Betsy Scholl, the reporter from *Rolling Stone*, at the Mandarin Oriental Hotel, not too far from the Suttons' home. The journalist rented a private room and came prepared with photographers.

"What are your plans?" she asked.

Lucille smiled. "I thought you were given a copy of our itinerary."

"Oh yes, but that's the public stuff. Any side trips? How about a Broadway show?"

Lucille went on to talk about our plans to visit a special exhibit at the Met featuring Dutch master-pieces. Off the record, she explained that we were going to visit a homeless shelter in the city that was near to Lucille's heart.

"Tell me more," Betsy said.

Lucille shook her head. "What makes it special is that no one knows. It's easy to do good for public recognition." She reached for my hand. "The prince and I aren't here for that. We care about the people in the States and those in Molave. We will do the activities for the cameras and also do what we can for the people behind the scenes."

"Tonight, you're going to an NBA game?"

"We are," I said, looking to Lucille and grinning. "The Knickerbockers?"

Betsy laughed.

"Just Knicks," Lucille corrected.

"Yes. Knicks." At one time, I'd had season tickets. The lineup had changed, but I was looking forward to the game, more than a Molavian prince would.

"I have seen your itinerary," Betsy said. "I also read that you, Princess, are a fan of the fictional universe UDARVIS."

Lucille's grasp of my hand tightened. "I used to be."

"I asked your secretary, Lady Larsen, if I could

surprise the two of you with tickets to the premiere. It will be happening when you are in California." Handing Lucille an envelope, she was smiling as if she were giving us golden tickets to the chocolate factory. "I've been in contact with your secretary; security is being worked out. The cast is excited and hope that they may be granted a small audience after the premiere."

Taking the envelope, Lucille opened the flap. "This is very generous." She looked to me. "We will need to check with our offices."

"And the royal security," I said.

"Yes, yes," Betsy said. "I can't wait. I've only seen the trailer, but the studio is guaranteeing some major surprises."

Such as they killed off one of the main characters.

A warlord—one in particular.

Lord Divisto.

Me.

I cleared my throat. "I believe I'll need to catch up. Is this the second film in the franchise?"

"No," she said. "It's the fifth. I could have DVDs delivered to your hotel."

I forced a smile. "That won't be necessary." I looked at the tickets in Lucille's grasp and back. "Thank you, Ms. Scholl. This is very kind of you."

"It isn't often we have the Prince and Princess of

Molave in the United States. I wanted you to know that I appreciate the opportunity to work with you and get to see the real couple." She shook her head. "Everyone loves a good second-chance love story. Now with the news of the demise of your sister's marriage, the whole world is watching you."

CHAPTER
36

Roman

The evening of the premiere arrived. Lucille's and my offices were elated with the publicity. The prince and princess attending one of the most sought-after events in modern entertainment. Our presence showed the world the new generation of the monarchy. Roman and Lucille weren't all about stuffy dinners. Tonight, we'd walk the red carpet along with the cast—movie stars the world welcomed into their homes on their televisions, in merchandise, and in apparel. According to Dame Williamson, all the people of Molave were staying up into the early morning hours to watch the broadcast live.

My stomach rolled and my skin felt tight as Lord Martin put the finishing touches on my attire. This was the worst case of stage fright I'd experienced in decades. No, since I walked the corridors of Molave Palace to attend a child's birthday party. Much like that afternoon, a bubbling sense of dread brewed within me.

The difference was that at Rothy's birthday party, my fear was self-centered.

My job.

My future.

My success.

The repercussions of failing during tonight's extravaganza were cataclysmic in comparison.

Molave.

King Theodore.

Lucille.

Our future.

"You look regal, sir," Lord Martin said as he stood back and scanned from my head to my shoes. The custom suit was deep blue. The shirt was black and the tie a lighter blue. If I'd been attending the premiere as Oliver Honeswell, I couldn't have selected better attire. Social media would be filled with pictures. Threads would be filled with the assessment of my fans. Women tended to be the most outspoken.

Funny how that never registered with me before.

Andrew, my agent, paid more attention to those things than I did.

A memory surfaced. It was the night after the premiere for the fourth film in the UDARVIS universe, Rita and I lay in bed, drinking and reading comments on social media. We read the best and the worst about ourselves and each other, discussions about our attire, body language, and interactions with others. At that time, our relationship was back on, and the fans were ecstatic.

"Regal is an interesting choice of words," I said.

Lord Martin nodded. "Accurate, sir." He brushed the shoulders of the suit coat and peered over my shoulder into the mirror. "Reflections are what everyone sees."

My lips quirked into a lopsided grin. "You're being poetic. Should that frighten me?"

He shook his head. "Not poetic, factual. Mirrors are believed to have existed since the fifth century BCE. Handheld mirrors were the rage for elegant Greeks." He scoffed. "It was believed narcissistic by some to desire to see oneself." My assistant shook his head. "I believe our reflection is important not due to a desire to see oneself, but because it gives us a means to see ourselves as others see us—inverted though it may be. Pictures and films accomplish the same."

I turned and faced him. "You know...who I am?"

"Yes, Your Highness, you are Roman Archibald Godfrey, Prince of Molave, Duke of Monovia." He nodded toward the mirror. "That is who I see. Who do you see?"

Swallowing, I again took in my reflection. It took a few seconds, time to wash away my fear, time to remember who my father was, and time to accept the choices I'd made.

When I didn't speak, Lord Martin did. "Royal reflections, sir. See yourself that way and others will too."

Before I could respond, the door to my bedroom in our hotel suite opened. Lord Martin's words sank in as I gazed at the most stunning woman I'd ever met. From her elegantly styled dark hair, her piercing blue stare, and down over her floor-length pale blue gown, Lucille exuded royalty. Born an American, she'd taken on the royal role with compassion and grace. Those qualities and more were why she was adored—by the world and by my whole heart.

"Your Highness," she said with a curtsy, a shimmer in her sparkling gaze.

CHAPTER
37

Lucille

The sear of Roman's gaze peppered my skin with an intensity he rarely showed in front of others, even our assistants. My gaze met his and in mere milliseconds, I assessed more than lust within his tumultuous eyes.

I looked to Roman's assistant. "Lord Martin, please leave us."

"Yes, Your Highness," he said with a neck bow and a quick look to Roman.

Once we were alone, I went closer, taking my husband's hands in mine and peering up at the face I'd come to love. The conflict he had in front of him was visible in his strained brow, concern lines near his eyes, and the chiseled edge to his clenched jaw. "My prince, we will survive this."

He shook his head. "What if we don't? What if I'm discovered?"

"We will deny." I pressed myself against him. "You are King Theodore's son."

Roman's eyes closed and his nostrils flared.

I took a step back. When the dark brown of his orbs returned, I tilted my head. "Have you changed your mind about remaining in Molave? Do you want to take the queen's escape route?"

"What? No." His hand went to his dark mane, mussing what had been perfect only seconds before, as he turned all the way around.

"I understand if being here has brought back memories of a life you miss. I get it. I've been there."

Roman shook his head. "My princess, I won't lie to you. I've been remembering many things, people, places...the list goes on and on. I'm not missing them. I'm reflecting on them."

"The queen gave us the choice to be free of all of this."

"I don't want that. Do you?"

"At one time, I did," I confessed. "When I was terribly lonely." My cheeks moved upward as my smile grew. "I'm not lonely any longer. It's a different life, being royal. Not at all like anyone can imagine. Tonight, you will see people you knew, friends...lovers."

There was no denial as Roman nodded.

"That old life," I went on, "it was filled with different people—many people. Being prince or princess is much more solitary." I took his hands in mine. "But solitary doesn't have to be lonely. You are loved by more than only me. King Theodore and Queen Anne love you, not because of who you represent but because of who you are. Noah represented the same person, and he wasn't loved." I laid one hand over my stomach. "This child will love you."

Roman cupped my cheek. "I'm not lonely with you. I don't need a soundstage of people. Papa and Mum have accepted me, even care for me. I feel it. I think I felt it before I knew. It was that pull to Molave and for Molave that I couldn't understand. It was there." He sighed. "Lord Martin said something earlier."

"What did he say?"

Roman turned us until we were both standing before a full-length mirror. We were truly the stunning couple Betsy Scholl described—the Prince and Princess of Molave.

"Basically, he said," Roman began, "that the way we see ourselves in a reflection is the way others see us." He nodded. "He's right. I've seen myself as many different characters throughout my life."

I tilted my forehead to his sleeve and watched his expression in the glass.

"When I was on Broadway," Roman said, "I didn't see myself as Oliver Honeswell playing Billy Flynn. Before the curtain rose, in that mirror backstage, I saw

Billy Flynn. The same with Lord Divisto, the warlord."

Smiling, I said, "I see the Prince of Molave."

Turning, Roman kissed my head. "I see the Prince and Princess of Molave."

I lifted my hand, palm up. "Then let us show them to the world."

"Yes, my princess."

I wasn't unaccustomed to fanfare. Even with Noah, when I was paraded around the world on his arm, there were crowds, cameras, and bright lights. As we waited for our car to make it to the end of the red carpet, I saw the unmatched jubilance of a premiere. The adoring fans, many dressed in costume, were out in force, filling the sidewalks. As our car moved closer, at a snail's pace, I began to see the others dressed in their finest, walking the red carpet.

As we sat in the back seat waiting for our turn, I softly asked, "Who is that?"

Roman scoffed. "Ronald Estes."

"What character does he play?"

"He's the producer."

As the car moved forward, I saw the red-headed woman at his side. "Is that his wife? She's beautiful." I recalled the trailer I'd watched. "No, she's in the movies, right?"

"Yes, Rita has one of the lead roles. She's a super-hero named Mercury."

"Oh," I said, "what is her superpower?"

CHAPTER
38

Roman

Her superpower is fucking people over.

Before I could answer, the car door next to me was opened. Taking a deep breath, I stepped out of the sedan. A hush fell over the crowd. Nodding, I turned back and offered Lucille my hand.

Taking it, Lucille stepped out.

"Prince and Princess of Molave. Prince Roman and Princess Lucille," came from a loudspeaker.

Thunderous applause ricocheted as flashes snapped and the crowd chanted our names.

With two bodyguards a step behind and Lucille's hand in mine, we made our way along the carpet, stopping in front of the UDARVIS backdrop for our picture. With Ronald and Rita only two couples ahead, I found a strange sense of appreciation when Betsy Scholl called us over to a private interview area.

"Your Highnesses," she greeted with a smile. "We're honored you accepted our invitation."

Lucille's blue eyes were filled with wonderment. "This is spectacular."

"Oh, wait until you see the film." She lowered her voice. "I was given an early screening and let me say, there wasn't a dry eye in the house."

Lucille straightened her neck. "Oh dear. I didn't expect a comic universe to be emotional."

"If you don't have tissues, get some before you're seated." She motioned to the cameraman. "Do you mind if I ask you a couple of questions?"

I nodded. "We're present as your guests, Ms. Scholl. It would be our pleasure."

She started with similar questions to the ones she asked the other day, questions about our States tour, how we enjoyed the exhibit at the Metropolitan Museum of Art. "One last question," she said. "Can you share with the world who your favorite character is in the UDARVIS universe."

"That is difficult," I replied.

"Mercury," Lucille said.

"Oh, she'll be excited to hear that." Betsy looked up at me. "Your Highness?"

"I'm going to have to say Leo Twist. He made a big impression in the first film." Leo was played by an actor named Brett Parkland. Rita had invited me to his house for a wrap party. Brett was an okay man and could be a lot of fun. He's also the character who killed me.

"I'm surprised," Betsy said, "that neither of you named Lord Divisto. You know, the warlord with a heart of gold."

My expression stayed unreadable.

Lucille looked up at me. "Which one is he?"

Betsy laughed. "Okay, it's good he won't know you said that." She motioned for the camera to be turned off. "Enjoy your night. After the film, Lady Larsen said you were willing to attend a small party with the cast and crew."

"It's our plan," I said. "It will depend. The time difference hasn't been kind to Lucille."

"Oh," Betsy said, looking to Lucille. "It doesn't show. You're absolutely ravishing."

Lucille laid her hand over her midsection. "Thank you."

Betsy's eyes grew wide, and she leaned closer. "Princess, do you have an announcement?"

"If you agree to keep our secret," Lucille said, "we will invite you to Molave for an exclusive."

Betsy enthusiastically nodded.

Placing her hand in the crook of my elbow, I led Lucille into the theater.

She peered around at the décor. TCL or the more recognized name, Grauman's Chinese Theater, was iconic, steeped in rich Hollywood history, and not far from where I used to live.

Royal.

Regal.

I repeated those words as we entered a large room filled with attendees. We garnered looks from those present, yet no one approached us. The two large men pretending to be our shadows was mostly likely one deterrent.

Fuck.

Laying my hand over Lucille's, I whispered, "We have company."

She looked up in time as Ronald Estes came closer. After an awkward bow, he offered me his hand. "Welcome, Your Highnesses."

Nodding, I didn't take his hand.

The Prince of Molave didn't shake hands.

There was more than a bit of pleasure watching his uncomfortable exchange with royalty.

"Thank you," I said, my accent thick.

"My name is Ronald Estes. I'm the producer of this franchise. It's an honor to have you with us." His beady eyes narrowed as he looked at me.

"I've never been to a premiere," Lucille said, focusing his attention on her. "What should I expect?"

The sleazeball scanned the princess up and down. "Princess, you should expect to be entertained beyond belief. UDARVIS boasts a star-studded cast, award-winning cinematography, and only the best production staff."

Fuck, does he think we'd invest Molave's money into his work?

What is with the sales pitch?

My breath caught as Rita appeared, laying her hand on Ronald's arm.

"Ron, there's someone—" Her eyes met mine and the color drained from her painted face.

"You are Mercury, right?" Lucille asked.

Rita's gaze went to Lucille. "Yes, I'm sorry..."

Ron proceeded as if we were old friends. "Rita, this is Prince Roman and Princess Lucille of Molave. Your Highnesses, this is the star of our show and my wife, Rita Smalls."

Wife.

Fuck.

I clenched my jaw. At least she kept her own name.

Rita offered a neck bow. "It is a pleasure to meet you. We'd heard you might fit us into your schedule."

"It is very exciting," Lucille said, gazing around. "I don't recall the last film I saw in a theater."

"It doesn't get better than TCL," Ronald said.

Rita's gaze was back on me. Nodding my head, I said, "If you'll excuse us."

Rita nodded as Ronald rambled on about something. The buzzing in my head didn't stop until we were settled in our seats in the fourth row. The next hour was filled with speeches, recognitions, and then, finally, the lights dimmed.

Lucille reached for my hand.

This was the first time I would initially witness my work at a premiere. In the past, I'd been involved with early screenings and going over scenes, and while I might not have watched every frame of the finished product, I wasn't going in cold.

This was cold.

The theater reverberated with the familiar overture. I caught Lucille's grin during a love scene between Mercury and Lord Divisto. My teeth ached from the pressure of my clenched jaw as Leo turned the laser on Lord Divisto. Despite the audience containing members of the cast and crew, the theater filled with a collective gasp as the warlord fell to his knees, gave one last, longing glance to his true love, and vanished before our eyes.

Lucille opened her purse and removed a tissue.

I leaned close to her ear and spoke as low as possible. "I have a secret. He's not really dead."

Her smile was breathtaking.

The final frame lingered on the screen.

This film is dedicated to the memory and career of Oliver Honeswell.

Before I could react, the red curtain came down

and the lights went up. We all remained seated as Rita Smalls walked onto the stage. "As many of you know, the decision to end Lord Divisto was a difficult one. What was even more difficult was learning of the unfortunate demise of our beloved castmate, fellow actor, and dear friend."

I didn't realize how tightly I was gripping the arms of the seat until Lucille's hand covered mine.

"Oliver Honeswell was not only a talented entertainer, but he was a good man."

As Rita continued speaking the curtain opened, and a montage of photos displayed behind her. Photos of me throughout my career.

Rita went on, "Sometimes I think I still see him." She inhaled. "Estes Production is honored to have Oliver's sisters with us today."

The theater clapped as a spotlight shone on seats behind us.

My sisters.

"Today," Rita went on, "Julie and Sally Cofield joined Ronald and me for the unveiling of Oliver's star on the Walk of Fame."

The screen filled with a picture of the four of them standing by a star on the Hollywood Walk of Fame. Consumed with the faces of my sisters, I didn't notice the entire theater standing until Lucille tapped me.

Joining my wife and the rest of the attendees, I too clapped for a career cut short.

"I'm sorry," Lucille whispered as we waited to exit.

"I sure as hell don't feel like a party."

Lucille clasped my hand.

We were on our way out of the theater when a man I used to know handed me an envelope. My gaze met his.

"Your Highness," Dustin Hargraves said.

I looked at the envelope. "Sir?" My Molavian accent was intact.

"Save it for later." He nodded. "Long live the king."

Tucking the envelope into the inside of my suit coat, Lucille and I continued our way toward the exit. Our bodyguards had a car waiting. I'd had enough of this premiere.

"You aren't leaving?" Betsy Scholl said, pushing her way through the people.

Lucille nodded. "I'm sorry. I'm so tired." She reached out to Betsy. "And you were right. I had tears."

"Thank you for coming."

"Lady Larsen," Lucille said, "will be in touch for your exclusive."

Betsy offered a neck bow. "Thank you. I look forward to seeing you again."

Once we were in the car on our way back to the hotel, Lucille asked, "Who was that man?"

"His name is Dustin Hargraves."

By the light coming through the windows, I saw her questioning expression.

"Why does that name sound familiar?" she asked.

"He was my voice coach."

Her eyes widened. "The one who called about your agent."

I nodded.

"What did he give you?"

Patting my fingers over the suit coat, I shrugged. "We will see when we get to the hotel."

"Do you trust him?"

I thought about her question. "I do."

CHAPTER
39

Lucille

A fter we returned to the hotel, I gave Roman time with his thoughts. I couldn't imagine what tonight had been like for him. To know his sisters were present and they believed he was dead. The death of the warlord. The fitting tribute. Even the star on the Walk of Fame.

It was a lot to take in.

I waited until Lady Buckingham and Lord Martin retired to their own rooms before I made my way to Roman's bedroom. Turning the knob, I slowly opened the door. The lights of Hollywood shone through the unblocked windows, creating the only illumination in the room.

Roman came into view, sitting in a corner chair, enveloped in shadows.

"My prince?"

He stood. His silhouette came toward me. I recalled the warlord on the screen, his strength, power, and determination. That was the man coming near me now. He was still wearing his shirt and pants. The shirt was untucked and unbuttoned; the sleeves were rolled.

"My princess," he finally said as he snaked one arm around me and pulled me close.

The aroma of bourbon was thick on his breath combined with the fading scent of his cologne. His hair was messed and wavy, probably from his habit of running his fingers through it.

With my hands on his chest, I looked up. "Are you all right?"

"I'm dead."

I dropped my forehead to his t-shirt-clad chest. "I'm so sorry."

"I think I knew. After what Noah told me. Even suspecting didn't make it any easier to learn, especially in such a public manner."

I took a step back. "What did Dustin give you?"

Roman went to the desk and turned on a lamp. I blinked, trying to make sense of the items on the desktop. There were two blue booklets, drivers' licenses, other papers.

"Oh my God," I said, lifting the passports and opening each one.

Ryan Mahoney.

Cassandra Mahoney.

"Those are our pictures," I said in disbelief.

"There's more," Roman said.

Shifting the papers, he handed me a folded page. Opening the folds, I found a letter, handwritten and on both sides of the page. My eyes skimmed to the bottom, looking for the signature. I looked up. "It's from Rita —Mercury."

Roman pressed his lips together as he nodded. "You'll get the gist when you read it, but in the interest of full disclosure, Rita and I had an on-and-off relationship. It was off when the Firm called Andrew."

My pulse increased as I pushed the page his direction. "No, Roman, this is personal. I don't need to read it."

"Princess, I have no secrets from you."

Inhaling, I nodded, pulled out the shiny desk chair, and sat. Placing the letter under the circle of light, I began to read.

You promised me the last time we talked you would return for the premiere. Either you have, or you think I'm some strange American stalker. I won't use your name in case this isn't you.

I want it to be you.

I want to think of you happy, with someone special, and enjoying life.

The alternative is too painful.

I've cried too many tears over the way things ended,

not only between us but with the studio too. You should know, Ron was offered a substantial contribution to write you out of the series. He said he didn't know who it was from. Something about LLCs and shell companies. Shocker, he took the money.

Speaking of money, do you remember making me your sole beneficiary in the event of your death? Imagine my shock when I received the call.

Thank you. Thank you for your friendship, encouragement, support, and for sharing part of your life with me. If this isn't you...at least I got to say goodbye.

As for that insurance money, find the attached information. It explains how to access an offshore account. (I've learned a few tricks from Ron's schemes.) Again, in the event you have no idea who this is, please put the funds to good use for SGA, community theater, or whatever charity you deem fitting.

If you're wondering how I know what I think I do, Andrew Biggs mentioned it once. No worries, I never told a soul and after his death, I feared and hoped he was right. I approached the man who handed you the envelope (again, not using names), and he agreed to help me.

Know you are loved and missed.
Long live the (future) king.
Rita

. . .

There were fresh tears in my eyes by the time I finished. Without looking up, I knew Roman was nearby. He stood with his arms crossed over his chest, staring out the windows. Standing, I went to him, reached for his hand, and uncrossed his arms. Stepping to him, I inhaled his scent and relished the warmth he radiated. "She still loves you."

He jutted his jaw toward the desk. "She gave us our out. There's enough money in that account for a normal life."

My hands trembled as I looked at the passports, papers, and identifications, and then back up at Roman. "A normal life."

"Walks in Central Park."

"Privacy."

"Spending all day at the Met without bodyguards." He swallowed. "I believe Queen Anne was serious in her offer, but history says that they don't let Romans go." He motioned to the desk. "This is our ticket."

My heart ached and tears came to my eyes. Reaching up, I cupped his cheek. "I don't want to live without you. You. Roman. Oliver. Ryan." I shook my head. "I don't care what your name is. I'll go where you go."

Roman held me close as his lips took mine.

Savage and possessive.

His fingers intertwined in my hair, pressing me

toward him, bruising my lips in his ruthless desperation to be closer. Not to be outdone, I pushed the shirt from his wide shoulders, securing the hem of his cotton t-shirt, I broke our kiss long enough to pull it over his head. My fingers roamed his solid chest, defined abs, and strong arms.

Lord Divisto to Prince Roman.

This was the man I was meant to live my happily-ever-after with—the inscription in his wedding band.

I wasn't in love with a title or a job. I was in love with *this* man and the woman I was when I was with him. I was in love with the idea of forever with him and with our children. I'd long ago given up on fairy tales, yet in his arms, I knew I'd found mine or it had found me.

As our passion erupted, there was no need for words. We both knew the answer and what our future would hold. It didn't need to be said—the time for words had passed.

EPILOGUE

Lucille
Six months later

The sun shone beyond the nursery window. Fluffy white clouds floated through the cobalt-blue sky. Below a velvety green lawn contrasted the flowers of varying colors, stretching their petals in the warm summer air. I was drawn to the bassinet, cloaked in layers of white tulle. The hallways beyond the room were less busy than those of Molave Palace.

I ran my touch over the handmade adornments. This particular bassinet had held generations of Godfreys, all the way back to King Theo's grandfather, Theodore I.

The infant within had recently fallen asleep. Her cheeks were pink, little hands were balled into fists, and her lips were drawn into a bow. Princess Polina

Anne was the perfect combination of her father and mother, with a faint crown of dark hair and eyes that were growing bluer each day.

Confiding to Mr. Davies that I knew about the various Romans, I asked for a DNA test. It wasn't that I'd love another man's child less. I wanted to know. The results came back with 99.9 percent assurance that my Roman was Polly's father.

While I'd told myself it wouldn't matter, seeing the results took my breath away. I couldn't wait to share the news with Roman. He'd said it wouldn't matter, but I saw the relief in his gaze the moment I told him.

Hearing a sound, I spun toward the door to the nursery as it opened and lifted my finger to my lips.

Roman came to my side, also peering down at our daughter. "You got her down," he said in a deep baritone whisper.

"For now."

Wrapping his arms around me, he held me tight within his embrace. The beat of his heart thumped in my ear as I closed my eyes, ready to sleep standing up. As my body relaxed, Roman stepped back, and took my hand.

"You, Princess, need to rest."

I peered once and then twice over my shoulder. "I don't want to leave her."

"There is a monitor in our bedchamber. Lady Buckingham has a monitor. Lady Louise" —our nanny — "has a monitor. Polly will not be left unattended."

With my hand in his, we made our way across the connecting parlor. No longer did we move between two bedchambers; we shared only one. My old bedchamber was Polly's nursery.

Despite the time of day, Roman led me to the bed and pulled back the covers. My irregular sleep patterns had me too exhausted to argue. I slipped off my soft slacks and climbed inside the blankets wearing my jumper and bloomers.

"Mum and Papa are coming tomorrow," Roman said after tucking me in.

"I know they want us in Molave City." I looked around our bedchamber at Annabella Castle. "I want time with Polly here."

He smiled. "Your wish is my command."

I sighed. "And my parents will be here a week from Friday."

Roman nodded. "The senator got the bill signed. I guess that's something in his favor."

I shook my head. "My dad is a good man."

"I hope Polly says the same thing one day."

"I have no doubt."

Roman kissed my forehead. "I'll tell Lady Buckingham you're resting. She'll take care of everything else."

As Roman started to move, I reached out. "I hope you don't regret our decision."

"This is my life—*our* life. I'm not only committed, but I also don't want anything else."

"I love you."

"I love you, too," he said, brushing my lips with his before closing the drapes and leaving me to sleep. At the side of the bed was a small screen with an overview shot of Polly's bed. I was almost asleep when I heard Roman's voice.

Smiling, at the sight of his strong hands along the side of the bassinette, I listened to the monitor.

"Princess Polly, your Mum and Papa will keep you safe. Always know that you're loved."

Sighing, I looked around our bedchamber. If anyone questioned why we chose to stay on Roman's side in our Annabella home, no one mentioned it. Only the most meticulous observer would notice the difference in dimensions.

Even with our sharing of secrets with the king and queen, Roman and I chose to keep the contents of the hidden room to ourselves. The countless journals still remain. We haven't taken the time to read any more, but they're there for the future if either of us wants them. There were also the tubs, the one with the escape clothes Noah had prepared. We'd added a few more items: lady's clothes, boots, as well as children's essentials. The information to access the funds Rita hid for us and the alternative passports are also in the room.

Neither of us talk about it.

We know in our hearts we made our commitment to one another, the king, and Molave. I also recall the stories of my mother's family's escape from Letanonia. Borinkia wasn't the only concern on the world stage. Disdain for monarchies was growing.

Roman vowed above all to keep our family safe. The content behind the bookcases was part of that plan—our insurance.

And no one will ever know.

Our bedchamber was merely a skewed reflection of the royal nursery.

Thank you for reading Royal Reflections.
When I began this series, I thought it would end with King Roman and Queen Lucille. As the story developed, I realized that Roman truly gained a father, and I didn't want to take that away from him, not yet.
The series is done for now. Maybe one day, we can revisit Molave and learn how the next generation will rule.
Will it be ruthlessly or relevantly?

In the meantime, check out all my titles: stand-alones, duets, trilogies, and series all ready to BINGE and available to read on Kindle Unlimited.

NEW romantic suspense duet coming. Check it out.

What to do now

LEND IT: Did you enjoy RELEVANT REIGN? Do you have a friend who'd enjoy RELEVANT REIGN? RELEVANT REIGN may be lent one time. Sharing is caring!

RECOMMEND IT: Do you have multiple friends who'd enjoy my dark romance with twists and turns and an all new sexy and infuriating anti-hero? Tell them about it! Call, text, post, tweet...your recommendation is the nicest gift you can give to an author!

REVIEW IT: Tell the world. Please go to the retailer where you purchased this book, as well as Goodreads, and write a review. Please share your thoughts about RELEVANT REIGN on:

*Amazon, RELEVANT REIGN Customer Reviews

*Barnes & Noble, RELEVANT REIGN, Customer Reviews

*Apple Books, RELEVANT REIGN Customer Reviews

* BookBub, RELEVANT REIGN Customer Reviews

*Goodreads.com/Aleatha Romig

Books by
ALEATHA

**ALL AVAILABLE TO READ ON KINDLE
UNLIMITED**

ROYAL REFLECTIONS SERIES:

RUTHLESS REIGN

November 2022

RESILIENT REIGN

January 2023

RAVISHING REIGN

April 2023

READY TO BINGE:

SIN SERIES:

RED SIN

October 2021

GREEN ENVY

January 2022

GOLD LUST

April 2022

BLACK KNIGHT

June 2022

STAND-ALONE ROMANTIC SUSPENSE:

SILVER LINING

October 2022

KINGDOM COME

November 2021

DEVIL'S SERIES (Duet):

DEVIL'S DEAL

May 2021

ANGEL'S PROMISE

June 2021

WEB OF SIN:

SECRETS

October 2018

LIES

December 2018

PROMISES

January 2019

TANGLED WEB:

TWISTED

May 2019

OBSESSED

July 2019

BOUND

August 2019

WEB OF DESIRE:

SPARK

Jan. 14, 2020

FLAME

February 25, 2020

ASHES

April 7, 2020

DANGEROUS WEB:

Prequel: "Danger's First Kiss"

DUSK

November 2020

DARK

January 2021

DAWN

February 2021

* * *

THE INFIDELITY SERIES:

BETRAYAL

Book #1

October 2015

CUNNING

Book #2

January 2016

DECEPTION

Book #3

May 2016

ENTRAPMENT

Book #4

September 2016

FIDELITY

Book #5

January 2017

* * *

THE CONSEQUENCES SERIES:

CONSEQUENCES

(Book #1)

August 2011

TRUTH

(Book #2)

October 2012

CONVICTED

(Book #3)

October 2013

REVEALED

(Book #4)

Previously titled: Behind His Eyes Convicted: The Missing Years

June 2014

BEYOND THE CONSEQUENCES

(Book #5)

January 2015

RIPPLES (Consequences stand-alone)

October 2017

CONSEQUENCES COMPANION READS:

BEHIND HIS EYES-CONSEQUENCES

January 2014

BEHIND HIS EYES-TRUTH

March 2014

* * *

STAND ALONE MAFIA THRILLER:

PRICE OF HONOR

Available Now

* * *

STAND-ALONE ROMANTIC THRILLER:

ON THE EDGE

May 2022

***

THE LIGHT DUET:

Published through Thomas and Mercer Amazon exclusive

INTO THE LIGHT

June 2016

AWAY FROM THE DARK

October 2016

* * *

TALES FROM THE DARK SIDE SERIES:

INSIDIOUS

(All books in this series are stand-alone erotic thrillers)

Released October 2014

* * *

ALEATHA'S LIGHTER ONES:

PLUS ONE

Stand-alone fun, sexy romance

May 2017

ANOTHER ONE

Stand-alone fun, sexy romance

May 2018

ONE NIGHT

Stand-alone, sexy contemporary romance

September 2017

A SECRET ONE

April 2018

MY ALWAYS ONE

Stand-Alone, sexy friends to lovers contemporary romance

July 2021

QUINTESSENTIALLY THE ONE

Stand-alone, small-town, second-chance, secret baby contemporary romance

July 2022

MY ONLY ONE

Stand-alone, small-town, best friend's sister, grump/sunshine contemporary romance.

July 2023

* * *

INDULGENCE SERIES:

UNEXPECTED

August 2018

UNCONVENTIONAL

January 2018

UNFORGETTABLE

October 2019

UNDENIABLE

August 2020

ABOUT THE
AUTHOR

Aleatha Romig is a New York Times, Wall Street Journal, and USA Today bestselling author who lives in Indiana, USA. She has raised three children with her high school sweetheart and husband of over thirty years. Before she became a full-time author, she worked days as a dental hygienist and spent her nights writing. Now, when she's not imagining mind-blowing twists and turns, she likes to spend her time with her family and friends. Her other pastimes include reading and creating heroes/anti-heroes who haunt your dreams!

Aleatha impresses with her versatility in writing. She released her first novel, CONSEQUENCES, in August of 2011. CONSEQUENCES, a dark romance, became a bestselling series with five novels and two companions released from 2011 through 2015. The compelling and epic story of Anthony and Claire Rawlings has graced more than half a million e-readers. Her first stand-alone smart, sexy thriller INSIDIOUS was next. Then Aleatha released the five-novel INFIDELITY series, a romantic suspense saga, that took the reading world by storm, the final book landing on three of the top bestseller lists. She ventured into traditional publishing with Thomas and Mercer. Her books INTO THE LIGHT and AWAY FROM THE DARK were published through this mystery/thriller publisher in 2016.

In the spring of 2017, Aleatha again ventured into a different genre with her first fun and sexy stand-alone romantic comedy with the USA Today bestseller PLUS ONE. She continued the "Ones" series with additional standalones, ONE NIGHT, ANOTHER ONE, MY ALWAYS ONE, and QUINTESSEN-TIALLY THE ONE. If you like fun, sexy, novellas that make your heart pound, try her "Indulgence series" with UNCONVENTIONAL. UNEX-PECTED, UNFORGETTABLE, and UNDENIABLE.

In 2018 Aleatha returned to her dark romance roots with SPARROW WEBS. And continued with the mafia romance DEVIL'S DUET, and most recently her SIN series.

You may find all Aleatha's titles on her website.

Aleatha is a "Published Author's Network" member of the Romance Writers of America and PEN Amer-ica. She is represented by Kevan Lyon of Marsal Lyon Literary Agency and Dani Sanchez with Wildfire Marketing.

facebook.com/aleatharomig

twitter.com/aleatharomig

instagram.com/aleatharomig

Made in the USA
Middletown, DE
20 June 2023

32881063R00203